Field

Hole 3: Open Area

Families

Gate
Shuttle

J G

A

D

B

E

C

K H

F

Listings

I

L

Dean,
Niko,
Astrid,
Alex,
Sahalia

M

Hole 11: Open Area

N

Kids' Play Fort

O P S

Q T V

Fence

R U W

X

Quilchena
Refugee Camp

MONUMENT 14: SAVAGE DRIFT

MONUMENT 14:
SAVAGE DRIFT

EMMY LAYBOURNE

FEIWEL AND FRIENDS
NEW YORK

A Feiwel and Friends Book
An Imprint of Macmillan

MONUMENT 14: SAVAGE DRIFT. Copyright © 2013 by Emmy Laybourne.
All rights reserved. Printed in the United States of America by
R. R. Donnelley & Sons Company, Harrisonburg, Virginia. For information,
address Feiwel and Friends, 175 Fifth Avenue, New York, N.Y. 10010.

Feiwel and Friends books may be purchased for business or promotional use. For information
on bulk purchases, please contact the Macmillan Corporate and Premium Sales Department
at (800) 221-7945 x5442 or by e-mail at specialmarkets@macmillan.com.

Library of Congress Cataloging-in-Publication Data Available

ISBN: 978-1-250-03642-1 (hardcover) / 978-1-250-06207-9 (ebook)

Book design by Ashley Halsey

Feiwel and Friends logo designed by Filomena Tuosto

First Edition: 2014

2 4 6 8 10 9 7 5 3 1

macteenbooks.com

For my sisters,
Herran and Renee

LETTERS TO THE EDITOR

THE MONUMENT 14
How I escaped from the epicenter of the Four Corners Area Disaster with my friends

To the Editor:

I've read some amazing stories in your paper about survivors of the Megatsunami. Up here in the Quilchena refugee camp in Vancouver, Canada, they sometimes read the letters aloud after lunch. Sometimes people cheer. But I've noticed that almost all the letters you run are from people on the East Coast.

Maybe that is because your readers are more interested in people from their own area. Or maybe it is because the mail is messed up and you are not receiving the letters from out here. Nevertheless, I am sending you our story, in the hopes that after you print it our parents will be able to find us.

On the morning of September 28, 2024, I was on the bus to school when a monster hailstorm came up. Our driver, Mrs. Wooly, drove the bus through the front doors of our local Greenway superstore, to get us out of harm's way. All together, there were 14 of us.

Mrs. Wooly went to get help, and while we were waiting, the riot gates came down, trapping us inside. It was only then that we found an old-fashioned TV set in the store and found out about the

Megatsunami. When the earthquake hit the next morning, and the chemicals spilled out into the air, we sealed off the door and holed up in the store.

We stayed in the store for two weeks, and would have stayed there longer, only to die in the air strikes, but one kid in our group, Brayden, was shot. We had fixed up the school bus, so some of us decided to leave to try to make it to Denver International Airport.

My brother, Dean Grieder, stayed behind along with a pregnant girl named Astrid Heyman and three of the little kids, Chloe Frasier and the twins, Caroline and Henry McKinley. Dean and Astrid are both O and were scared they would be exposed again and attack us, as they had done before.

We set out into the pitch black and it was terrifying. Niko Mills, our leader, was driving. There were eight of us on board, ranging in age from 17 to 8 years old. [See complete list below.] We saw bodies on the road and terrible things.

We were more than halfway there when our bus was ambushed by Air Force cadets. They threw us off the bus and didn't let us take any of our supplies, except for one backpack Niko was wearing.

On the way, we lost one of our group. Josie Miller took off her air mask and went O on purpose, when we were being chased by a deranged soldier. She gave her life to protect us.

Another man helped us, Mario Scietto. We fell into a pit trap that a father and son had arranged. They were trying to steal our air masks and water. Mario helped us get out and let us rest in his bomb shelter.

We walked until we came to the DIA collection point. At the airport, we found Mrs. Wooly, who is in the National Guard and had been called to serve. Niko and I told Mrs. Wooly about my brother and the rest of the kids back at the Greenway. When we learned about Operation Phoenix (the Air Force strike that destroyed the MORS compound and the

RAVEN blackout cloud and also leveled the Four Corners area), we tried to help Mrs. Wooly find a pilot willing to go on a rescue mission. We were begging one pilot to help us when another one came up and said he'd take us. He was the father of the twins who had stayed behind with Dean and Astrid.

We went racing back to Monument in Captain McKinley's Wildcat helicopter. As we were landing on the roof, we saw the first bombs drop over NORAD. At first, we panicked. Dean and the rest weren't in the store! They had left to try to make it to DIA just before we'd landed. But Dean, my brother, saw us up on the roof. He came running back and we rescued all of them.

Scorching hot winds from the air strike almost blew us down and we could see bombs punching holes in the black sky on all sides of us, but we made it out.

Of the fourteen of us, twelve made it out alive. Eleven are here at Quilchena, but out of all of us, only five have found our parents, or have had any news about them at all.

We are:

Alex and Dean Grieder, ages 13 and 16

Jake Simonsen, age 18

Astrid Heyman, age 17

Niko Mills, age 16

Sahalia Wenner, age 13

Chloe Frasier, age 10

Batiste Harrison, age 9

Max Skolnik, age 8

Ulysses Dominguez, age 8

Caroline and Henry McKinley, age 5

and

Josie Miller, age 15, presumed dead.

Brayden Cutlass, age 17, deceased.

Please, if you have any information about our parents or family members, call the Quilchena Refugee Camp Relocation Coordinator.

Sincerely,

Alex Grieder

CHAPTER ONE

DEAN

NIKO'S EYES FLASHED TO OUR FACES, ONE BY ONE.

"Josie's alive!" he repeated. "She's being held against her will in Missouri!"

We all boggled at the newspaper he was holding out. It was Josie. He was right.

"I'm going to get her. Who's coming with me?"

I didn't know what to say. I'm sure my mouth was gaping open like a beached fish.

"Let us see the thing, Niko. Are you sure?" Jake said. Ever the politician, he stepped forward and took the paper from Niko.

"Is it really Josie? Are you sure?" Caroline asked. All the kids swarmed to Jake.

"Hold on, hold on. Let me set it down."

Jake put the paper down on the bedsheet that Mrs. McKinley had laid down as a picnic blanket. We were out on the green, celebrating the twins' sixth birthday.

"It's Josie! It's Josie, it really is!" Max crowed. "I thought for sure she got blown up!"

"Careful with the paper!" Niko said. The kids were pushing and jostling for a better look. Luna, our fluffy white mascot, was up in Chloe's arms, yipping and licking anyone's face she could reach. She was just as excited as the rest of us.

"Somebody read it out loud, already!" Chloe complained.

"Now, Chloe. How would you ask in a polite way?" Mrs. McKinley reprimanded her.

"Somebody read it out loud already, PLEASE!"

Good luck, Mrs. McKinley.

Mrs. McKinley started to read the article. It said that the conditions at the type O containment camp were negligent and prisoners were being abused. It said that there was limited medical aid reaching the refugees inside. It said that if Booker hadn't given the power to govern these containment camps to individual states, none of this would have happened.

But I was just watching Niko.

He was bouncing on the soles of his feet.

Action. That's what he'd been missing, I realized.

Niko was a kid who thrived on structure and being productive. Here at the Quilchena luxury golf club turned refugee containment camp, there was plenty of structure, but almost nothing to do besides watch the twenty-four-hour cycle of depressing news from around the country and wait in lines.

Niko'd been wasting away—consumed with grief and guilt about losing Josie on the road from Monument to the Denver International Airport evacuation site. And he'd been starving for something to do.

And now he thought he was going to rescue Josie.

Which, of course, was completely absurd.

Niko started to pace as Mrs. McKinley finished the article.

The kids had a lot of questions. Where is Missouri? Why is Josie being hit by that guard? Can they see her soon? Can they see her today?

But Niko cut through the chatter with a question of his own.

"Do you think Captain McKinley can get us to her?" he asked Mrs. M. "I mean, if he got permission, he could fly us, right?"

"I think if we go through proper channels, we should be able to get her transferred here. I mean, obviously you children cannot go down there and get her yourselves," Mrs. McKinley said.

I shared a look with Alex—she didn't know Niko.

He'd already packed a backpack in his mind.

He turned to me.

"I think if you and me and Alex go, we'd have the best chances," Niko told me.

Astrid looked at me sideways. Don't worry, I told her with my eyes.

"Niko, we need to think this through," I said.

"What's there to think through? She needs us! Look, look at this picture. There's a man hitting her! We have to get there NOW. Like, tonight!"

He was ranting, a bit.

Mrs. Dominguez edged in.

"Come, kids. We play more football." Her English was a mite better than Ulysses's. She led the kids away, out onto the green. Her older sons helped, drawing the little ones and Luna out onto the field.

Mrs. McKinley joined them, leaving us "big kids"—me, Astrid, Niko, Jake, Alex, and Sahalia—standing next to the picnic

DAY 31

blanket and the remains of the twins' birthday feast. (It featured a package of chocolate-covered doughnuts and a bag of Cheez Doodles.) There had also been some rolls and apples from the "Clubhouse"—that was what everyone called the main building of the resort. It housed the dining hall, the offices, and the rec room.

Astrid, who seemed more pregnant by the minute, had eaten her share, my share, and Jake's share. I loved watching her eat. She could really put it away.

Her stomach looked like it was getting bigger every day. She had definitely "popped," as they say. Even her belly button had popped. It stood out, springy and cheerful, always bouncing back.

When Astrid would let them, the little kids took turns playing with her belly button. I sort of wanted to play with it too, but couldn't bring myself to ask.

Anyway, the little kids didn't need to hear us fight, so I was glad they herded them away. Mrs. McKinley worked hard to arrange this little party and the twins should enjoy it.

Niko's eyes were snapping and there was a little flush of color on his tan face. That only happened when he was really mad—otherwise he's kind of monotone. Straight brown hair, brown eyes, light brown skin.

"I can't believe none of you care," Niko said. "Josie's alive. She should be with us. Instead, she's locked up in that *hellhole*. We have to go get her."

"Niko, she's thousands of miles from here, across the border," I said.

"What about your uncle?" Alex asked. "Once we get in touch with your uncle, maybe he can go get her himself. Missouri's not so far from Pennsylvania, compared with Vancouver."

4

"It won't work," Niko interrupted. "We've got to go get her now. She's in danger!"

"Niko," Astrid said. "You're upset—"

"You don't even know what she did for us!"

"We do, Niko," Alex said. He put a hand on Niko's shoulder. "If she hadn't gone O, we'd be dead. We know that. If she hadn't killed those people, we'd be dead."

"Yeah," Sahalia added. She was wearing a set of painter's coveralls rolled up to the knee, with a red bandanna around her waist. She looked utterly, shockingly cool, as usual. "Whatever we have to do to get her back, we'll do it."

"Fine," Niko spat. He waved us away with his hands, as if to dismiss us. "I'll go alone. It's better that way."

"Niko, we all want Josie free," Astrid said. "But you have to be reasonable!"

"I think Niko's right. He should go get her," Jake announced. "If there's anyone on this black-stained, effed-up earth who can get to her, it's Niko Mills."

I looked at him: Jake Simonsen, all cleaned up. On antidepressants. Working out. Getting tan again. He and his dad were always tossing a football around.

Astrid was so happy about how well he's doing.

My teeth were clenched and I wanted *so* badly to punch him.

"Come on, Jake!" I said. "Don't do that. Don't make Niko think this is possible. He can't cross the border and get to Missouri and break her out of jail!" I continued. "It's crazy!"

"Says Mr. Safe. Says Mr. Conservative!" Jake countered.

"Don't make this about you and me!" I shouted. "This is about Niko's safety!"

"Guys, you have to stop fighting!" Sahalia yelled.

DAY 31

"Yeah, watch it, Dean. You'll go O on us."

I took two steps and was up in his face.

"Don't you ever, EVER talk about me going O again," I growled. His sunny grin was gone now and I saw he wanted the fight as bad as I did.

"You guys are a-holes," Astrid said. She pushed us apart. "This is about NIKO and JOSIE. Not you two and your territorial idiot wars."

"Actually, this is supposed to be a party for the twins," Sahalia reminded us. "And we're ruining it."

I saw the little kids were watching us. Caroline and Henry were holding hands, their eyes wide and scared.

"Real mature, you guys," Sahalia said. "You two had better get it together. You're going to be dads, for God's sake!"

I stalked away.

Maybe Astrid would think I was being childish, but it was either walk away or take Jake's head off.

Niko's uncle's farm was the common daydream that kept Niko, Alex, and Sahalia going. And me and Astrid, too, to a degree.

Niko's uncle lived in a big, broken-down farmhouse on a large but defunct fruit tree farm in rural Pennsylvania. Niko and Alex had schemes for fixing up the farmhouse, reinvigorating the crops. Somehow they thought the farm could house all of us *and* our families *when* and not *if* we found them.

It was a good dream anyway. Unless the farm was overrun with refugees.

6

CHAPTER TWO

JOSIE

I KEEP TO MYSELF.

The Josie who took care of everyone—that girl's dead.

She was killed in an aspen grove off the highway somewhere between Monument and Denver.

She was killed along with a deranged soldier.

(I killed her when I killed the solider.)

I am a girl with a rage inside that threatens to boil over every minute of the day.

All of us here are O types who were exposed. Some of us have been tipped into madness by the compounds.

It depends on how long you were exposed.

I was out there for more than two days, best we can piece together.

Myself, I work on self-control every moment of the waking day. I have to be on guard against my own blood.

DAY 31

I see others allow it to take over. Fights erupt. Tempers flare over an unfriendly glance, a stubbed toe, a bad dream.

If someone gets really out of control, the guards lock them in the study rooms at Hawthorn.

If someone really, really loses it, sometimes the guards take them and they don't come back.

It makes it worse that we're just a little stronger than we were before. Tougher. The cycle of healing, a bit speeded-up. Not so much you notice, but old ladies not using their canes. Pierced-ear holes closing up.

More energy in the cells, is what the inmates say.

They call it the O advantage.

It's our only one.

The Type O Containment Camp at Old Mizzou is a prison, not a shelter.

The blisterers (type A), the paranoid freaks (type AB), and the people who've been made sterile (type B) are at refugee camps where there's more freedom. More food. Clean clothes. TV.

But all of the people here at Mizzou have type O blood and were exposed to the compounds. So the authorities decided we are all murderers (probably true—certainly is for me) and penned us in together. Even the little kids.

"Yes, Mario," I say when he starts to grumble about how wrong it all is. "It's unjust. Goes against our rights."

But every time my fingers itch to bash some idiot's nose in, I suspect they were right to do it.

I remember my Gram talking about fevers. I remember her sitting on the edge of my bed, putting a clammy washcloth on my forehead.

"Gram," I cried. "My head hurts."

I didn't say it aloud, but I was begging for Tylenol and she knew it.

"I could give you something, my baby girl, but then your fever would die, and fever's what makes you strong."

I would cry, and the tears themselves seemed boiling hot.

"A fever comes in and burns up your baby fat. It burns up the waste in your tissue. It moves you along in your development. Fevers are very good, darlin'. They make you invincible."

Did I feel stronger, afterward? I did. I felt clean. I felt tough.

Gram made me feel like I was good through and through and I would never do wrong.

I'm glad Gram is long dead. I wouldn't want her to know me now. Because the O rage comes on like a fever but it burns your soul up. Your body it makes strong and your mind it lulls to sleep with bloodlust and you can recover from that. But after you kill, your soul buckles. It won't lie flat; like a warped frying pan, it sits on the burner and rattles, uneven.

You can never breathe the same way again because every breath is one you stole from corpses rotting, unburied, where you left them to bleed out.

It's my fault that Mario is here in "the Virtues" with me. The Virtues are a quad of buildings with inspiring names: Excellence, Responsibility, Discovery, and Respect, as well as a dining hall and two other dorms, all contained by not one but two chain-link fences, each topped with razor wire. Welcome to the University of Missouri at Columbia, post-apocalypse edition.

I remember when Mario and I first passed through the gates. I wondered what the gates were protecting us *from*. Stupid.

DAY 31

At the screening and sorting, we had placidly submitted to the mandatory blood typing. We had told our story. Mario could have gone to a different camp—he's AB. But he wouldn't leave me.

A tall guard with bright blue eyes and not much hair signed off on us.

He looked at Mario's paperwork.

"You're in the wrong place, old-timer," he told Mario.

"This girl here is my responsibility. We prefer to stay together."

The guard looked us over, nodding his head in a way I did not like.

"You 'prefer,' do you?" he said, pronouncing the words slowly. "Little girl found herself a 'sugar daddy'?"

"Come on now, there's no need to be crass," Mario grouched in his way. "She's fifteen years old. She's a child."

The smile slipped off the guard's face.

"Not in here," he said. "In here she's a threat. I'm going to give you one last chance—you need to go. You think you're being high and mighty, protecting the girl. But this camp ain't no place for an old man like you. You should go."

"I appreciate your concern, but I'll stay with my friend."

I didn't like this. A six-foot-tall bully looking down on frail, elderly Mario like he meant to flatten him, and Mario looking back with undisguised contempt.

I got antsy, started making fists and releasing them. Maybe I shifted from foot to foot.

The guard took hold of my jaw and forced me to look up into his face.

"How long were you out there?" he asked.

"She was out for just a short while," Mario said.

"I DIDN'T ASK YOU, OLD MAN!" the guard shouted.

He tightened his grip on my jaw, gave my head a shake.

"My name's Ezekiel Venger, and I'm one of the head guards here. Now, how long?"

"I don't remember," I said.

He let me go.

"I know you're trouble, Miss Fifteen. I can tell which ones are dangerous. That's why they put me in charge. You better watch yourself. I'm not gonna give you an inch of wiggle room. Not one sorry inch."

"Yes, sir," I said.

I know when to call someone sir.

You call someone sir if you respect him. If he's older than you. If he's in a position of authority. Or if he's got a nightstick and a chip on his shoulder.

Mario is my only friend.

He thinks I am a good person. He's wrong, but I don't argue with him. He tells me he believes in me.

We share a two-person suite with four others. I am not the only one Mario is protecting. He volunteered to sponsor four kids, and this is why they allowed him to be with us up on the second floor of Excellence. All the other suites on the second floor are just women and children.

It's only men on the first floor and it's rough down there.

I share a bed with Lori. She's fourteen. She has brown hair and white skin and huge brown eyes that look so sad sometimes I want to punch her in the face.

She's told me her story. She's from Denver and she and her folks were hiding out in their apartment but they ran out of food. By

DAY 31

the time they made it to the airport the evacuations had begun. They were among the last of the people there so when the rioting began—with people clawing and trampling one another as the sky over Colorado Springs lit up—her mother was killed. Then her father fell between the Jetway and the door of the plane as he shoved her in.

I didn't want to hear her story. I wanted it to fall away from my ears, like beads of water on wax paper, but the words stuck in. Water, water, water. Lori is all water.

Lori lies against me at night and weeps and gets the pillow wet.

I know, I know I should comfort her. It wouldn't take much. What? A pat on the back. A hug.

But there is no compassion left in me.

Like I said, that Josie is dead.

What do I give to her? I give her the warmth of my sleeping body. That's all she can have. Escaping heat.

I should tell you about the other three. Yes, I should name them. Tell you about them and tell you what they look like and their sweet, scared smiles and how Heather looks like Batiste, her oval face very sincere and serious. Half Asian. How one of the boys is always getting words wrong. Nemolade for lemonade. Callerpitter for caterpillar. Bob wire for barbed wire. Cute, innocent, annoying, traumatized. Sweet, demanding, lost, and present. There is nothing I can do for them and I want nothing to do with them.

Every day I wish Mario had not taken them in. The orphan Os.

They were fending for themselves and getting roughed up. I know it was the right thing to do.

There should never have been kids in here in the first place.

As I understand it, the national government brought us here, but the state of Missouri is running the camp. The locals don't want us released, but don't care to pay for us to be properly cared for, either. And the national government has been slow to provide for us.

The result: not enough guards, not enough food, not enough space, not enough medical care. And they won't let us out.

There were petitions circulating, when we first arrived. People trying to get the stable O's separated from the criminal ones. But the guards made life hard for the signature gatherers.

Now we're all just waiting it out.

Every week a rumor drifts through the camp that we're to be released.

The hope is dangerous. Makes you care.

I have to watch out for the men. Some of them are handsy.

I'm not so worried about what they could do to me—I'm worried about what I could do to them.

You do not want to get in trouble.

There was a scuffle a few days ago near the fence. Some reporters got the idea to talk to us about life inside the compound. Were shouting questions to us.

I begged Mario to stay away. But he insisted. He gets all red in the face when he talks about the conditions here. He wants justice and he wants his rights and all I want is to get out of here.

I went over with him, to the gates, because I knew there'd be trouble and there was.

There were maybe twenty inmates standing there, shouting to the dozen or so reporters who were yelling things like

DAY 31

"Do you feel your rights have been violated?"

"Are the rumors of gang violence true?"

"Are you in danger?"

Some of the prisoners shouted answers. Others yelled, "Get us out of here!" and "Contact my uncle so and so! He'll give you a reward!" and "In God's name, help us!"

Then a couple of Humvees came to herd the press away and out came two guards, with their semiautomatic tranquilizer dart guns.

Venger was one of the guards.

I saw delight flash across Venger's face when he saw me and Mario at the fence. The guards waded into the throng of people, pulling them from the fence and pushing them toward the dorms.

"I knew it!" he shouted. "I knew you two were trouble! Nobody *chooses* to be in here!"

Venger pushed through the crowd and grabbed Mario's frail arm.

And VRAAAH, my rage amped up. Like a car getting on the highway, zooming up to speed.

"Don't touch him!" I spat.

He poked me, hard, in the center of my chest with his nightstick.

I grabbed it.

"You little black poodle skank!" he snarled.

Then he raised up his stick to hit Mario. Not me, Mario.

I raised my arm and took the blow to my forearm.

I shoved myself between them and felt Venger's body warm and tall and powerful up against me. And I caught his eye.

I saw euphoria there. The delight of using your body to hurt others. Swinging an arm, breaking a skull.

Venger may be O or he may not be. But he knows the joy of the kill.

Of course, it was a huge mistake, to defy Venger.

I don't know what bothers him most, that I'm young, that I'm a girl, or that I'm black.

But I kept him from cracking the skull of an eighty-year-old man.

Now I'm his favorite target.

DAY 31

CHAPTER THREE

DEAN

I STORMED UP TOWARD THE HOUSING TENTS.

The leaves on the trees that bordered the golf course were in the final stages of falling. Red, gold, and many browns, from ochre to chocolate.

It was hard to stay mad in the presence of that kind of boastful, exuberant natural beauty. But I managed.

"Dean!" Alex called. "Wait up!"

I turned and watched him sprint up the incline to me.

"Jake was really laying it on," he said. "It seems like it's getting worse between you two."

"He's such a jerk!" I said. "He acts like he's still her boyfriend! It's insane."

"I agree," Alex said. He had to walk double-time to match my strides.

"Jake always acts so entitled. Like he deserves her—like I don't."

"But she's really into you, right?" Alex asked me. "Astrid?"

I nodded.

Trust Alex to cut to the chase.

"Yeah," I said. "I think so. I mean, I'm her boyfriend. That's clear. But . . . sometimes I feel like she holds me at a distance."

"That's just her personality though. She's not a real showy kind of person," Alex offered.

"She's not showy at all," I said. And I probably sounded as miserable as I felt.

"Jake's just messing with you. You know that. He sees that you're worried about Astrid and he's playing you."

I shrugged.

"I heard him telling Astrid that he and his dad are going to go back to Texas soon, and saying she should go with them," I told Alex.

"That's harsh."

We walked.

"Look," Alex said. "Remember what Mom always used to say? About, like, manifesting reality?"

I looked at him.

His face was changing, it seemed to me. Growing leaner.

"Yeah," I said.

"Well, think about what you're manifesting with all this fighting and the self-doubt."

"You mean if I spend time worrying about Astrid turning to Jake, she will?" I asked.

"I mean, if you spend a lot of time being *afraid* of it, you could make it happen."

I took that in.

"Because who wants to be with a guy who's afraid all the time, you know what I mean?" he continued.

"Yes," I sighed. "I know exactly what you mean."

DAY 31

"Cheer up," Alex said. "There could be some good surprises headed your way."

He had a kind of a cat-that-ate-the-canary smile lurking around the side of his mouth.

"That'd be a change," I said.

It was good to be alone in Tent J for a while. Well, alone in our five-person cubicle bedroom. The massive tent was divided down its long center by a corridor. Off the corridor were little "rooms" made by low, dividing screens. Two bunk beds stood on either side against the screens, and one single bed was set under the plastic window.

That bed, we had all decided, was Astrid's.

Other orphaned teens were messing around in their rooms, but I had ours to myself—this was the refugee camp definition of alone time.

I wrote in my journal. Always helped.

Maybe a half hour later, Astrid came in, trailed by Jake.

They seemed to be fighting. Good.

"I just want to rest," she told Jake.

Astrid was holding her round belly. Her face was twisted in a grimace of pain.

"What's wrong?" I asked. I sat up too fast and bonked my head on Alex's bunk above me. Jake rolled his eyes.

"It's a pain. Down low. Feels like cramps. I just want to rest," Astrid said.

"I told her she's gotta hustle over to the clinic. They probably have a pill made just for crap like this," Jake said.

"And I told him I'm not going!" Astrid said. "They're taking pregnant women away, Jake. I know they are."

"Astrid, I know you're not supposed to say this to a pregnant lady, but sweetie, you're acting nuts!"

"Jake, I think Astrid just wants to rest," I said. I had my hands out, trying to get them both to calm down.

"How do you explain Lisa?" Astrid fumed.

Astrid had met a few other pregnant women at the camp. They would all get together and talk about swollen ankles, stretch marks, I don't know. Two of them had left suddenly, in the last few weeks. Both of them had been exposed to the compounds back home and now some of the pregnant women had a theory that the government was taking them away for testing.

Conspiracy theories were one thing we had an unlimited supply of in the camp.

"She probably found her relatives and left! People are leaving all the time," Jake said.

"Lisa was my friend. She would have said good-bye," Astrid maintained. "Dean thinks so, too."

"What's important is how you're feeling," I said. I was trying to sidestep the whole issue.

"Exactly," Jake agreed. "You're feeling crampy, so we gotta go over to the clinic."

"I'm not going, Jake. I just need to lay down," Astrid insisted. She dropped down onto her cot.

"If they're taking pregnant women who were exposed, why haven't they come for you already?" Jake asked.

"Let it go, Jake," I said.

"Maybe because two thousand people came on the same day as we did," Astrid continued. "Maybe they lost my file. Maybe it's sitting at the bottom of a stack, but I don't want to call attention to myself."

"So, you're not going to see the doctors here?" Jake asked. "Like ever? What, is Dean going to deliver the baby out on the eighteenth hole?"

DAY 31

He was right. I hated him for being right.

"The baby's not due for another three months," Astrid said. "We'll be somewhere else by then."

Astrid had received a sonogram the first day we arrived. The ultrasound technician had told her that the baby looked really healthy and big for 4 ½ months old. He said the baby's so developed, he thought that Planned Parenthood was wrong when they told Astrid the date of conception and she was more like 6 and ½ months pregnant.

He said the baby would come in January. We had thought it would be in March.

Jake turned to me. "Dean, tell her. She has to go. I mean, come on. You don't buy this 'army taking people away' nonsense, do you?"

Astrid looked at me, her mouth set in a hard line.

"Well . . ." I said. "I met Lisa. She seemed really nice. I think it is a little weird she didn't say good-bye to Astrid. She kept saying she had some maternity clothes she wanted to give her—"

Jake rolled his eyes, scowling in a way that let me know he thought I was whipped.

"And it's Astrid's body," I continued. "I'm not going to put pressure on her to do something she doesn't want to do."

"Geraldine, tell me, do you have any actual opinions of your own?" Jake asked.

"Just because I'm sensitive to Astrid's feelings doesn't make me a woman, Jake!"

"Go away, the two of you," Astrid growled. "Sometimes, I think I'd be better off without the both of you!"

"Fine. Catch you later," Jake said. He walked away.

Astrid shifted on her side, stuffing a pillow under her belly to prop it up.

Seeing the hurt on my face, her steely gaze softened. A little.

"I didn't really mean that," she apologized. "I just . . . I need a nap."

"Okay," I said. I turned to leave.

"Hey," she said. "Number one: Please don't go away mad, and number two: Would you get me a sandwich at dinner?"

I smiled. She smiled back.

"Okay and you bet," I said. I bent down and kissed her on the top of her head.

I had found Alex and Niko strategizing in front of the Clubhouse. I joined in, figuring that the more support I could give to Niko to use diplomatic channels, the better.

At Quilchena, there was a whole office filled with bilingual signage and mild-mannered Canadian social workers who spent the day placing calls and taking calls and scrambling to help us refugees connect with family outside the camp.

I heard a joke here, Q: "How do you get 100 Canadians out of a pool?" A: "Would everyone please exit the swimming pool?"

Funny, because it's true. I'd never seen one of them lose their temper.

But Niko gave the woman we ended up talking to a run for her money. She was a pasty lady named Helene with short hair that was gray at the temples.

"I thought Josie was dead," Niko told Helene. "She was O, and she was off in the woods and I hoped that our friend, Mario, would somehow be able to get her into his shelter, but I didn't really hope."

Niko laid out the newspaper on Helene's desk and pointed to Josie's photograph. "And look, there she is. She's alive and she's trapped in one of those concentration camps!"

DAY 31

"Oh, now, whoa there," Helene said. "concentration camp? That's just not right."

"They rounded up all the Type O's who had been exposed to the compounds and put them in a camp. They're treating them like criminals! We have O's here in Quilchena who've been exposed and you're not segregating them, locking them up."

"Well, that's true."

It was true, but it was also true that they had been forced to take some O's away. People who flew into a rage at the slightest insult, who couldn't stop getting in fights, who couldn't handle the crowds, the lines, the waiting.

"Look at my friend Dean, here. He's O and he was exposed. He's fine."

This made me kind of nervous. It wasn't that I was afraid of them knowing about my past, exactly, but I didn't want to be singled out, either.

Helene gave me a weak smile and a little nod.

She thought for a moment.

"It is certainly not the policy here in Canada to contain people this way, but listen, I will take your case to the review board and I will personally make a case for a transfer for your friend," she told Niko.

"Hey! That's great!" I said. I clapped Niko on the shoulder.

"We just need to fill out some forms, and I'll also need to get a petition slot," Helene told us. "There's a bit of a waiting list for new requests."

"How long?" Niko asked.

"Probably a week or two," Helene said.

"And after that?"

"After that?"

"How long would the transfer take?" Niko asked. He was very quiet then, very calm.

"Another week to ten days to process the transfer."

"Thank you," Niko said. His voice was cold, almost robotic.

"Oh, good," she said. "I was worried that wouldn't be fast enough for you. But it is?"

Niko gave an indistinct nod. "If that's the fastest way . . ."

"It is, short of you and me driving down there and getting her out ourselves!" she joked.

Alex and I exchanged a look.

"Let me get you the forms," Helene said and she scurried out of the room.

Niko looked at us.

"Captain McKinley," he said.

As it happened, the shuttle to the Air Force base was done for the day.

"Sleep on it, Niko," Alex advised him as we walked toward the dining hall. "That's what you always tell me. You need to make a careful plan. Don't go rushing off."

"She's alive, Alex. All this time I thought she was dead. I want to see her. I want to tell her—"

Niko choked up, then corrected his course, getting back to the issue at hand: "Here's my plan—I'm going to go see Captain McKinley and I'm not going to leave his side until he says he'll fly me out of here. When I get to the States, I'll hitchhike."

The hitchhiking was actually the only good part of the plan. It wasn't as dangerous as it used to be. With the gas shortages, it was actually against the law to drive your car with less than three people in it.

Not that we knew, since we were only allowed off the camp in the shuttle bus, but from what I'd read in the papers, it was making for some very weird car rides stateside.

DAY 31

"I'm going to need an air mask," Niko said, thinking. "Do you guys know anyone who has one for barter?"

"Why? For the drifts?" Alex asked, shocked. "Niko, do you think they're real?"

This was the biggest source of gossip and rumor in the camp.

In the last weekly radio address from whatever undisclosed secure location the government of the United States of America was operating out of, President Booker had assured us that as far as he knew, the drifts were just rumors. He said that the military had assured him that the clean-up of the compounds was completed and the Four Corners area was safe. (Burned and bombed into a giant, black desert, but safe.) He promised that if he ever comes to find out there's been some sort of cover-up, he will take swift action.

But then he went back to talking about the efforts to house and feed and clothe the seven million displaced victims of the megatsunami up and down the East Coast, and I got the feeling he just wishes the Four Corners would disappear.

"I can't afford to gamble," Niko told Alex. "I don't know what route I'm going to take. I could get close to the area."

"You don't need to get anywhere near the Four Corners," I broke in. "You stay north, way north, and then dip down to Missouri. They put the camps in those Midwestern cities to keep them far away from the Four Corners. There's no reason for you to—"

"If the drifts are real, and if I run into them, I'm dead meat," Niko said. "So, I'm going to find a mask. It's part of the *careful plan* I'm making."

Niko cast Alex a pointed look and walked away.

"He's not the same," Alex said. "He never used to be like that. Sarcastic?"

I shrugged. "A lot of us are different now."

CHAPTER FOUR

JOSIE

AS HUNGRY AS THEY ARE, THE KIDS ARE SKITTISH AT MEALTIMES. They're scared to go to the dining hall for breakfast. It's called Plaza 900. I don't know why it has the fancy name of Plaza 900. Maybe it's a Missouri in-joke. I'm not from here. I don't know.

"Quiet! Quiet down now!" Mario shouts today. It's Freddy who gets them riled up. Always Freddy, who is sort of unhinged and shrill. Can't settle down. He's like a flea, always jumping and even biting sometimes.

"Settle down, here we go," Mario tells the kids.

Once, of course, Excellence had been a nice dorm. Color scheme of cream and aqua. Flecked carpet and artful paintings on the walls. Like a nice hotel chain.

Now everything that could be pried off the walls has been. There are stains on the walls and the floor—coffee, blood, tobacco spit, urine, who knows.

The men are out already. Now we pass through their hall on the way to the front door.

DAY 31

Design flaw.

We have to go through the first-floor Men's hall to get into the front hall and get outside. The Men's hall is a zoo, these men being more animal now than they ever thought they'd be.

We walk, single file, down the Men's hall, along with the seventy other women, children, and old people from the second floor.

"Stick together now," Mario says, more to offer reassurance to Heather and Aidan than instruction.

"Sssstick together," says a wild-eyed creep, lurching from his room.

Heather screams and the man laughs.

He's smelly and skinny with just a few wisps of hair.

"Back off," I growl.

He sticks his tongue out at me and I can smell his stanky breath. God-awful.

"All right, all right," Mario says. "Out we go."

We step out into the cold, clean morning air and cross the courtyard.

Autumn's in effect and it's getting cold. I feel it as we walk across the deadland stretch of dried grass and cement that is the courtyard.

None of us have real winter clothes. I gave my jacket to Freddy, in a moment of softheartedness, so I now wear the two shirts I have at all times. Along with my dirty jeans and the EZ-on mules that used to belong to Mario's wife. They fit me, almost.

Mario gave his sweater to Lori, perhaps more for safety than for warmth. She's chesty and had only her one paperweight thermal top. She was a little nipply.

I think of all the clothes we used to donate through our church. Where are the cast-off clothes of the free citizens of America? Do they feel no pity for us?

We'd wear anything—doesn't have to fit. Doesn't have to be clean. People would kill, truly kill, for a change of underwear.

The guards give clothing to their favorites. We are nobody's favorites.

So now Mario and I feel the cold, as we head to Plaza 900 for breakfast.

The sky is the color of silt, with a creamy peach band at the horizon. It's the prettiest thing we'll see today, no doubt.

I breathe it in, but the beauty catches in my lungs, like I inhaled a bit of gravel.

"The drifts come in the night, I heard," Heather whispers to Aidan and Freddy, with her lisp on the *s*.

"Wrong," Freddy blurts out. "They LOOK like night. They're black clouds that zoom in."

He darts ahead, arms raised like a vampire's closing in on prey. "And then *BOOM*, they hit a town and everyone's dead."

Lori scoffs, "That's not how the compounds work, Freddy."

"Says you," he snorts. "I was out there, too, you know."

"Shut it, you two," Mario says. "Those drifts are rumors, nothing more. Josie and I saw the bombs go off. They blasted those compounds out of the air. Right, Josie?"

The kids look to me.

I shrug.

Mario keeps trying to get me to talk to them, to take interest.

I think he thinks it would be good for me.

I stuff my hands in my pockets.

"Can I go ahead?" I ask. "It's cold."

"Nope," Mario says. "We stick together. That's what we do."

As if. As if this little band of kids could ever matter in the face of this hellish prison. As if this little group of kids is any kind of group at all.

DAY 31

We go in together.

"Find a table, kids. Lori, take Heather by the hand," Mario says. "Josie and I will bring the eats."

He has to talk loud over the bedlam.

(Because Mario is officially the sponsor to all of us, he works the system a bit. According to the rules, the little kids should stand in line with us. But he waves their passes and they don't have to brave the lines, which can get rough. Also the ladies serving the food have a soft spot for Mario. No surprise there— he's the only nice person in the whole camp, salty as he can be.)

Even without the fights and the brawls that inevitably break out (we're all type O, after all), the sound of six hundred–plus people eating and talking and clattering their silverware always gives me a headache and an anxious knot in my stomach.

The kids go off to find a table in the corner and Mario and I get on line.

I keep my eyes on the floor. That's the best way not to engage.

Before the disaster, Plaza 900 was probably a very cool place to be. Luxurious, even with different food stations scattered in the giant hall. From the signage, you can see that before it was Pizza Time! Or diners could have Zen Gen Sushi, or Tío's Burritos or Omelets Your Way!

They all serve the same dishes now: Everyone Eats Oatmeal! And for lunch, Always Soup! And for dinner, Eternal Spaghetti!

They serve us in shifts.

Excellence and Responsibility eat from 6–7 a.m.

Discovery and Respect eat from 7–8 a.m.

Gillett and Hudson from 8–9 a.m.

There is pushing in the food lines, and fighting. Every meal. Over oatmeal. (Actually the fighting isn't over the oatmeal, but over the sugar we get to put on the oatmeal. Two packets apiece and people are always accusing one another of taking more.)

We get in line.

I'm shoved. I take no notice. Mario's shoved. My head goes up.

"Good morning, Mr. Scietto," comes a voice from behind.

It's Carlo. The leader of the Union Men, one of the three gangs of idiots that vie for control of the Virtues.

One's all Latinos and is run by a guy named Lucho. There's the Clubbers out of the Discovery dorm. They have clubs they hit people with. They also have a way with words.

And the one based in our dorm calls itself the Union, and its members are called Union Men.

I don't want to take them seriously. I want to blow them off, pretending that they are just men playing at being hoodlums. But they hurt people.

Sometimes they hurt people in public. While the guards look away.

Carlo puts his hand on one of Mario's thin arms.

My blood amps up for a fight, immediately.

The sounds from the rest of the room seem to dim and my sight somehow takes in only Carlo, and the three Union Men with him. One broad, one tall, one teenager.

"It's time for you to start paying your share," Carlo murmurs. He's dark-skinned. Shaved head. Has watery brown eyes and a calm, dignified "comportment" that seems fashioned after some Bond villain. He almost speaks with a British accent.

He wears a mostly clean button-down shirt every day, tucked into tight black jeans. A mostly clean shirt takes a lot of resources here.

"You're holding up the line," Mario grumbles.

"Mario Scietto, you're a mystery to me. Do you know who gives us tribute? Do you? The old and the weak," Carlo says.

DAY 31

"Maybe you should look in a mirror, Scietto," says the teenager. He has a thin, wispy mustache and the teeth of a smoker.

"Brett's right," Carlo says. "You truly fit the description. Both old and weak. And those kids rely on you. Mr. Scietto, what if something happened to you?"

"Leave us alone," I choke through gritted teeth.

"Oooh," Carlo purrs. "She speaks. We were beginning to think you were a mute, little sister."

"I've heard her talk," says the homely Brett guy.

I have no memory of him whatsoever.

"Someone tried to take a towel away from one of her brats and she nearly took his head off."

I do remember the jerk who'd tried to snatch one of our two towels from Heather, but I have no memory of this Brett.

"Yeah," he continues. "She's feisty."

I hate that word. It's used to describe any woman with an opinion.

"Move the LINE!" some deranged someone shouts from behind us.

I push forward, taking Mario gently by the shoulder, trying to move him away from the Union Men, but they push through the milling people to catch up with us.

We put our trays on the line and the cafeteria workers set out bowls for us.

"You got four little ones, right, *mi amor*?" the lady asks Mario.

"Good morning, Juanita. Yes. There are six of us total."

Juanita spoons the porridge into six bowls and starts sliding them across the glass to us.

"All we want today is a percentage of your rations, Mario," Carlo says, lifting a bowl off Mario's tray. God knows what they would want tomorrow.

"That's not for you, *pendejo!*" Juanita bellows.

"It's okay," Mario tells the serving lady. "I'm not hungry today."

Juanita slips me our twelve sugars as Mario and I move forward. I put them in my pocket.

We push past the Union Men. I see the kids at a table in the corner. They look small and scared as usual.

"And I'll take those sugars." Carlo holds out his hand.

"Go to hell," I say.

Carlo steps close and puts his foul-smelling face up in mine.

"We're already there, sweetmeat," Carlo murmurs.

"Give him the sugars, Josie," Mario directs. "Go on, now."

BAM, BAM, BAM goes my heart. Oh, the bloodlust is up and I want to hurt Carlo. I could hurt him so much. And Brett. Entitled, arrogant idiots. Hurt them both.

And I see Mario there, standing next to me, a light, God help me, shining in his eyes.

I take our sugars, most of them anyway, and shove them into Carlo's hand.

"See? She knows what's good for her," the creep Brett says with a smile.

He slides his hand onto my hip and pulls me to his body.

"We got a table, Uncle Mario!" chirps Heather, pushing through the crowd to us.

I see Lori standing, craning her neck, watching us anxiously.

"Come on," Heather insists. I follow Mario as Heather leads us away.

"Don't worry, Uncle Mario," Carlo calls. "You're under our protection now."

Mario's hands shake with the tray.

He glances at me and sees my expression.

"Never mind," he says. "One less bowl of mush. Big whoop."

DAY 31

"We need the food," I say.

"We do what we gotta do to stay safe," he murmurs. "Heck, maybe it'll do us some good."

I let him think that and I swallow down what I know to be true: give in to a bully and he always wants more.

CHAPTER FIVE

DEAN

WE LIKE TO EAT EARLY, ALL TOGETHER. IT'S FUNNY HOW QUICKLY we found a routine here—all the refugees have. When your life is utter chaos, you cling to little things like sitting at the same spot at dinner each day. Fistfights have broken out about the seating. I'm not kidding. Alex and I found the group at our regular table.

The little kids were writing and drawing. Who knows how Mrs. McKinley got hold of the construction paper and markers. They keep saying they're going to set up classes for the kids, but everything's still in a state of flux.

"How do you spell 'celebrity'?" Chloe asked as we sat down.

I told her and leaned over to read her letter: "Luna is famous here. Everyone loves her so much. Becawse I walk her I am basically a selle . . ."

"We're writing letters and doing drawings for Batiste!" Max said, his cowlick bobbing like a rooster's comb.

DAY 31

Batiste is at a refugee camp in Calgary. We found him at the listings. Every day, they update these thick notebooks filled with old-fashioned computer printouts with a record of the refugees at each camp. People line up for hours to pore over them, hoping to find a loved one. It felt so good to see his name printed on the register. He's there with his mother and father. I'm glad for him. We all are.

Ulysses's picture showed a family playing on green grass under a blue sky.

Max's drawing was of a boy with spiky yellow hair, sitting on some kind of a car, being pushed by a taller figure. The boy was crying—big tears drawn as blue dashes shooting out of his eyes.

Caroline was drawing big circle people sitting at a campfire and Henry was just sitting on his mother's lap, twirling her hair around his index finger.

"See, this is us around the fire at Greenway," Caroline said. "Remember when Uncle Jake made us s'mores and cowboy soup?"

Henry nodded, serious. "That was fun."

Max held up his drawing and I saw he had added red over the child's black boots.

"This is me when Niko was pushing me in that stroller just before we got to the bus station," he told me.

Jeez, I had missed a lot, holed up in the Greenway.

"That was a good stroller," Max said wistfully.

Ulysses showed me his picture.

"This is us now," he said with his beautiful no-front-tooth grin.

"Batiste is going to be psyched," I told them.

Alex took a piece of paper and started to write a letter.

"You're writing, too?" Caroline said, happy.

"Of course. Batiste is my family, too."

"Just like all of us?" she asked.

"Yup," Alex said, nodding.

Caroline looked to Chloe. "I told you, Chloe. We're all family now. For real. Not 'just a saying.'"

She shrugged. "Whatevs."

Sahalia came up with her tray and I watched the smile hit Alex's face. It was bright, unprotected.

Aaah. Made me nervous for him. Sahalia's not always been the most dependable person.

But the wattage on her smile equaled his. That was good. Very good.

"Dean," Max said, pushing a piece of paper toward me. "Can you concentrate a story for me?"

"How do you mean, concentrate?"

"Well," Max began. "This one time I asked my mom to write down a letter to my uncle Mack who was in the pen, doing five to ten for salting batteries. I wanted to tell him about how I was sitting out in the car at Emerald's, waiting on my dad because he had some business arrangements to straighten out and I wasn't allowed to go in there anymore on account of all the G-strings.

"Anyway I was just sitting there, doing my multiplication tables homework when a cop car glides in, real quiet.

"And I see a cop get out, walking over to a car that's way over at the end of the parking lot and he's moving real slow and suddenly he opens the door and an actual lady, a mom I actually knew, fell right out on the asphalt. It was my used-to-be best friend Channing's mom and she didn't have any pants on!"

DAY 31

Sahalia laughed out loud and then buried her face against Alex's shoulder.

Max continued.

"It turned out Channing's mom was doing lap dances on the side. And that's illegal! So she got arrested into the cop car and the man she was sitting on was, too."

"Oh boy," said Mrs. McKinley.

"What's a lap dance?" Henry asked.

"Max, sweetie, I'm not sure this story is for little ears," Mrs. McKinley said.

I wanted to tell her that Max's stories never are, but he held up his hand, holding her off, and barreled on.

"So anyways, I wanted to tell all that, about what I saw to my uncle Mack, because he used to hang around Channing's mom a lot and sometimes buy her things like baby diapers and stuff when she ran out. So I told that whole story to my mom and she was supposed to be writing it down and she only wrote one sentence on the paper. And I said to her, 'Mom, why didn't you write down my story?' and she says, 'I did, hun. I just concentrated it.'"

"What did she write, your mom?" asked Henry.

"She just wrote, 'Natalia Fiore got arrested for prostitution.'"

He shrugged.

"Huh," I said. "And what story did you want me to concentrate?"

"The story of what happened to us!" Max said. "So Batiste will remember us."

He tapped the paper, like I should get to work.

I looked at him, his blue eyes sparkling and ready to roll.

"You know what, Max? That would take me a really long time to write."

"You're a good writer. It won't take too long."

"How do you know I'm a good writer?"

"You better be. You write in your journal every day!" Max exclaimed.

"Hey, do you write about me in your journal?" Chloe demanded.

"I do," I told her.

"Do you write good stuff or bad stuff?" she asked, her mouth set in an expectant curl.

"About you? Only good."

"Will we be in the story, too?" Caroline wanted to know.

"I'm sure you'll all be in the story," Mrs. McKinley said. She kissed Caroline on the top of the head. "Now it's time to put the markers and papers away and go get our trays."

Back in Tent J, I handed Astrid the meatloaf-on-a-roll sandwich I'd managed to smuggle out under my sweatshirt.

Watching her face light up was worth the glaze stain I now had on the inside of my shirt.

"Mmm," she said, digging in. "Thanks."

I handed her the apple I'd pocketed as well.

"Apple a day . . . ," I said.

Slightly lame, but I wasn't entirely sure where I stood with her.

"I'm sorry about me and Jake," I apologized. "I know it drives you crazy when we fight like that."

She waved it away with her sandwich.

"Do you think I'm being ridiculous?" she asked after she took a sip of water.

She looked up at me.

When she looked at me like this, when she really focused on me, it made me shy for a moment. She was so smart and so perceptive, I felt like she could see right through me.

DAY 31

How could someone as beautiful as she was like me at all? Would she ever feel the same reckless love that I felt for her? The do-anything kind of love?

"Do you think I'm being ridiculous?" she repeated.

I looked away.

"You know that woman, the one from the line?"

I nodded.

"I've looked for her every day. At the listings, in the Clubhouse, I've never seen her again."

"You think they took her away," I said.

Astrid nodded, her blue eyes wide with fear.

I remembered the woman.

We had been on line for breakfast.

It was a really beautiful morning, the Clubhouse was filled with the scent of maple syrup and Astrid was being funny.

"How's my hair?" she asked me.

I had given her possibly the worst haircut in the history of personal grooming back at the Greenway when we all got lice. Sahalia had since done her best to shape it up. But still . . . Astrid now basically had a blond faux-hawk, a style from around 2002 that our old barber had always tried to sell me and Alex on. Some of Astrid's hair curled but in other places it just frizzed out.

"You look like a deranged baby chick," I told her.

"Nice," she said. She ran her hand through the blond mess of it. "Don't you know you're supposed to flatter pregnant women shamelessly."

"I meant, a beautiful, radiant, deranged baby chick," I said. "Obviously."

Astrid winked at me and pulled on the knit green ski cap I'd given her back at the Greenway.

"Maybe it's better for everyone if I wear this," she said.

"Yeah, I think it's for the best," I agreed.

We put our trays on the metal serving table and slid forward. Suddenly I was jostled from behind. Pushed aside and some woman was grabbing for Astrid.

"Barbie! Barbs?" the woman was saying, her voice frantic.

She was thin, maybe in her twenties, with blond hair. Wearing a baggy sweater.

The woman spun Astrid around.

She looked at Astrid's face and gave a cry.

"I'm sorry," she said. "I thought you were my sister."

"It's okay," Astrid said kindly. "I think we all hope to find our lost family members here—"

"No!" the woman moaned. "It's not that. It's not like that at all!"

The woman kind of slumped and swayed. I put my hand on her shoulder.

"Are you okay?" I asked. She seemed like she might faint.

"Come over here." I led her to a table and sat her down.

Astrid sat down next to the woman and took her hand.

"I saw your belly and I thought you were my sister Barbie," the woman said.

"Where did you see her last?" I asked, expecting her to say Castle Rock or Denver or Boulder.

"At the medical center," she said. "Just two days ago. She had some pains and she went in to be checked and they took her!"

"Took her where? To a hospital?" I asked.

"I don't know! These men from the US government went and talked to her and told her she was needed in the States for medical testing. But she wouldn't go. She was scared to leave me and she said she just wanted to stay here."

DAY 31

Astrid's breathing was speeding up. I saw her put a hand to her throat, absentmindedly.

"What does she look like, your sister?" Astrid asked.

"She's thin, like you, and is carrying the same way. But she's a brunette."

"Does she wear an eyebrow ring?" Astrid asked.

The woman nodded.

"Oh my God, I know her! She's in my pregnancy group."

"When we woke up in the morning, she wasn't in our tent!" The woman went on. "I think they just took her. She said they were asking her all kind of questions about the time she was exposed to the compounds. It was only for a few minutes. I was there, with her. We're both type AB. We were only exposed for a few minutes before my husband found us and got us back inside. Why would they take her?!"

"Ooh, I don't feel good," Astrid said. She was wheezing now.

"And now no one will talk to me or tell me anything!" the woman said, nearly shouting now.

"I need air. I can't breathe," Astrid gasped.

It was a panic attack. I'd seen her have them before.

"I'm sorry," the woman said. "God, I'm sorry. I didn't mean to upset you—"

But we were moving away from her then, Astrid leaning on me and me telling people to get out of our way.

It *was* scary. But . . .

But the woman had said she was type AB—that's the blood type that suffers from paranoid delusions when exposed to the compounds.

That fact made it hard to give her full credit. She seemed a little crazy, was acting a little crazy. I'd assumed she was a little crazy.

But Astrid had assumed she was telling the truth.

It was a little tricky, knowing what to say to her.

"I know you're scared," I said. Wrong thing to say. Astrid's eyes blazed.

"It's not that I'm scared, Dean. It's that I believe they are taking pregnant women who've been exposed away for testing. And I don't want to be taken away."

"We're in a bind." I tried to reason with her. "Because, eventually, you're going to have to go to the clinic. Even if it's just for your checkup."

She shrugged and turned her attention back to the meatloaf sandwich.

"How are you feeling? Are the cramps better?"

"Yeah," she said. "It just happens when I'm stressed out. I'm too hopped up. Sometimes I can't get myself to calm down."

"I get that same way. It's why I get so out of control with Jake. This energy comes up in me out of nowhere."

"I know exactly what you mean," Astrid agreed.

We were getting along again. It was a relief, and I should have let it be, but I pushed it.

"When Jake edges me on like that, it's not cool!" I said. "He's always pushing me, trying to make me lose my temper."

It was like a shutter closed behind her eyes.

"Don't talk about Jake," she snapped. "I'm sick of you both putting each other down to me all the time. It's exhausting."

Oh, so Jake was putting me down to her? I'd suspected but now I knew.

And before I could tell myself to chill out, I realized my hands were in fists.

I looked over to Astrid and she was watching me.

I shrugged. "I'm sorry," I said.

Her eyes flitted away, as if she was embarrassed by what she was seeing in me.

DAY 31

"Well, thanks for standing up for me, even if you think I'm being paranoid," she said. She bit into the apple.

"Do you want to go for a walk before lights out?" I asked.

She shook her head.

"Hey!" Sahalia called. She and Alex were making their way toward us through the bunks. She held up a guitar.

The Canadians had distributed a few musical instruments this way—and sometimes little jam sessions broke out, which was amazingly nice, actually.

Other teens and kids were returning from dinner all around us. Some of them seemed really nice—some of them seemed rotten—just like you'd expect of any group of kids.

But I'd not made friends with a single one.

I didn't want any new people to worry about—I had my family of friends.

"It's my night with the guitar!" Sahalia said happily. "Is there anything you want to hear?"

"Do that Jamaican song!" Alex requested.

Sahalia rolled her eyes.

"You have the worst taste in music," she teased.

"You're the one who knows the song!" Alex replied, grinning. "If it's so bad, why did you memorize it?"

Sahalia launched into an old reggae song, "No Woman, No Cry." It had been one of our dad's favorites.

Had Alex told that to Sahalia? Had they started to share personal stuff with each other from the past?

Astrid got under her covers, clothes and all. She watched Sahalia playing. Her face relaxed.

Kids from all around us were listening, too.

Seriously, the Canadians were genius.

Sahalia played a couple more songs, but was interrupted

when Niko came over and practically threw himself down on his cot.

"I tried to get to the base. Stupid guards wouldn't call a shuttle for me. I said I'd walk and they threatened to arrest me!"

"Hey, Niko," Alex called. "You have to hear this new song Sahalia wrote."

"Alex, no!" Sahalia groaned. A smiling groan.

"Come on, you have to. It's so good, you guys."

"It's kind of personal," Sahalia said.

"What is there about you to know that we don't already, Sasha," Astrid teased. "I mean, really!"

Sahalia looked around at the four of us.

"Okay, if you really want to hear it."

She clearly wanted to play it for us and wanted us to make her play it for us.

"We do," I said.

"We really do," repeated Astrid. She gave me a smile. Thank God.

Sahalia started to play. The song was slow and thrumming with a steady rhythm, really pretty. And the words broke my heart.

He says there is a place
He says that there'll be light
I know not to trust a boy
But I think he's all right.

He says that we'll be safe
He says they take in strays
I don't believe in God
But I listen when he prays.

DAY 31

Let there be a place that's good.
A green oasis in a hidden wood.
Take us far out of harm's way
And find us shelter so that we all may
Stay together.

He says we have to hope
He says we must not fear
He doesn't know I'm fine
Just as long as he is near.

Let there be a dream come true.
A broke-down farmhouse on a shaded lane.
Take us far out of harm's way
And find us shelter so that we all may
Stay together.
Together.
Together.

A stillness fell in our corner of the tent. All the kids around us had stopped to listen to Sahalia's raw, raspy, beautiful voice.

When she finished, everyone burst into applause.

"That's a really good song! You wrote it?" I asked.

She nodded, blushing. Alex was all red in the face, too. Man, they had it bad.

"Sahalia, that song could go on the radio in a heartbeat," Astrid gushed. "You guys should make a video for it someday."

It was nice to see Astrid so excited.

"Niko, did you hear how it's about your uncle's farm?" Alex asked.

Niko nodded.

He was looking up at the roof of the tent.

"Didn't you like that part so much?" Alex wanted Niko to join in.

"I liked the part where it says we're supposed to stay together," Niko said.

Then he turned his back on us.

DAY 31

CHAPTER SIX

JOSIE

"DADDY! DADDY! DAAAAAAADDY!" LORI SCREAMS.

"Shut up." I elbow her in the ribs.

She sits up, taking the whole blanket with her. Her breathing is jagged and full of sobbing to come, like a ripe thundercloud waiting to spill.

I slide off the bed and stalk into the bathroom.

Our two towels are dirty but I'd rather sleep on the floor with them than with broken-up Lori.

Under the bluish LED lighting, my skin is the color of gunmetal.

Back a million years ago, I used to be proud of the color of my skin. The glow, the depth and light in it. And smooth—never a blemish, never a scar.

Who is that girl in the mirror now?

Sunken cheeks, dark blackish circles under my eyes, and creases on either side of my mouth. Scar on my forehead from the ancient bus crash.

My hair is tied up in my knots, but it's dirty, dirty, and if I don't get a hold of some shampoo soon and a comb, it'll just dread into two clumps.

I look like a zombie avatar of myself.

I think of Brayden, so handsome. That jaw of his and how I liked to push my face into his neck, and feel his stubble. It was a fling, and I know we were only together because we were trapped in a store, but still, it was thrilling to be with someone so ruggedly gorgeous.

I think about Niko, with his utter seriousness. Almost unable to be lighthearted, even for a moment. And who so believed he loved me.

I loved him, too. Maybe at times I felt smothered by his adoration. But I did love him, too, I did.

Maybe the only kind of love that can thrive now is a desperate, crushing love.

Anyway, it's lost now.

Did he make it? Did the kids make it?

I do not allow myself to think about them.

I might as well throw myself off a cliff.

I open the medicine cabinet. There are two old Q-tips, stuck to the metal with yellow residue. A safety pin lying askew to its rusted shadow.

What was I hoping for? Nobody snuck in and put a pair of scissors there.

But if they had I would take off my knots.

Maybe I'd take off my face.

(See, 0, 0, 0 is rising and begging for release.)

Sometimes I ask God if I should kill myself.

I ask Him to send me a sign.

Am I asking Him to send me a sign as I stand there, staring into the empty glass?

DAY 31

I don't remember, but Lori appears in the mirror. The ghost of Lori. Standing behind me and shivering, miserable in her stupid thin thermal.

"I'm sorry," she says. "Please come back."

"Can't sleep without me?" I ask, as mean as I feel.

She shrugs. She runs her hands over her goose-bump arms.

"Do what you want. I'm just trying to be nice," she says.

I know I'm hurting her with my callousness and indifference. Sometimes it feels good to hurt someone.

She shuffles back to our mattress and naked pillow and our charity blanket and grubby, coarse bottom sheet.

Rising in my throat is an apology and the tears to wash it out of me.

I'm sorry, Lori, that you have nightmares.

I'm sorry your daddy died getting you on that plane.

I'm sorry they locked up all the Os together—you don't deserve to be here.

I'm sorry that I have nothing for you or the others.

I am sorry about the dead.

I am sorry I am the dead.

I swallow my apology and go back to bed.

My feet are like ice.

I don't let them touch her.

CHAPTER SEVEN

DEAN

AT DAYBREAK A SOUND WOKE ME UP. IT WAS NOT THE KIND OF sound you want to wake up to: the sound of your girlfriend stifling a moan into her pillow.

I slid out of bed. My feet made the platform floor squeak.

"Cramps?" I asked her.

"Yeah," Astrid said. "Not as bad as yesterday, though."

The paleness of her face made me pretty sure she was lying.

"I know you don't want to go, but I really think we should go to the clinic."

"I know," she said.

I leaned in and kissed her. Little tears were pooling at the corners of her eyes.

"Do you really think it's safe to go?" she asked me. She sat up. Her hair was poking all over with its wayward curls.

"I was thinking, what if we just give them a fake name? We could say you've just arrived. You're not in the system . . ."

DAY 32

"Yeah," she said. "Maybe. But what if they recognize me from before. What if it's the same guy?"

"You could say you prefer a woman? You're shy?"

"That's a good idea. Yeah." She smiled, then grimaced. "It hurts."

"Let's go."

"Dean," she said. "Thank you. I know I'm not always as, like, girly or gushy or girlfriendy as somebody might want. But the way you take care of me, it means a lot to me. I just wanted to say that."

That made me feel great. It wasn't quite "I love you forever," but I guess that was her point. She wasn't that kind of girl.

I put my hand on Niko's arm.

He was instantly wide-awake.

"Hey, I just wanted to tell you—Astrid's not feeling well so we're going over to the clinic."

"Okay."

"When we get back, I'm going to help you figure out about Josie."

"Okay."

"I didn't want you to think I forgot."

He nodded.

The early-early birds were up and headed to the Clubhouse for breakfast. We saw them crossing the greens, alone and in small groups. Rising early was a good way to beat the lines.

The field hospital was housed in a series of tents behind the Clubhouse.

Alex had found out these tents were made by a Canadian company called Weatherhaven that had a manufacturing plant right here in Vancouver. It explained why the tents were so new and nice.

In the first tent, we had to register to get an appointment. A pleasant-faced woman sat behind a desk. An old-fashioned desktop computer took up a good portion of the space. Wires ran out of the back and down onto the floor, where they snaked back across the floor, collecting into a rubber tube. Hard-wired into the system. Very quaint.

She handed us a clipboard with several sheets of paper. A ballpoint pen swung off a string.

For whatever reason, Network coverage up here in Vancouver was nonexistent. We'd been told about some new WiFi systems being rigged up in other places, but here at Quilchena, it was a computer with a hard line or it was good old pen and ink.

We sat down with a couple other early stragglers. One woman was clutching her jaw and groaning. An older man had his arm in a cast and watched us with suspicion.

Maybe it was because Astrid's hand was shaking as she filled in all the blanks on the form. She filled them with lies. Mostly lies.

Name: Carrie Blackthorn (Carrie was the name of her first pet—a bunny. And Blackthorn was her mother's maiden name.)
Social Security or Taxpayer ID number: 970-89-4541 (The first nine numbers of her home phone number.)
DOB: 07-04-2007 (The Fourth of July of the real year she was born.)
For Previous Address, she put her best friend's house.
For Intake (this meant the day we were entered into the system at Quilchena), she put the day before.
Then she got into the medical data—previous surgeries,

DAY 32

immunizations, etc., etc., and for all that stuff she told the truth.

Chief complaint (that was the reason we were there): cramping. Approx 28 weeks pregnant.

"If they ask, I'm your fiancé," I said as she finished the forms.

"*What?*" she asked, with her eyebrow cocked to the heavens.

"In case they won't let me in with you. Because I'm just a boyfriend."

"Okay," she said, in a slightly "whatever" tone of voice.

"Never mind," I said.

Why couldn't I keep my mouth shut? Why couldn't I ever be cool?

The woman took Astrid's forms and typed them into her computer.

"Oh dear," she said. "I don't have your number in the system."

"Ugh. They had the same problem yesterday," I told her. "When we got in, at the registration. The lady said she'd try to sort it out and we should come back today to see."

"Can we see someone anyway?" Astrid said. "I'm scared for the baby."

The woman studied Astrid with a kind look on her face.

"Here's what we'll do. I'm going to have one of the nurses take a look at you. Tomorrow, or later today, once the paperwork is all settled, I want you to come back and book a proper appointment. They'll do a physical, blood work, the whole thing."

She picked up a telephone.

"Sylvia, I'm sending a young couple to you. Could you ask Kiyoko to take a quick look?"

After she hung up she turned back to us.

"Kiyoko's one of my favorites. She used to be a labor and delivery nurse. She's your gal."

We went back outside with directions to Tent 18. The tents were laid out in a grid, very orderly. Tent 18 had rows of examining tables standing against the walls. Cabinets with medical supplies and equipment stood between the tables, separating them into little examination cubicles. Each cubicle had a white curtain that could be drawn for privacy.

A woman in fatigues saw us.

"You here to see Kiyoko?" she asked us.

We nodded.

"Come this way. I'm going to put you in a cube with an ultrasound machine."

In the exam cubicle Astrid and I stood there uneasily. I could see why the idea of coming here had made her uneasy. It was all very organized and efficient—but it was also very military. I felt strange, standing there in my dirty sweatshirt and jeans. Like I was messing the place up.

The curtain whisked open and we both jumped.

"Hello, Carrie?" a Japanese woman in scrubs asked Astrid in a thick accent. She was tall, with wire-rimmed glasses and a ponytail.

"What seems to be the problem?"

Astrid explained about the cramps.

Kiyoko read her intake form.

"Only twenty-eight weeks?" she asked.

"I think so," Astrid said.

"Let's have a look." She helped Astrid lie back onto the examining table. Astrid lifted up her shirt.

Her belly was taut and improbably round, like a dwarf watermelon. Pink stretch marks lined the area under the belly near her hips. I hadn't noticed them before. They ran in messy parallel lines, like indistinct claw marks.

DAY 32

"Mmph, baby's growing fast," the nurse noted, pointing to the stretch marks. "Skin can't stretch fast enough."

She took out a tube and squeezed a clear gel onto Astrid's belly.

"Are you the daddy?" she asked me.

I didn't know what to say.

I decided on yes.

Astrid reached out her hand to me. That was nice.

The nurse put a handheld wand on Astrid's skin and the screen of the ultrasound machine came to life.

In shades of green, shapes moved around the screen and I had no idea what we were seeing. Blobs moving and then Kiyoko pointed to the screen.

"Here's baby's heart," she said. She clicked a mouse on the computer attached to the screen and took a measurement of the beating shape.

We could hear it, too.

"This is the coolest thing I've ever seen," I blurted out.

Astrid squeezed my hand. She looked so proud and relieved.

"Baby's fine," Kiyoko said. "Do you want to know the sex? Boy or girl?"

"No," Astrid and I said at the same time.

"Mmph," she grunted. This seemed to be a part of her vocabulary, this strange little mmph. It conveyed "Yes, I see," and also, "Maybe."

The screen moved with the wand. As she traced it over Astrid's belly, the image changed. I thought I was seeing things I could recognize, arms, legs, but who knows.

"Here's the face," the nurse said. "Look, Mama. The face of your baby."

There it was, in silhouette.

"It's a real baby. It's a real baby in there," I said like an idiot.

"I know. It's beautiful, isn't it?" Astrid asked me.

I nodded, awed by the glowing swimmer on the screen.

"This baby is big," Kiyoko said. "You were exposed to compounds?"

"No," Astrid choked out. "Never."

"Mmph," she said. "I think maybe so. Your uterus is small, but the baby is big. Growing too fast."

"No," Astrid said.

"These cramps. The body is surprised by the baby. Growing so fast."

"We're from Telluride," I lied. "The compounds never reached us. But we had to evacuate anyway. We had to leave everything behind." That was the story of a teenage boy I'd met in our tent.

"My mom said I was a really big baby," Astrid protested.

It struck me that she was afraid of the baby being too big.

"Mmph," Kiyoko said. She wasn't making eye contact with us now. She was making notes on "Carrie's" file. "US government's doing study on pregnant women. They pay well."

"I'd never let them do tests on me," Astrid said. Her voice was cold.

"Lots of women say this. But when they learn more, they change their mind. Very good money. Low risks."

"They're taking people away against their will," Astrid said. I tried to tell her to stay quiet with my eyes.

"For you, you need rest, okay, Mama? Take rest. Take vitamins."

Nurse Kiyoko wrote a prescription on a pad. I thought only doctors could do that, but maybe things were different in Canada.

"Vitamin D. This will help."

Around this moment we heard a shrill voice yelling outside the tents. A kid.

DAY 32

"I will just check dilation, next, mmph," Kiyoko continued, but we hardly heard her.

"Astrid?" came the voice outside the tent. Jesus, it was Chloe. "Astrid? Dean? Where are you?"

She had to be right outside the tent.

"Chloe! What's wrong?" I yelled.

What had happened? My heart was up in my throat in an instant.

"Where are you?" I shouted.

"Where are *you*?!" Chloe snapped back.

I stepped out of the curtain in the main passage of the tent and saw her pass by outside the open door. She had something in her hand.

"Chloe!" I yelled.

She stepped in, pushing right past the nurse in fatigues.

"Oh my God, guess what?!" she gushed. "We're FAMOUS! Like really, really famous!"

Chloe held up a newspaper.

"Alex wrote a letter to a newspaper and they printed it and it tells our whole story, about how close we were to NORAD and everything!" She glanced at Kiyoko. "Hi."

There was a slugline reading: THE MONUMENT 14.

"That's really cool," I tried to cover. "We'll read it all together with the others back at the tent. We're in the middle of something here—"

Chloe didn't even hear me. She barreled on.

"Look, it's all about us and how we made it from Monument to Denver and about Mrs. Wooly and everything. Astrid, look, here's the part about you."

Chloe pointed to a paragraph.

"Now's not the time," Astrid said. She pulled her shirt down, getting the gel all over it.

I helped her off the table.

Kiyoko took the newspaper from Chloe.

"But it tells our whole story! About the compounds and the black cloud and how the others went to Denver in a bus and came back for us. And now anyone can find us. Everyone can know where we are!" Chloe exclaimed. "It's how our parents will find us!"

"Let's go read it outside," I said. I took the paper from Nurse Kiyoko. "Thanks again for everything."

She looked pissed.

"Lying to a nurse is very bad," Kiyoko said sternly. "Pregnant women, exposed to compounds, need special care."

I grabbed Astrid's arm and steered her away from her.

"I don't need special care. I'm fine," Astrid said.

We were at the door to the tent now.

"You guys! You should be happy!" Chloe complained, trailing behind us. "I thought you'd be psyched."

"Wait!" Kiyoko called. She turned around and called for the other nurse. "You need to tell me the truth! And we need to do some tests."

We sped away from the medical tents as fast as we could.

"I still don't understand why you're not excited!" Chloe whined.

Astrid turned around and grabbed Chloe by both arms.

"I didn't want them to know my real name!" she snapped.

"Why?" Chloe asked. "That doesn't even make sense? I mean, how am I supposed to know that?"

We left her behind.

"You know, Alex and Sahalia were really psyched about the letter. They kept it a secret and everything."

We were headed toward, I don't know where. Away from Chloe.

"Try a little gratitude sometime!" she yelled after us.

DAY 32

CHAPTER EIGHT

JOSIE

SOMETIMES WE GET A MOMENT OF REPRIEVE AND THIS AFTERNOON, in the courtyard, it's a blue-sky Indian summer kind of day and someone lends Freddy a Frisbee.

We all play, even me.

Heather's shouting, "Throw me the Frithhhbee!"

Aidan, who's the youngest—just 8—is somehow really, really good at it and can place the Frisbee wherever he wants.

Freddy is hyper, like always, but in the sun, on an unusually warm day, it's okay. Everything is okay.

Inmates are watching us play now. I don't like the way some of them look at Lori and me, but there's nothing I can do about it.

Then Venger comes into the courtyard and I can feel him watching us.

Somehow I know to tone it down, to make it seem like I'm not having fun.

And then my instincts tell me, nope, he's watching me too closely. I'd better stop.

"I'm out," I tell them. "I'm just going to watch."

And I sit down next to Mario, on the cement bench.

I'm breathing hard. My adrenaline is up and suddenly I have the feeling that if I could exercise this way every day, maybe I could get rid of some of the rage.

I feel a little jab of hope in my heart. *Maybe I could get rid of some of the rage.*

"You're looking good out there," Mario tells me.

I roll my eyes, and I smile. He can usually get a smile out of me.

Then I see that Aidan is holding his crotch a little between throws. He's doing that shifty little thing with his legs that boys do when they need to pee.

I nudge Mario and point.

"Aidan needs to go."

"Aidan," Mario shouts. "Go take a leak."

"In a minute," he calls back.

I don't blame Aidan. It's the best moment we've had. Who wants to leave and go into the cesspit of a bathroom, to fend off God knows what perverts are lurking in the stalls?

"Lori okay?" Mario asks me.

"I don't know," I tell him.

"Don't like her?"

"It's not that."

"Must be something. That girl would do sorcery if she thought she could get you to like her. Throw a friendy spell on you."

I sigh.

The sun feels so good on my face. I don't want to talk.

"Hmmm?" Mario prods.

"I don't want to be responsible to anyone, Mario. I am not . . ."

"Not what?"

DAY 32

"Not safe," I answer. My stupid voice cracks.

"I want you to remember something, Josie Miller. What you did, it was to protect your friends. You saved those kids when you attacked that soldier."

"Killed him."

"What?"

"I didn't just attack him. I killed him," I say.

"Yeah, okay, you killed him."

"The other guy, too. The dad."

"No-good Tad Mandry. He deserved what he got, trapping a bunch of kids the way he did. I think when you get to Niko's farm, you're gonna let go of all that junk. Move on. We just gotta get you outta here."

I have the note from Niko about the farm in my pocket. He had given it to Mario, in case Mario somehow found me. The note is on a small scrap of graph paper. The paper is soft and degrading at the folds and edges. Sometimes I would just put my fingers on it, just touch it to remind myself it's here.

In Niko's square print, it reads:

Josie—You can trust this man. Meet me at my uncle's farm in New Holland. Red Hill Road. I love you always. No matter what.
—Niko

No matter what *you do.*

You do are the unwritten words.

Also unwritten: no matter who you kill.

I keep my eyes on my EZ-on mules. No way am I going to let myself feel anything, out in the courtyard. Venger standing at the fence watching us.

"You saved your friends. That's what counts. You gotta let the rest go."

I look at my feet so I won't see the compassion in Mario's eyes.

Sometimes it makes me want to break things.

Venger drifts off around the side of Excellence and I decide I can play again.

Courtyard period is almost over and the sun is starting to go down when Aidan suddenly begs Freddy to come to the john with him. And Freddy, of course, refuses, and Aidan starts to race for the building and wets himself.

He stops running, aghast. His chinos are turning dark brown and there's a puddle underfoot on the cement tile deck.

"Scietto!" Venger's voice booms out across the courtyard. "Look what your boy did!"

And Mario's already up, crossing to Aidan as fast as he can hobble. Which is not fast. He's old.

I get there first. "It's okay," I say to Aidan.

Venger is on us.

"How old are you, boy?" he sneers.

Aidan sniffles. "Eight," through his tears.

"Eight years old and messing yourself like a toddler, aren't you ashamed?"

My pulse is banging in my neck now.

"All right," Mario says, drawing near, taking short, gaspy breaths. "Little accident. We'll fix it."

Mario puts out a hand on my shoulder to steady himself.

"Can the boy go inside and get cleaned up?"

"Courtyard period's almost over," Venger snaps. "He can wait out here with everyone else. It will teach him a lesson."

DAY 32

A little sob/sigh catches in Aidan's throat. His face is twisted in misery.

Venger's a sadistic a-hole and I wish, I wish, I wish I could teach *him* a lesson.

"But this mess can't stay on my courtyard," Venger says.

"I'll clean it up," Mario says.

"Darn right you will," Venger growls. "You're his sponsor."

"No problemo," Mario says. "Say, can I send the girl for a rag?"

"I'd recommend it," Venger says. "This puddle better be gone by dinner bell or you're all docked."

None of the kids can stand to lose a meal. We're all stick-skinny as it is.

Dinner's in maybe ten minutes so I run.

My feet slide on the linoleum in my stupid house shoes. Not the first time I've cursed these things.

I nearly crash into a fat man in stained overalls who's gazing listlessly out of a frosted window.

"Watch it!" he yells.

I skid away, not bothering with an apology.

When I return to the courtyard, with one of our two towels, it's maybe three minutes to the bell.

Mario and the kids are standing there. Aidan's shivering and crying. Heather's crying now, too.

I drop to my knees and begin to wipe up the puddle.

Then, *bam,* there's a foot pushing me over.

"I said SCIETTO was supposed to clean it up!" Venger says.

"She's sorry, she's sorry!" Mario sputters.

For his sake, I speak. "I'm sorry," I say.

The dinner bell rings.

"Yeah, you're sorry," Venger spits. "Seeing as you're so eager to clean, I guess you can stay out here and clean it good."

Venger pushes Aidan and Heather toward Plaza 900.

"Say, Mr. Venger," Mario stammers. "I've been meaning to apologize about that mess at the fence a few days ago—"

"Go on," Venger says. "Scietto, take your brats and feed them!"

"Josie wanted to apologize, too, didn't cha, hun?"

Mario is telling me to beg.

He knows Venger's been waiting for some way to pay me back for my defiance at the gate.

I am not going to beg.

I drop to my hands and knees and start to scrub.

"No, she's too proud to apologize," Venger says. "It's okay, Scietto. I'll take care of your girl. Go on, now, go have your supper."

Mario says nothing in reply, and for that I am glad.

He gets the kids out of there, before Venger changes his mind.

DAY 32

CHAPTER NINE

DEAN

ASTRID WAS SAYING, "OH MY GOD," ON REPEAT.

I seemed to be stuck on, "It's okay."

"It's not okay!" she finally snapped. "She's totally going to track me down. With that letter she has my real name, my whole story. She's going to rat me out!"

Her face was flushed and her breathing shallow. She was going to make herself sick with this, I thought, and then I burst out, "Enough! Stop! We have to think about what she said."

I held her two arms and got her to look at me.

"She said that most women who hear about the testing refuse at first but then change their minds when they hear about the money."

Her expression shifted into doubt.

"And she said pregnant women who've been exposed need special care, Astrid. I think we should come clean with her and listen to what she has to say. We need to think about the health of the baby."

"Do you think that I'm not worried about the health of the baby?" She was furious now. "I lie there at night and I feel it moving inside me. And I worry so much about what might be wrong! I just want to get somewhere safe."

"But it is safe here!"

Astrid looked away from me. I went on. "I just . . . I can't think that the US Army would take women away without their consent. It would be totally illegal, Astrid. It would be immoral. Wrong."

I waited for her to say something like, "It's illegal for them to keep the Os locked up at Mizzou." Or, "Wasn't it immoral when the US government made the compounds in the first place?"

Instead she just looked me in the eye and said, "I want to find Jake."

I fumed.

We searched the camp for Jake and I fumed.

Here I was, totally supporting her, trying to help her to calm down and think rationally, and she was going to turn to Jake at the first disagreement.

Maybe Jake was right. Maybe I was whipped. Maybe I gave in to her all the time. Why else would she shut me down when I tried to talk sense to her?

The man of the hour, of course, was nowhere to be found.

Not in the dining hall. (Thankfully they were still serving breakfast. I wolfed down two bacon and egg sandwiches while Astrid stood waiting irritably, almost tapping her foot with impatience. She wouldn't eat anything but a banana. Said the smell of eggs made her want to puke.)

He was not on the grounds—that we could see.

And not in the rec hall.

We couldn't find Alex and Sahalia, either, for that matter.

DAY 32

Finally, we ran into Mrs. McKinley and Mrs. Dominguez, out with the little kids, way, way down on the eleventh green. They were building a playhouse in a thick stand of trees at the edge of the course that bordered the road.

"Astrid! Dean!" All the kids besides Chloe clamored. "Did you see the letter? Isn't it cool?"

"Yeah," I told them. "Very cool."

"Alex says it's going to help find your parents!" Caroline chirped. "I can't wait to meet them!"

"Look at our fort!" Max said.

"We building a wall!" Ulysses said, pointing to a wonky construction of sticks leaning against the trunk of a large maple tree.

"Very cool," I said.

"What's wrong, Mommy Junior?" Henry asked Astrid.

Either because she was pregnant, or because they had their "big" mom back, they'd taken to calling Astrid Mommy Junior. Usually it got a smile out of her, but not today.

"Have you guys seen Jake?" Astrid asked the moms.

"Yes," Mrs. McKinley said. "We saw him at breakfast. He said he was going to go with Niko over to the Air Force base."

Astrid threw up her hands.

"Is everything okay?" Mrs. McKinley asked.

Astrid looked away from her. I knew the expression—if she started to talk about it, she was going to cry.

My heart melted for her. But only a little.

"I just need to talk to him," Astrid said.

"And I'm helping Astrid find him." I couldn't help myself. "See, I take care of Astrid, and I help her get whatever she wants. That's my job. I do what I'm told."

Surprise at my sarcastic tone of voice flickered onto Mrs. McKinley's face.

"Ignore him," she said. "He's being a jealous jerk."

Astrid turned on her heel and headed up to the Clubhouse. A shuttle for the Air Force base left once an hour.

I followed her.

"You don't have to come with me," she said.

"I know that," I answered.

"So don't come."

"I need to talk to Niko anyway," I said.

It was sort of the truth.

But mostly I went because . . . because I was a jealous jerk. I was worried about what Jake might do or say without me around.

From what Alex had learned, the main reason that the refugee camp had been established at the Quilchena golf course was that it was a large area of open space close to the Vancouver International Airport South, which was acting as a temporary Air Force base for the USA.

Part of the reason that Captain McKinley had gotten us all brought to Quilchena was that he knew he'd be able to see a lot of his family if we were here. This improvised base was the center of the US Armed Forces effort to support the hundreds of thousands of American refugees housed across the west coast of Canada.

Supplies came and went from this base, refugees arrived and departed on a daily basis, and there were Army offices where you could go to file petitions for transfers and the like.

All you had to do to take a shuttle over to the base was give them your social security number. They wanted to know who was where at all times.

Security was tight at the base, and guards patrolled the outskirts of the camp, so I guess they weren't worried about us escaping.

DAY 32

I wondered what Astrid was going to do, as the shuttle approached. Would she use her own number or the made-up one that she'd used in the medical offices?

I felt too pissed off to ask.

She entered her real SS number on the sign-in sheet the driver held out.

She looked at me and shrugged.

"They know everything else about me," she said.

She was giving me an opening.

But I was still too mad. What did she think Jake would say that was different from what I had said? He wouldn't be any nicer or more understanding about it. What did she want from him—now or ever?

At the base, it didn't take long to find Niko and Captain McKinley, but Jake was nowhere to be seen.

The captain looked really annoyed. Niko was basically trailing behind him as he did some kind of equipment check on a large transport helicopter.

"You don't have to approve of my plan to help me," Niko was arguing as we approached.

"I'm not risking my job to help a seventeen-year-old kid go on some wild goose chase," McKinley snapped.

Niko was sixteen, but I wasn't about to correct him.

"Hey, guys," I said as we drew near.

"Is Jake with you?" Astrid asked.

"He's visiting someone he knows at the motor pool," Niko said. "It's out behind this building."

"Ugh," Astrid said, rubbing her back. She looked miserable.

"Hey," I said. "Why don't you sit down and I'll go get him?"

"No. I'll go. I want to talk to him alone."

Okay, fine.

I exhaled through my mouth, trying to keep my cool.

She headed back outside.

"What's going on?" Niko asked. "You fighting again?"

McKinley ducked away to the chopper, probably happy to have Niko off his tail for a moment.

"Yeah, I guess. Hey, did you see the letter?"

"No, what letter?"

I told Niko and Captain McKinley about it.

"Do you think it could help me get Josie out?" Niko said, getting excited.

"Maybe," I said.

"I bet if I brought it to the press at Mizzou—showed them that the 'presumed dead' girl from The Monument Fourteen was actually inside—they could put pressure on them to let her out. Captain McKinley, don't you think?"

"I think that the publicity might help you to get her transferred here. Which would be safe and legal," McKinley said.

Niko threw up his hands.

Captain McKinley stopped what he was doing and came around to the front of the chopper.

"How's Astrid?" he asked. "Kara said she's not been feeling well?"

"She's been having some cramps. I got her to go over to the clinic today."

"She didn't want to go?"

He was leaning on the nose of the chopper now.

"Ahh. . . . ," I stalled. I didn't want to tell the captain about Astrid's paranoid fantasies about the Army. It seemed like he would be insulted.

"She's heard about some women being pressured to do testing."

That was the least direct way I could put it.

DAY 32

"But she's feeling all right?"

"She's had some cramping. The nurse said she needs more vitamins and rest. I got to see the baby on the ultrasound."

"Isn't it amazing?" McKinley asked.

"Blew my mind!"

"I remember seeing the twins, all nested in together. Arms and legs all a jumble. Once they were sucking their thumbs! Both of them!"

There was a glow on his face as he remembered the sight.

Astrid came back with Jake then.

She looked furious.

"Dean!" Jake said, cheerfully, and I instantly saw he was drunk. "I hear we're famous!"

"Is it even noon yet?" I asked.

"Never too early for a friendly game of cards," he drawled. "And look, I won!"

He had a fistful of cash.

He tried to put his arm around Astrid.

"Don't touch me," she nearly shouted.

"Whoa, whoa, calm down," Jake said.

"Astrid, I think we should go back," I said.

"To where?" she asked, her frustration spilling over. "There is nowhere safe for me to go! That nurse is probably waiting at the tent!"

"Really," I insisted. "We should go."

I didn't want her spouting the abduction stuff in front of Captain McKinley.

"Niko." Astrid turned to him, begging. "Would you take me with you? Take me out of here to go get Josie? We can leave tonight! I'll go with you!"

Niko didn't know what to say.

But then Captain McKinley came around the corner of the chopper.

"Astrid, what's wrong?" he asked.

"There's a nurse who knows my name, she knows I was exposed, and she was pushing me to sign up to let the Army scientists do experiments on me and the baby—"

"Are you sure—"

"And NO ONE will help me! Everyone thinks I'm being paranoid."

Captain McKinley rubbed his hands over his face. Then he dropped them.

"I'll take you," Captain McKinley said. "I'll take you both tonight."

"What?!" I cried.

"I'm supposed to fly this afternoon, but I'll push it back a few hours," Captain McKinley said, his voice calm, quiet, and dead serious. "Go back to Quilchena. Pack your stuff, say your good-byes."

"Wait a minute, wait. What?" Jake said.

"They've been running women out. At night," Captain McKinley told us. "I've seen them do it, a couple of times. I asked about it and they said that it was none of my business, and that the women have all consented to testing, et cetera, et cetera."

Astrid swayed on her feet. I reached out and held her arm.

"But?" she asked.

"I've been asking myself. If they had given consent, why were they all drugged?"

We agreed that Captain McKinley would drive past the eleventh hole, where the kids' play fort was, around 10 p.m.

What we couldn't agree on was how many of us were going.

DAY 32

CHAPTER TEN

JOSIE

"YOU WANTED TO CLEAN," VENGER SAYS. "SO CLEAN."

Well, of course, to clean—to *properly* clean a urine puddle off a courtyard floor—you'd want a bucket and a mop. A sponge would do it. Hot water. Some Mr. Clean, maybe, or at least some bleach.

Take it back even more and start by sweeping up the dirt, so it wouldn't cake all up in the bucket.

What did I have?

I have a dirty towel.

On our first day, Mario had given me a four-word mantra to get by: "Look down. Look dumb."

He said that would get me through life in the Virtues.

Look down, look dumb.

I scrub the stone pavers with the towel.

Most of the pee had run into the cracks anyway.

There was no way to get it out. It was just going to have to dry up. You'd never see the urine in the morning.

But Venger wants to see me scrubbing so I scrub.

The skin doesn't come off my knuckles right away. It starts coming off about a half hour in.

I have to be more careful; somehow the wiring is messed up in my brain. Things don't hurt the way they should anymore.

How do you know you've grated the skin off your finger bones? They hurt and then you look and see blood on your towel.

I feel my knees, though. They ache. The cold from the stone is setting into my bones, that's how it feels.

I hear our group come back from mess.

I hear Heather cry, "She's still there." And hear her shushed.

Venger takes out a pack of cigarettes.

"Hard to get cigarettes in here. Know how I got these?" He is chatting to me like I am a barkeep in his regular haunt.

"Every week, we ship off about fifteen, twenty prisoners. All type O. All people who've been exposed for longer than a couple hours. Bunch of brass. They ask me for the worst of the lot."

He lights a smoke. I can smell it.

My knees are numb now. They feel like they are made of cold metal. But my back is screaming.

"They take them away. I don't know where. And do experiments on them."

It is getting cool, now, but that isn't why I feel my flesh shivering.

"I just wanted you to know that, so the next time you think about disrespecting me, or showing off for Scietto and the snot pack, or just doing anything even the littlest bit out of line."

He is standing over me and I can smell his god-awful breath intertwined with the cigarette smoke.

DAY 32

"Here's what I want you to keep in mind: I can send you somewhere even worse than this."

I can't help it. I laugh.

I say the word, "Really?"

The thought is so absurd.

And I hear a sound from him and it sounds like a laugh.

I dart a look over my shoulder and he is laughing, too.

Somehow I think this means I can get up. The ordeal seems over.

I lean back on my heels. Wipe off my brow.

"What're you doing?" he asks me, still chuckling.

"I thought . . . I thought we were done."

"No," he says. "Not yet. I'm gonna keep you out here till the last group goes in. Safer for you if we wait until after lockdown."

"I think . . . please," I say. "Can I go now?"

He leans down to me, nodding, liking what he is seeing, I guess. That I am broken.

He opens up his maw and says, "Not. Just. Yet."

I hear the next group go over to Plaza 900.

I hear them come back.

My knees are bleeding now.

Crickets somewhere start singing. It isn't too cold for them, I guess.

Soon they will die.

My left hand keeps cramping up.

The last group goes over for dinner.

Forty-five minute shifts.

Then another thirty minutes to get everyone locked down.

My hips feel raw in their sockets.

Tears fall from my eyes and that is fine, I use the water for my cleaning. Spot, spot, drip, drip, drip. The dark little tear-marks vanishing under the arc of my towel.

I didn't know I could cry, anymore. I nearly thought they were rain.

I should have stayed out of it.

"I can take care of myself, for Pete's sake," Mario had grouched the day after I kept Venger from cracking his head open at the fence. I was supposed to let the guards bust his head like a melon, if it came to that.

I was supposed to keep my head down until I was set free.

"I'm an old man," he had said. "I'm not afraid to die—but you, you're my project. You're my last good deed on this earth and you're making it out of here alive."

Ha-ha. I saw the trick.

I should take care of myself for his sake.

The stain is long gone and the towel, now, shredded into long, sinewy strings that I hold cupped between my palms.

I ask God if this might be a good time to get it over with.

I know all I'd have to do is rise to my feet and take a weary swing at Venger and he'd put me down.

He wears a gun. He wears it so we can all see the leather holster.

It isn't the kind of riot-control gun the other guards wear. Those ones are big, semiautomatic guns, loaded with tranquilizer darts.

Venger's gun is a pistol loaded with bullets.

God, I pray. Send me a sign if I should get this over with.

There is no sign.

DAY 32

"Send me a sign if I should *not* get this over with." I must have mumbled aloud.

"What's that you say?" Venger asks.

"I said, God, please send me a sign if I should not end this!" I sit back on my heels, holding my wet face in my hands.

Venger leans over and grabs me by one of my hair knots. He pulls up and I rise to my knees, my neck taut.

"I guess you're feeling pretty sorry for yourself," Venger says. "Maybe by now you're thinking, 'This a-hole Venger, he's serious. He MEANS what he SAYS. Maybe I won't PUSH him anymore.'"

I start shaking now. And the poor sucker thinks I am shaking scared.

No, my blood is rising and I am keeping my weary self from trying to kill him.

Battered, bleeding, wrung out as I am, I want to wrap my two hands around his neck and SQUEEZE.

"Excuse me, Mr. Venger," comes a voice and the sound of heels clicking across the courtyard. "Is this really necessary?"

Venger releases my hair and I fall forward, catching myself on my bleeding knuckles.

"You've been forcing this young girl to scrub this same spot since I left to make my rounds, two hours ago."

"She might look harmless to you, Dr. Neman, but this one's a real animal."

"I find that hard to believe."

You're making it worse, lady, I want to tell her. Just leave us be. It's almost over.

"She's just about done now, right, Josie?" Venger asks.

I nod.

Head down.

The doctor leans over. I bow my head, avoiding her inquiring gaze.

"You come by the clinic tomorrow and we'll get some gauze on your knuckles," she says.

And I sigh as her heels click away.

Now I couldn't get Venger to kill me.

Because that doctor was a sign from God and I couldn't ignore it.

DAY 32

CHAPTER ELEVEN

DEAN

"YOU THINK YOU SHOULD GO AND NOT ME?!" JAKE HISSED TO ME on the shuttle. "I'm the baby's father. Me. You're just a boyfriend. You're a temporary condition."

"Stop it, you two," Astrid said. "Captain McKinley said he'll take all four of us. Why are we still discussing this?"

An elderly couple at the front of the bus glanced our way.

"Because Jake was drunk before noon!" I said, struggling to control my voice. "He's a liability!"

"STOP!" Astrid said. Her eyes were flashing and there were red spots of angry blush on her cheeks. "If you can't be nice to each other, then I don't want either of you to come. I mean it. Niko will take care of me just fine, if you two can't get it together."

That shut us up.

Though that whole time, Niko was just staring out the window. He didn't even seem to hear us.

He was smiling, for the first time that I could remember

since the last time I'd seen him with Josie, before they left the Greenway.

Our plan was to go to the tent so Astrid could rest for the afternoon. She would sleep, and in the meantime, Jake, Niko, and I would pack up. We'd also call a meeting of the kids to tell them the plan. And I had to take Alex for a walk.

Just imagining me telling him I had to leave made me feel like I'd eaten a loaf of lead.

But when we got near Tent J, Niko suddenly motioned for us to follow him and he darted back down toward the greens.

I saw why—two guards were stationed inside our tent.

"Do you think they're looking for Astrid?" I asked.

"I have no idea," he answered, looking over his shoulder. "But there's no reason to risk it."

So instead of lying on her cot, Astrid was lying on an odd little pallet of tree boughs Niko showed us how to make. A little Boy Scout daybed.

The kids had chosen a good spot for their playhouse. The woods were thick, and there was a small rolling hill in between the stand of trees and the golf course, which meant it was out of view from the Clubhouse.

One silver lining to the whole disaster was that the kids' imaginations seemed to have grown back much stronger than before.

I remembered them in the Greenway, how bored they were with the toys, after the initial feeding frenzy wore off.

And now, because they had basically nothing—no toys except for a lone soccer ball and a ratty doll Chloe had conned out of some younger kid—they played outside. With leaves and branches and bits of bark and moss.

DAY 32

We had all agreed that Jake, Astrid, and I should stay hidden until nightfall; Niko left us in the woods while he went back to pack.

The kids would come for a meeting at 4 p.m. and Niko would come back after dinner with as much food as he and the others could smuggle out.

Niko was specifically going to tell the other kids not to come down and see us until the meeting time. He didn't want there to be a lot of going back and forth during the hours when everyone was usually waiting on line at the listings or watching the afternoon movie.

There was one exception, though—Alex. I told Niko to send Alex to me. I needed to tell him alone.

He came bounding down the lawn, newspaper in hand.

"What do you think?" he asked. Then he saw Astrid lying on her stick bed. Jake was sitting on the ground, drafting a good-bye note to his dad. "What's going on? What are you guys doing down here?"

I took him by the arm.

"Let's go walk," I said.

"Hey, Alex," Jake drawled. "How's it going?"

"Did you see the letter?" Alex asked him, holding it out. "We haven't had any calls yet, but there's a nice woman in the office who promised to let me know as soon as we do—"

Jake took the paper.

"Cool, man."

"Let's walk," I repeated. Astrid was asleep and I didn't want her to wake up and say anything bad about the letter to Alex. Not until I could explain what had happened to Astrid.

* * *

His first response was just what you'd think it would be: "What?"

I laid it out again. That the letter had identified Astrid as a pregnant O who had been exposed multiple times, and that Astrid was afraid she'd be taken away for testing against her will and that Captain McKinley basically agreed.

It was horrible to watch his face fall. Like seeing a kid who made a Mother's Day breakfast realizing he'd lit the house on fire.

"What did Captain McKinley say, exactly?" he asked.

"He said she should leave here, tonight."

"But what did he say about the testing? Where are they taking the women?"

"I don't think he knows. But he confirmed that they're drugging pregnant women and taking them away. That's all she really needed to hear."

"Wow," he said. "This is really tough. Where is she going to go?"

Mmmmmm. Now for the hard part.

Our feet crunched on the leaves for a moment, while I tried to think of how to say it.

And I guess the pause itself conveyed the information because he said, "No."

He grabbed my arm.

"You can't go with her. You and I made a promise to each other to stay together. And now . . . and now our parents are going to find us, Dean. Thanks to the letter—"

"I have to go," I told him. "I can't let her go alone."

"She won't be alone. She'll be with Niko."

"Niko's going on a rescue mission!"

"Jake should go. He's the baby's father."

"We went to go find him today. Do you know where he

DAY 32

was? He was drunk at a poker game! At, like, ten in the morning! He's a total screw-up. He won't keep her safe!"

Alex sputtered. "All she needs to do is get somewhere safe! Niko can leave her and Jake in some motel somewhere—"

"Just listen to the plan. Me, Astrid, Jake, and Niko are going to go—"

"This is stupid!"

"We're all going to help Niko make it to Mizzou, which is on the way—"

"I hate this plan!"

"It's on the way to Pennsylvania. Then we'll all meet up at Niko's uncle's farm! And when those calls start coming in, from the letter, you can tell our parents to meet us there." That was the part I thought he might like.

"You're going to become a fugitive, just because Captain McKinley has some unfounded fear about scientists?"

"We're not fugitives, we're just leaving here. People are doing it every day."

"Those people have papers and are allowed to go home."

"We are going early," I said. Alex rolled his eyes. "Look, they took another pregnant woman from her bed, at night. Her sister told us so. Then Captain McKinley gets all freaked out about them wanting Astrid? There's something bad going on and we can't let Astrid get sucked into it."

Alex stopped, rooting his feet into the ground.

"I've heard you the past few days, telling Niko how dumb it would be to go after Josie. What about the drifts? What if they're real? Now you're going to go with him?"

"We have Captain McKinley helping us. He says he'll get us as close as he can. It's really not that dangerous. I'm going to go to keep Astrid safe and to get her to the farm. We're taking no risks. None at all."

A maple leaf, orange like a flame, landed in his hair.

"I hate to leave you, Alex. You know I do."

He was looking down. I picked the leaf out.

"But I love her. I have to take care of her."

"She doesn't love you the same way!" Alex protested.

That hurt. I won't pretend it didn't. But I knew he was mad.

"Alex, look, Jake is a drunk and Niko's only concerned with getting to Josie. Astrid has these cramps. She's stubborn and she doesn't rest enough. She needs someone to look after her and it's me. I'm the guy. It's my job."

Alex's face crumpled. "I don't want you to go. I don't want to be away from you, again."

I hugged him to me and he cried into my shirt. "I'm sorry," I said. "But you'll see, we'll meet up in Pennsylvania. This is no big deal. You'll see. We'll all be together at the farm."

One day ago I had wanted to poke some holes into his dream to let reality in.

Now I was using his dream against him to convince him to let me go.

When we got back, Niko was there with the little kids. They seemed delighted we'd taken an interest in their playhouse.

Henry was seated at Astrid's side on her stick pallet, his hands on her belly. And Chloe was on the other side.

Chloe put her cupped hands to Astrid's belly. "Hello?" she said. "Can you hear me, baby? KICK IF YOU HEAR ME!"

"Come on, Chloe," Astrid said. "Give me a break."

"Yeah," Max added. "You don't want to give the baby a shock or he'll come out nalbino."

Max was using Jake's pocketknife to whittle a stick into a spear.

"A nalbino?" Chloe asked.

DAY 32

"Yeah, a baby with no hair and pink eyes."

"We didn't have hair when we were born," Caroline said. "Are we nalbinos?"

"Guys, it's *al*-binos," Astrid said.

"Albinism is caused by a genetic mutation," Alex interjected. "It has nothing to do with scaring a pregnant woman."

As mad as he was at me, he still wanted the kids to have the facts straight.

I felt my throat start to get tight. It was hitting me that we were really going to leave.

"He's right," Astrid said. "Thanks, Alex."

She was trying to catch his eye, but he wouldn't look at her.

"I guess I owe you an apology for the article," he said stiffly.

"No, no," Astrid interrupted. "I owe you the apology. You must be so pissed at me—"

"What the hey are you two talking about?" Chloe asked. "Is it about the letter?"

"Are we really going to be famous?" Caroline asked me. She slipped her tiny hand into mine. "I think I just want to be regular."

Finally Sahalia came, holding a backpack of Astrid's belongings that Niko had apparently asked her to pack. Sahalia slung the pack down along with the three Niko had packed with stuff for me, him, and Jake.

"What's going on?" Sahalia asked.

"Are we having a sleep-out?" Caroline added. "Are we going camping?"

"I'm afraid not," I said. "We've learned that some scientists want to take Astrid away for testing."

All eyes turned to Astrid. Caroline hugged her and buried her head in Astrid's neck.

"No!" "Never!" "You can't go!" was the chorus from the little kids.

"Listen up!" Niko said. "This is important. We've decided that Jake, Dean, and I are going to leave and get Astrid to safety and go get Josie, too."

I saw misery spread across Sahalia's face. Her eyes flashed to Alex with concern.

The kids began to erupt into wails and protests again but Niko cut them off.

"We could have not told you guys, but we wanted you to know the truth because we're all family. You understand? We're treating you guys like big kids, so you have to act like it."

"When are you going?" Ulysses asked.

"Tonight."

Henry walked over, taking something small out of the pocket of his corduroys.

"Take this," he said. Henry handed me five dollars.

"But your dad gave you that for your birthday!" Chloe exclaimed. "That's *birthday* money!"

Caroline spoke for him, as she sometimes did. "Daddy Junior might need it, Chloe. Like, really."

That made my heart hurt. Astrid was Mommy Junior. I guess I didn't know I was Daddy Junior.

"Thank you, Henry," I said. "We'll need this on the road."

"How are you getting there anyway?" Chloe asked. "Are you going to walk?"

Niko put up his hand. "We're not going to talk about the details, because people might come to you guys and ask a lot of questions. If anyone talks to you tonight, you haven't seen us. But tomorrow, if they ask, you can tell them the truth. We left because we were scared for Astrid's safety."

"But we will be together again," I said. "I promise."

DAY 32

"Tell Josie I say hi, okay?" Max asked. "When you get her?"

"Of course," Niko said.

"Tell her I said quack, quack," Chloe added. "She'll get it."

"Tell her I miss her," said gap-toothed Ulysses.

Alex had a hard time looking at me. His eyes were red. Sahalia kept patting him on the hand. He wouldn't meet her eyes, either.

Caroline pulled back, in my arms, and looked at me. Her freckled face was full of concern.

"You have to take very good care of Mommy Junior," she told me. "Because moms need a lot of help."

Alex came alone, to bring us a plastic bag filled with the bits of dinner that everyone had managed to smuggle out for us.

He handed me a wad of money.

"What's this?" I asked.

"It's what I was saving, plus a hundred and five from Mrs. Dominguez. She says God bless you."

Alex looked away, over the greens to the dark blue sky.

There was at least three hundred dollars in there.

"Hey, you don't have to give me all the money you've earned," I said. He'd worked hard fixing small electronics for people.

"Take it," he snapped.

"I just feel bad—"

"Dean, I'd give every cent I'll ever make in my whole life to keep you safe. This will buy you guys food and water and gas. Who knows what you're going to need!"

"I'm sorry," I said, for the hundredth time.

"You get there safe," he told me. "Or I will never forgive you. I mean it, if you die out there, or you don't show up, I'm going to go around for the rest of my life telling people that my brother was an a-hole."

He was acting tough, covering up the pain, and I really started to hate myself.

Alex stormed away, up the lawn, toward the tent city that was our home.

It was hard to wait, after that.

I kept wondering if I was doing the right thing.

Was it stupid to leave? What would my parents think? I tried to channel my dad—he was so logic driven—what would he say about my choice? When I thought about my mom, my throat got tight. She'd want me to protect Astrid, wouldn't she?

I stood against a pine tree. The wind played in the branches around us. The golf course was beautiful at night.

Captain McKinley would come for us soon.

Astrid came and leaned up against me. Jake was sleeping on Astrid's pallet and Niko was sitting closer to the road, watching for the captain.

"I have an apology to make," Astrid said quietly. I glanced sideways at her. She was wearing my old green cap and a white Irish sweater that didn't cover her belly quite all the way.

Her breath made a little cloud when she spoke.

"The reason I wanted to find Jake before . . ."

She took my hand.

"Is that I was going to ask him to take me to Texas."

I breathed this in. It felt like a punch to the gut. I closed my eyes and put a hand up to my face.

"I was scared and you weren't taking me seriously and I was desperate," she said, it all spilling out in a confession.

She sounded sad, worried, pained to be hurting me.

"But as soon as I saw him I gave up that plan," she said, begging me almost. "I'm sorry."

"It's time," Niko said. "Come on, guys."

DAY 32

My heart felt like it was in the grasp of some iron-gloved fist.

"Please don't be mad," she pleaded. "I do love you. I really do. And I'm scared to go without you."

I grabbed her, maybe more roughly than I meant to, and I kissed her on the mouth.

"I love you, too. And there's no way I'd let you go without me," I told her.

CHAPTER TWELVE

JOSIE

"TOOK YOU LONG ENOUGH, BUT YOU GOT THE MESS CLEANED UP," Venger says.

As if he could see the spot anymore in the dark night. As if the spot hadn't dried up two hours ago.

The last shift had returned from dinner. The nine o'clock bell had rung.

"Get on back to your room, now," he orders me. "Lights out in a few."

I can't get up, not at first. My joints are too sore, too cold.

He drags me to my feet, and even then, I can't get my knees to firm up and support my weight.

Venger releases me and I stagger, trying not to fall over.

A little spark of conscience must have caught in his black, cancerous heart because his eyes flicker to mine, and away.

DAY 32

"Maybe this seems uncalled for to you," he says. "But every-one who saw you cleaning here knows I won't take disobedience from anyone, man, woman, or child."

There's nothing you can say to a man so stupid he thinks that publicly punishing a fifteen-year-old girl will earn him re-spect in people's eyes.

And I have bigger things to think about.

There is a curfew and everyone is supposed to be locked in their rooms after 9 p.m. And they usually are. But since the riots, some of the doors don't work right.

There is a chance I am about to run into some animals in the Men's hall.

Venger unlocks the front door for me and holds it open.

I guess I hesitate.

"Go on," he says. "They're all locked up for the night."

"But some of the locks are broken," I say.

"Oh, for Christ's sake." Venger grabs my arm and pushes me through into the vestibule.

In the front hall, where the co-eds had once checked their mail and gathered to watch live events on the bigtab, two skanky-looking guys are squatting against the wall, trading a cigarette back and forth.

Venger pushes me in and says, "You two leave this girl alone— she's just crossing through."

They look up at me. One of them smiles.

"Yes, sir," says another one. I see he's missing his two top teeth. I edge toward the hallway as Venger turns to leave.

If these are the only two guys out—I can outrun them . . .

They wait until Venger is gone.

The skinny creep opens his mouth. I expect him to say some-thing ugly to me.

Instead he yells, "RABBIT! Rabbit on the hall!"

* * *

My heart starts hammering and the adrenaline pumping. My joints instantly lubricate. Muscles ready to spring. O blood coming to my rescue.

Thank you, biological warfare compounds—the sports-enhancement energy shot that I carry in my DNA now and forever.

I take off at a sprint down the hall.

The two behind me come lumbering along like snarling undead.

"Rabbit on the hall!" the one repeats.

Most of the doors are locked, and inside I hear the men shaking the levers, trying to bust free.

But there *are* some doors open and several men come lurching from their rooms in front of me.

One of them is sweating and bald, and he works his huge hands like I am already in them.

"Easy now, girly," he coos.

"Leave her alone," says a man, coming out of another room in front of me. "She's just a child."

"Shut it, Patko," one of the men behind me snarls.

The man named Patko grabs the smaller of the two men in front of me and that is my moment to push forward.

Two from behind, one from in front, and another coming, now, down the hall—they swarm me.

The bald guy. Elbow to the gut. Stomp down on shin.

Wired, bug-eyed loser from front hall. Bash his nose in. Blood spurting out.

A bare-chested skinny maggot reaching for me and catching hold of the waistband of my pants.

He pulls me into his body, pressing his groin to my backside. Men swarming behind him and dragging me back.

I shift my hips and grab the maggot's male parts and pull hard.

He screams and falls. I turn and a hand is holding me. Pry

DAY 32

myself loose and scramble over bald-headed giant on the floor in front of me.

Released, I hurl myself forward, almost to the stairs, almost.

Then out comes Brett, the teenaged Union Man, ahead of me. God help me, ahead of me and I brace myself to hit him with my body.

He smiles and steps aside.

"Go, Josie, go," he says as I fly past. I slam into the stairwell door.

It is locked, it is locked, it is locked, of course, it is locked.

Now I will die, hopefully quickly, but suddenly the door opens.

Mario and Lori are there and they pull me through and slam the door behind me. Somebody's hand is in it, and a foot, and they slam it again, harder, and those parts are withdrawn and the door locks closed.

Lori pulls me to her, sobbing, and we sink to the ground.

Mario and Lori help me upstairs.

Adrenaline spent now, I am like a rag doll.

"Oh my God, oh my God, oh my God." Lori is on repeat.

"That SOB," Mario fumes. "He set you up—that monster!"

"I don't know," I say. Someone had hit me in the jaw, I am realizing. It is sore.

We get to our room. The kids are all waiting at the door.

They see me and burst into tears.

"I'm sorry, Josie, I'm so sorry," Aidan cries and hugs me. Heather and Freddy join in.

"Stop. Stop!" I growl. "Don't feel sorry for me. Don't! Get OFF me!"

It is too much. Their embraces are too much. Fear grips me— I'll suffocate—I will hurt the children.

I push them away.

"Don't get attached to me. Understand? I don't care about you and I don't want you. Any of you!"

I don't look at their stupid faces to see how they feel.

I am dead, don't they see it? I am dead meat. I am bait. I am a rabbit, tossed to the wolves to keep them at bay.

I don't want HELP. From a bunch of KIDS?

I pull away from all of them, even kind, loyal Mario and shut myself in the bathroom.

I run water in the tub.

Sometimes there is hot. Usually there is at least warm.

Tonight there is hot and that means steam. Hallelujah.

I take up our shard of soap. I am going to use some. I am going to use my share of lather tonight.

I realize I am shaking and I sit down on the toilet before I fall down.

"Hey!" and a rap at the door.

"Leave me alone," I say.

I feel bile in my throat. I make myself slow my breathing.

"Yeah, yeah. I know, you're too tough to need help. And none of us is allowed to talk to you or try to help you or even like you," Mario quips. "But you need to see something."

I open the door a crack.

"What?"

He slides me a quartered sheet of newsprint.

THE MONUMENT 14, reads the title. It is a letter to the editor.

They made it.

I am glad for the running water because I cry.

I feel joy for them and I miss them and I feel sorry, so

DAY 32

deathly sorry for myself and I feel angry at myself for feeling so sorry for myself.

I am presumed dead. My name is set down from theirs. Separated. Of course it is.

I remember our times in the Greenway. All the funny things the kids would do. How Chloe was always pissing off the other kids and how small and precious the twins were. Max's stories and Ulysses's front-toothless grins. And I cry to be missing being locked in a superstore.

I hadn't known how good I had it *before* we got locked in. And I hadn't even known how good we had it when we *were* locked in.

Now my whole life before the clanking shut of the gates around the Virtues seems like a fairy tale.

I cry at Alex's voice, laying out the story like a little salesman. Trying to get the editor of the paper to bite.

Alex would have known the letter was the best way to find their parents.

Since we have no TV, no radio, here at Mizzou, newspapers are like money. They are circulated, coveted, borrowed, and lent. It must be so in all the camps.

And have they found their parents by now? I cry for that, too.

Have they all met up with their parents and I am stuck at Mizzou?

Dead. Alex presumes I am dead.

I reach out of the tub and across the floor to my filthy jeans. I reach into the pocket and take out Niko's note.

I read it one last time.

Then I tear it to confetti.

I put my hands into the water and open them up, letting the pieces float out into the water.

I am lost, Niko. I pull my head under the water. I am lost to you forever.

The bits of paper rise to the top. Confetti scum.

My knees bleed into the gray tap water and I cry like the stupid orphan I am.

DAY 32

CHAPTER THIRTEEN

DEAN

CAPTAIN MCKINLEY WAS DRIVING A LARGE MILITARY PASSENGER-transport truck. A canvas cover was pulled taut over metal supports that arched overhead—sort of like a covered wagon. Two benches ran on either side.

We piled in the back.

"Hey," he said to us through the open back window of the truck cab. "Any problems getting out?"

"No," Niko told him.

He drove toward the base.

At any moment I expected, I don't know, guards to fire or a cop car to come screaming out of the dark.

But it was a still, moonlit night. The wind picking up the autumn leaves a bit. Quiet.

Before he turned the corner to head to the base, McKinley stopped and typed a message into his minitab.

He got an immediate answer.

"I have a friend at the gate," he told us.

He turned toward the base then, and waved at the guy on duty.

The guard patted the hood of the truck as McKinley slowed.

"Didn't see you, man," he told McKinley. "Didn't see you at all. Carry on."

"Thanks, Ty." And we were on the base.

McKinley drove the truck right out onto the landing strip, where his huge helicopter waited for us.

This wasn't the same machine that had rescued us from the Greenway. That one had been slick and state of the art. This was more like Army standard issue. No frills.

McKinley parked the truck with a screech of the brake.

"Now listen," he said. "I'm going to open the side door. I want you to keep low and hustle right in. I've got two friends here—one was at the gate. The other's working the tower. But there are people here who will stop us, if they see you. There are guards and there is brass, so be quick about it."

He got out of the truck cab and went over and opened the door to the chopper.

We all scooted down toward the back of the truck, getting ready to dash.

"Let's go," we heard his voice.

We filed out onto the moonlit tarmac and ducked down, scurrying to the chopper.

Niko went first and his feet on the rungs sounded like gongs clanging.

I looked around, sure soldiers would have heard. No.

One by one we filed up into the chopper, where we were all just jammed inside. There was nowhere to go.

"Jeez, move in," Jake whispered, pushing in behind me.

Heavy netting made out of thick bands of black nylon was strung from ceiling to floor and behind it boxes were stacked,

DAY 32

nearly overflowing into the tiny amount of space we had. There were two jump seats that didn't have boxes stacked in front of them—the seats were facing each other.

McKinley shut the door.

"Okay, good. We're doing well," McKinley said, climbing into the cockpit. He craned to look over his shoulder.

"Maybe not enough room back there, huh? Well, Jake, come up here, that's first off."

Jake carefully edged past us and stepped over the hand-shifters and levers in the cockpit. He got shotgun and didn't even call it.

"Astrid gets one seat and one of you gets the other and the third has to sit on the floor," McKinley called back.

"You take the seat," Niko told me. "My legs are shorter anyway."

"We can take turns if you like," I said.

I buckled myself in.

Astrid put her legs to one side and I put mine to the other and Niko, somehow, found space for his butt between our feet. He sort of rested his head on my knees, as a joke.

"Comfy?" I asked him.

"More or less."

Meanwhile, up in the cockpit, McKinley was radioing the tower.

"Delta-nine-bravo-seven, ready for takeoff . . ."

He paused, listening, tense.

Nothing.

"Repeat: delta-nine-bravo-seven ready for takeoff . . ."

Then a sound like a hand grabbing a microphone.

"What the hell is going on out there, McKinley? We have you DEPARTED at sixteen hundred hours!"

In the background was a voice, "Take it easy, Pete, I can explain."

McKinley cursed out loud and hit the dashboard.

"Sorry, Pete," McKinley said. "Got behind and Valdez was letting me slide."

"What's your cargo?"

McKinley shook his head, as if he was weighing options, none of which appealed.

"Should all be on the manifest, Pete."

"What's the mother-loving cargo, McKinley?"

McKinley sucked his teeth in frustration.

"Come see for yourself," he said.

"Roger that, you scumbag," this Pete said.

"Oh my God, what's going to happen?" Astrid said.

"I don't know," McKinley snapped. "Some of the pilots have been smuggling black market stuff in."

He tore off his headset and slid out the door.

Astrid held my hands.

"It'll be okay," I said. I hoped.

Moments later two figures approached the chopper. We could hear them arguing.

"I'm sick of you guys running scams left and right."

"That's not me, Pete. You know it's not."

"Yeah. This is different," another voice said. "McKinley's not into that crap."

"What's the cargo, McKinley?"

Suddenly the door swung open and there were three faces looking in at us.

It was easy to see which one was Pete. He was young, with a pronounced brow ridge and small eyes, set close together.

A fat, kindly-looking guy stood a ways back, hand on his hips.

DAY 32

"See that girl?" McKinley said. "She's seventeen years old and six months pregnant and USAMRIID is going to take her for testing."

"This is . . . this is big trouble, McKinley." The guy was practically spitting, he was so shocked.

"It's a two a.m. retrieval. I saw the order myself," McKinley added. "They're using a Blackhawk out of the Army side. They're planning on taking this girl."

"They have their reasons," Pete sputtered. "This is court-martial, right here, is what this is!"

"You know what happened to McMahon and Tolliver," the fat guy said. "Died in the line of fire? Two days after they took them to USAMRIID?"

He put his hand on Pete's back.

"All we gotta do is nothin,'" he said. "McKinley left at four p.m., gilled up with cargo. No big deal."

"Please," Astrid said, her voice small and scared. "Captain McKinley is just helping us to get across the border."

The guy looked at Astrid for a long, quiet beat.

He shut the door on us.

"I owe you, Pete," McKinley said.

"Shut up. You're not here," came Pete's voice, heading toward the tower.

The flight lasted three hours.

We couldn't see out the window. It was cold, and a little hard to catch my breath.

But we crossed the border.

And all the while I couldn't help wondering about what Captain McKinley had revealed. He had seen an order for Astrid's removal?

Had they been coming for her?

Had we just gotten out in time?

In less than four hours we were landing at Lewis-McChord Air Force Base in Washington State.

"Are you going to be in trouble?" Astrid asked Captain McKinley as soon as he shut the motor. It had been impossibly loud—way too loud to talk.

"I don't know," he said.

"Was that true? What you said about them having a plan to take Astrid away?" I asked.

"Guys, this is not the time for questions. Right now, I have to get you out of this cab. A buddy of mine named Roufa is going to come. At least, I hope he is."

McKinley took out his wallet.

"Assuming he does, give him this for his crew." He pulled out five or six twenty dollar bills.

"No," Niko said. "We have our own money. We'll give it to him."

"Are you sure?" McKinley asked.

"Yeah," the rest of us chorused in.

"You've done enough for us already," I added.

"All right then—that's good—just stay here and don't move." He removed his headset and climbed out of the cabin.

"Sweet ride, huh?" Jake said, grinning back at us. "I can't believe we did it! We're out!"

"I think my booty is iced to the floor," Niko said, groaning.

Something about it was funny—the way he said it, and suddenly I started chuckling.

I put my hand over my mouth.

"Dean!" Astrid shushed me.

DAY 32

I couldn't help it.

"It's just," I gasped. "The way you said 'booty'!"

Astrid giggled, Jake guffawed, and then the three of us were laughing.

"Shut up, you guys!" Niko hissed, but he was smiling, too.

Then the door flipped open.

A pilot stood there, in full uniform. Almost impossibly tall, with a crew cut that was straight and had a hard edge, like a broom.

"You the Monument four-*teen*agers?" he asked us in a thick accent—New Orleans, I thought.

We blinked at him, and finally I answered, "Yes, sir."

"Put these on. But don't bother with the headgear," he ordered, and threw in a duffel bag, which Niko caught. "Knock when you're decent."

He shut the door, and God help me, I almost burst into laughter again.

"Get it together, Dean," Niko said.

It took me a couple deep breaths, laced with last chuckles, to get myself together.

Niko opened the duffel. Inside were four shrink-wrapped packages.

We ripped into them and discovered they were some kind of ultralight hazmat suits. They had four parts—a jumpsuit, a face mask, gloves, and a belt that held round cartridges.

Niko took one of the cartridges out of his belt. "An air filter!" he exclaimed.

The material of the jumpsuit was in a dark-brown-and-gray-camouflage pattern and was incredibly light—almost like silk.

The headpiece was really weird. It sort of looked like bee-keeper headgear—with a large, clear visor and the rest of the head covered by the light material. But attached to the faceplate, on the inside, was a mouthpiece that you obviously would put in your mouth. On the outside of this mouthpiece, on the outside of the mask, was a slot for the round air filter to fit into.

The headpiece curled into the shape of a tube and there was an elastic holster on the thigh of the suit to hold the tube.

A little piece of paper fluttered out of each suit.

It showed a drawing of a soldier putting on the suit and then putting his boots on over the foot part of the jumper. There was copious writing in Japanese, but in English there were just two words: *boot over.*

On the other side it showed a soldier inserting a new cartridge into the face mask.

I was thinking about Japanese design ingenuity when Astrid asked:

"Why did he give these to us? I mean, is it for drifts? Are there drifts out there?!"

"Maybe it's a kind of disguise," Jake hypothesized.

"He said don't worry about the headgear," I said. "So Jake's probably right."

"Oooh, he said I'm right," Jake lisped, mocking me.

Getting dressed in the tiny chamber, along with three other people, wasn't easy.

When we were all geared up, and looking pretty ridiculous, I might add, Niko tapped on the door.

The giant pilot opened it up.

"Took y'all long enough," he said. "Come on out."

Niko must have looked timid, because he added, "Stand tall and proud. Confident. You've as much a right to be here as anyone else."

He helped Niko down, then me, adding, "As least that's what we want folks to think. My name's Edward Francois Roufa, the third. But y'all can call me Roufa. Everyone does."

DAY 32

Jake hopped down from the cockpit.

When Roufa took Astrid's hand he gave her half a smile, "Pleasure to meet you, miss. Hank's told me all 'bout you and the others."

Roufa looked Astrid over in the suit.

"Nice and baggy, just like I hoped," he said.

The protective suits were very loose, and because the material was so thin, they sort of bloused out. The belt was needed to keep the material close to the body, as well as hold the cartridges. Otherwise you'd be wearing a gauzy cloud.

There was lots of activity on the tarmac, even though it was the middle of the night now.

"Excuse me sir," Astrid ventured. "We were wondering . . . about the suits . . ."

"Protocol, sweetie. Everyone here is required to keep one on at all times. Waste of money, if you ask me."

Night crews were servicing helicopters around us.

I saw everyone had safety suits like ours. Most of them wore their safety suits tied off at the waist, instead of fully on, like us.

"This way," Roufa said, ushering us toward a metal hangar. Just as we walked away, a jeep with a flatbed pulled up to the back of McKinley's chopper. Two men went to the chopper and opened it, starting to inventory the boxes inside.

"Guess that timed out pretty well, considering," Roufa quipped.

"Can you tell us where we're going?" Niko asked. "Where you're taking us?"

"I'm taking the four of you to Lackland Air Force Base. Believe it or not, I rearranged my schedule to fly at this godforsaken hour. Running a bunch of medical supplies and more of these fancy ki-mo-nos you're wearing down to Lackland."

Soldiers and workers passed us as we walked. One or two shot glances our way, but most were busy.

How many Air Force and Army personnel had stuck their necks out for us so far? Roufa made four. No, five if you counted Pete.

I hoped they were good at covering their tracks.

"Lackland in San Antonio?" Jake asked.

"The very same," Roufa answered.

"San Antone is maybe three hours away from my mom's place in La Porte!" Jake said.

"Well, that's good, son. My advice is to get there, find yourself a good doctor, and hole up with your girl for a while," Roufa said. "I guess we're all pretty inspired by your story. McKinley told me what y'all did for his kids. I even saw your newspaper story. It'll be nice to get you settled somewhere nice and cozy."

"We're headed to Pennsylvania," Astrid said pointedly.

She gave me a smile.

I could've kissed her.

Jake rolled his eyes, pissed.

Roufa held up a hand. "Don't tell me your plans; I'd rather not know 'em."

We skirted a giant, truly gigantic hangar and went over to a row of parked vehicles.

Roufa got into a jeep and gave an underhanded wave, motioning for us all to get in.

"Hey!" came a voice. "Wait!"

It was Captain McKinley. He jogged over to the jeep.

"Roufa-man!" McKinley said. He was grinning. The two men hugged.

"I can't thank you enough for this," McKinley said.

"It's nothin' you wouldn't do for me," Roufa answered seriously.

DAY 32

He clapped McKinley on the shoulder and gave him a shake. They were really good friends, it was easy to see.

"They're asking questions inside. I gotta get back," he told us. "Ed will get you safe to Texas. From there you're on your own."

Everyone chimed in thanking Captain McKinley and saying good-bye, but he still hadn't answered my question.

He started to walk away, waving to us.

"Captain McKinley," I said, raising my voice. "Before you go, did you really see Astrid slated for removal? Were they going to take her away?"

Captain McKinley walked back to us, the smile slowly fading from his face.

"I did, Dean. They were going to take her tonight. If you'd stayed, she'd be drugged and on her way to USAMRIID right now."

"Oh," Astrid said and gulped. "Oh."

"Yeah. And . . . I couldn't let that happen to Mommy Junior," he said.

Captain McKinley's voice was full of emotion.

He patted the jeep.

"Good-bye, you kids. Good luck!"

Between Alex's nest egg, the cash Mrs. Dominguez had given us, Jake's poker winnings, and Henry's five dollars—we had a grand total of $418.

"How much do you think?" Niko asked us, counting off bills.

"Two hundred?" I said, unsure.

"One fifty," Jake cut in. "Trust me, one fifty's fine."

We drove away from the large planes, onto an outlying tarmac.

We stopped in front of a large beige cargo plane.

"This is for the crew," Niko said, holding out the little wad of cash.

"What? Well. That's very kind of you. They'll appreciate it."

There definitely were plenty of crew members around.

Two workers were running checks on the engine. The tail of the plane was flipped up to reveal the cargo space inside and there was a ramp leading out of it.

Another guy drove a jeep up into the belly of the plane. The jeep was fitted with a big, strange contraption. Two huge tanks were hooked up to some kind of compressor. Hoses and cables were wrapped in loops, hanging off the side. Most of them led to a giant funnel that sat on top of the machine.

What the heck was it?

"You all head to the nose. There's a gangplank there. My copilot will help you up. It's a lady copilot. Leslie Fox. She's nice."

Roufa headed off toward the crew with our money.

We climbed out of the jeep and went over to the gangplank.

Captain Fox, a thin, pretty blond woman in her late thirties, maybe, got us seated in the cargo area. She seemed okay. Hardly said a word to us, just showed us into the cargo area from the open cockpit door.

There were four more of those jeeps inside the body of the plane. That's how big it was.

There were jump seats on either wall of the plane. Most were folded up, but Fox folded them down.

The only thing Fox said was to Astrid.

"You need a special seat belt," and she switched out a part of the harness on Astrid's belt for one that wouldn't cut across her belly.

DAY 32

"Try to get some sleep," she told Astrid. Then she handed us all noise-blocking earphones.

And somehow, we did manage to sleep. At least I did.

"We're here," Roufa shouted over the engine's thrum. He nudged us awake with his boot. "Landing soon, sleepyheads."

I had drool on my shoulder. A big wet spot. I wiped it off.

Of course Jake saw me.

"Nice," he mouthed.

I mouthed back a popular two-word curse phrase.

The landing was bumpy. Not like flying in a jet airliner at all.

The jeeps bounced on their shocks, jostling the strange contraptions they carried.

"When we land, I want you four to just get out and walk directly into the brush. You'll see what I mean. Walk straight and you'll come out on a street near government housing. Take your suits off then. Keep walking and you'll find yourself in town."

He turned to go back into the cockpit.

"Mr. . . . . Captain Roufa!" I yelled.

He turned.

"Thanks! Thanks for taking us."

My friends added their own words of thanks and he nodded.

"Keep those suits handy," he told us sarcastically. "There's rumors of drifts."

Fox opened the door and let down the folding ladder that served as the gangplank.

The sky was light gray, shot through with thin, wafting peachy-colored clouds.

The plane was still far out on the tarmac, engines running. I saw Roufa meant to proceed taxiing down the runway to the base. He was letting us off so we could disappear into the brush.

I took Astrid's hand.

Niko went first, then Jake, then us.

We went down the ladder and darted across the tarmac into the tall weeds at the edge of the runway.

Fox pulled up on the folding stepway and it disappeared into the plane. She gave us a wave. The door shut and the plane moved slowly toward Lackland AFB.

Our feet crunched over grass and twigs, branches grabbing at our safety suits. The weeds were gold colored, all dried up, and there were larger bushes, too, also desiccated.

Around us the plumage of the grasses started glowing as the sunrise spread up, filling the sky, and I realized that the feeling in my heart was joy. Joy at being free and living in the beautiful, wild world.

We went through a mile or so of grass.

"I can't believe it," Astrid said, squeezing my hand. "We did it."

I was worried about her keeping up, but she seemed fine. She was smiling and much happier than she'd been in a long time.

"Captain Roufa was something, wasn't he?" Jake said.

"Roufa man!" Niko exclaimed, repeating McKinley's nickname.

Niko was grinning.

Niko wasn't a smiley guy, per se. But even back at the Greenway, he'd had moments of relaxing and hanging out with us.

I remembered once he'd made up a story about a girlfriend he had. An older girl who went to college.

He had dropped her—I'd never heard him mention her again. But he sure wasn't that way with Josie. It was clear to me that he loved her. He was devoted to her, no question. Here he was risking his life to rescue her.

DAY 33

"Is anyone hungry?" Astrid asked. "I'm starving."

"Mommy Junior needs some chow, people!" Jake announced. "Lord, do you think diners are running like normal? What I'd give for a short stack and a side of bacon extra crispy!"

"Mmmmmm," Astrid moaned.

"Make mine a Belgian waffle with strawberries—fresh strawberries and real maple syrup!" Niko said.

"You know what I'd like," I added. "A Spanish omelet!"

"Spanish omelet," Jake mocked me. "You can have anything in the world and you want a Spanish omelet?"

"Obviously you've never had a Spanish omelet," I answered.

"Please nobody say Spanish omelet again," Astrid said. "The idea of eggs makes me want to hurl."

We could see cars zipping by on the road.

"Can we take our suits off already?" Jake asked.

"Yeah," Niko said. "I mean, you should. I might just keep mine on. Just in case."

This was telling. Niko believed the drifts might be out there and was willing to keep the blousy safety suit on just in case. I didn't blame him—if he was exposed to the compounds for more than a few seconds, he'd blister up. If he was exposed for more than a minute, he'd be dead meat.

We changed quickly. The suits being so big actually helped getting in and out of them quickly. Once I took it off my shoulders, I just kind of stood there and the whole thing ballooned down, settling around my feet.

The suits did not take up much room in our packs, thankfully. I packed Astrid's and mine into my backpack, setting the masks, which were the most bulky parts, right on top. They were right there, if we needed them.

* * *

We reached the road. There was a Denny's sitting down a ways.

"Denny's!" Jake yelled. He whooped. "We made it back to the real world!"

We ambled toward the cheery signage and bright, squat building.

"God," I said. "What's it gonna be like?"

"What do you mean?" Astrid asked. She slipped her hand in mine. I shrugged.

"Denny's after the fall."

DAY 33

CHAPTER FOURTEEN

JOSIE

IN THE MORNING MARIO IS ALL OVER ME ABOUT THE LETTER.

"Imagine when those reporters find out you're in here," Mario tells me. For the first time since we had arrived, his eyes are twinkling again.

It reminds me of the long days we spent in his bomb shelter. He'd talk and plan and rub his hands together, so happy was he in anticipating Niko's face when we were reunited. Or how good it was going to be for me when we tracked down my parents.

Sometimes it seems like my future is the only thing keeping Mario Scietto going.

Now he has that same fire back. He wants to get the attention of the reporters.

"We'll hail them down and you start talking. You should say, 'I'm Josie Miller, from this article here about the Monument Fourteen!' just as loud as you can. Once they find out you're in here, they'll get you out. Special-interest story—absolutely. The power of the press! You're presumed dead! They love that stuff."

The kids are listening to us. Freddy bouncing on the bed he and Aidan share. Lori braiding Heather's hair.

My body feels like it has been backed over by a delivery truck. Everywhere aches. My knees are skinned raw. I feel them sticking to my jeans. My knuckles are a mess, already festering around the edges.

"And don't mind what happens to me," Mario continues. "I'm going to keep Venger off you until you catch the ear of one of those reporters."

"You can't," I say.

"Hell yes, I can!" he continues. "Maybe me and the kids can make a distraction."

"Yeah, yeah!" they agree.

"Maybe I could fall and trip someone and then I'll be like, 'I'm hurt! Somebody help me!'" Aidan suggests.

"No, no, I have it!" Freddy interrupts. "Can anyone vomit on demand?"

"Shut up!" I shout. "No one is helping me do anything."

Mario raises his hands to argue me down. He knows I will protest.

"It's not because I don't want help or I'm being tough," I say, cutting him off. "Look, last night Venger threatened me."

Just saying his name tightens my empty stomach into a knot of dread.

"He said if I step out of line he will send me away for some kind of medical testing. I don't know why he has it in for me, but he does."

Mario looks at me, his mouth set into a grim line.

"And if you guys help me, he could do it to you. He could send you away. No," I continue. "What we're going to do is lie low. Just like you say, Mario, 'Look down. Look dumb.' I'm going to play it really safe. I'm not going to provoke Venger. And we'll

DAY 33

get through this together. If, *if* I can get a completely safe chance to talk to someone, I will. Okay, you guys?"

I look to Mario.

He is studying me, trying to figure me out.

I am faking an interest in the group. Faking a new desire to protect the kids. Faking. No way am I going to let Mario get himself killed trying to talk to reporters on my behalf.

"You know," Mario says, scratching his head. "A better thing to do might be to try to talk to one of the cafeteria ladies. They like me."

"Maybe they would smuggle a note out!" Lori says.

"Yeah!" Freddy shouts.

Fine, let him sweet talk the lunch ladies.

Maybe it would work.

On the way to breakfast we have to pass through the Men's hall and I nearly bolt.

The men are already out, but still, my heart races to be there.

Lori takes my hand.

I don't want to hold her cold-fish hand, but I do.

We see Venger, too, out in the courtyard, talking with some guards.

I keep my head down. Don't make eye contact.

He can think me cowed.

That is just fine. Lori squeezes my hand.

I try to walk like I'm not falling apart at the joints.

As we enter Plaza 900, Brett sidles up alongside me.

My Gram used to call kids like him gankly—gangly and lanky. Awkward for sure.

And the ratty little mustache isn't helping his look.

"Hey," he says.

"Hey," I make myself say back.

"Can I talk to you a minute?"

Mario looks over, a question mark in his eyes.

I shrug.

"I'll catch up," I tell Mario.

My guard is up. He is going to make some demand. What does Carlo want?

Brett motions me off to the side, near the restrooms, where we can talk.

"You really know how to handle yourself," he says, his Adam's apple bobbing up and down as he gulps. Is he nervous, somehow? "I thought you were a goner last night."

I shrug.

"What do you want?" I ask. My mouth is dry.

"Look, this is a weird way to say it, but you should get with me. Like, be my girlfriend."

I must have shot him a shocked look, because he gets red in the face.

"I can protect you. Me and the Union Men. It's not such a stupid idea."

"No, no. It's not that," I stammer, stalling while my brain catches up with this bizarre situation.

What is bizarre is that the kid seems sincere. He is stroking his pathetic mustache.

"It's just—have you looked at me?" I ask him. "I look like the walking dead."

He smiles.

"You look pretty good to me."

He puts his hand on my shoulder and pulls me into his body.

I can't help it—I push him away. Elbow his ribs and pushing myself off him. My heart is pounding.

DAY 33

"Don't be like that," he says.

"Sorry," I mumble. "It's just—I'm not—"

And then I hear the other Union Men come into the entranceway.

"Watch yourself, Brett. She bites." Carlo laughs.

"She'll eat you for lunch, man," another one jokes.

Brett's face goes all red.

The moment slows down and with my eyes I try to say, I'm sorry. Wait. Of course I can't "be with him." But maybe . . .

Maybe we can be allies? Friends? Is that insane?

But the light in his eyes goes out. They turn flat and hard.

"Your loss, rabbit," he says.

I sag against the wall and he rejoins his gang.

CHAPTER FIFTEEN

DEAN

IN THE ENTRY FOYER THERE WAS ONE OF THOSE BLACK DRY-ERASE boards that you write on with neon markers.

It said in bubble writing:

> Welcome to Denny's!
> We have no vegetables or fruits
> except canned!
> No decaf ☺ No sodas! But we got milk!
> And we'll do our best to make it a great day!

"They sure do like exclamation marks," Astrid said wryly. There was an edge of nervousness in her voice.

"We're cool," I said. "No one would have any reason to question us being here."

"It is a little early for us to be out, don't you think?" she replied.

"We've been out all night partyin'," Jake said, throwing his arm around her.

"That's one word for it," she said with a laugh.

I rolled my eyes and pushed open the second door.

Inside it was busy. You could almost, almost forget there'd been a huge national emergency. Waitresses in uniform carried glass carafes of coffee (not decaf) to busy tables.

But there were a few striking differences.

There was a section of the wall near the restroom that was covered with bits of paper scotch-taped or pinned to the wall. Above it a sign made from three sheets of computer-paper taped together read:

RIDE SHARES.

There was also a big sign taped up over the register:

NOTICE: Prices are set as per printed menu. Report any discrepancies to the Price Gouging Hotline.

It listed an 888 number.

"Good morning, y'all," the bottle-blond waitress greeted us. Her roots were way, way grown in. "Who's paying this morning?"

We must have looked startled because she laughed.

"No offense, kids. We just need to see the cash up front."

"Oh, yeah, sure," Jake said. He fumbled to get some out of his pocket.

"Y'all want coffee?"

Astrid glumly said she'd just have milk, but Niko and Jake asked for coffee so I did, too.

I kind of wanted to ask for hot cocoa, but knew Jake would make some stupid crack.

When she returned with our coffees, she gave us the options. She said we could have eggs, French toast, regular toast, pancakes, or oatmeal. So much for my Spanish omelet and Niko's Belgian waffle.

Niko and I ordered eggs and toast. Jake and Astrid ordered French toast.

The coffee was watery and bitter, but I put a whole lot of milk and sugar in it. It made it drinkable.

Of course Jake had to look at my coffee and chuff disapprovingly.

"My granddaddy drank his coffee black, my daddy drinks it black, and I drink it black."

Imagine if I'd ordered the cocoa.

"Is it just me, or has Jake's Texas accent come back a thousandfold since we landed?" I asked Niko and Astrid.

"Would you two please shut it?" Astrid said.

"I'm sorry," I said. I put my hand on the back of her neck. She shook me off, putting her hand on her belly.

"Baby's doing back flips in there," she said.

"She loves Denny's, just like her pop," Jake said.

Did I mention Jake thinks the baby's a girl? And I'm sure it's a boy. Insert irony here.

I gritted my teeth and looked away. I was not going to let him bait me.

"I'm going to go check out the ride board," Niko told us.

He edged out of the booth.

Astrid leaned back and shut her eyes.

Jake and I sat there in silence, trying not to look at each other.

DAY 33

Before the catastrophes, I remember feeling left out, watching groups of kids from my high school out together, sitting in booths just like this one, laughing and teasing each other in a rough, jocular way. They seemed to know each other so well.

Now I was sitting in a booth with the very kids I had watched enviously and I was about as familiar with them as anyone could be, but everything was different now.

For a minute, a short minute, I felt the unfairness of it all. We *should* be sitting there after a long night out partying. Jake should razz me about coffee and I should come up with something sharp to say back and everyone should laugh and Astrid should put her head on my shoulder.

But the world that could have happened in had been wiped away. Scorched and gassed and washed away.

The waitress brought our food and Niko came back to the booth.

"There's a trucker going to Kansas City," he said excitedly. "That's close to Mizzou."

He started shoveling the plain eggs into his mouth. Didn't seem to mind there was no butter or jam for the toast.

Astrid and Jake each had a single container of maple syrup for their French toast servings.

Never mind, we ate and were happy for the food.

"He says cash or barter," Niko continued. "We get up there, we're really close."

"Hey man, what's the plan for getting Josie out, anyway?" Jake asked him.

"I'm going to go to the authorities and show them the letter to the editor and see if I can get her out the easy way," Niko said.

"But in case they won't let me do that, I'm also going to get a good look around, to see if I can find a way to break in."

Jake was sitting back as he listened. He didn't look entirely open-minded, but Niko didn't notice.

"I figure there are deliveries. They've got to bring in food and supplies, like at Quilchena. I mean, think about it. Who's going to be checking for someone breaking *in*?"

"What if you got stuck in there with her?" Astrid said. "What if you couldn't get back out?"

Niko took a sip of his coffee.

"Then I'll be with her and I can keep her safe until she's released," he said.

He wiped his mouth on his napkin.

"While you guys finish eating, I'm going to see if I can find the trucker."

"Wait," Jake said. "Hold up a minute. We need to discuss the plan for a second."

Niko looked surprised. "I know there are some aspects that are vague, but you know none of you needs to go with me to get her out of Mizzou. I mean, that's not even in any version of the plan."

"Well, I don't know about that," I protested. "I mean, obviously Astrid wouldn't go, but I could go to help you—"

"I don't think we should go with you at all," Jake interrupted.

Niko looked at him, startled. We all did.

"What do you mean?" Niko asked.

"Look, we're less than a couple hours from where my mom lives. Her place isn't a palace, but it's nice enough." He turned to Astrid. "And it's safe. I know she'd be over the moon to meet her grandbaby girl. Make us a place there to live with her. Her new husband's pretty nice. They'd make sure you have a really good

DAY 33

doctor," he said to Astrid. "I think you should have family looking after you."

Jake Simonsen. Always playing some kind of angle. Trying for the advantage.

"I'm sure *I*, for one, would be really welcome there," I said. "Here's your long-lost son. Here's the mother of his child. And here's her boyfriend!"

"You could go with Niko and then come back for Astrid when it's safe," Jake said.

"When are you going to get it that Astrid and I are a real thing?" I asked.

"I don't think you get it. I'll never be able to have another kid. What the compounds did to me is irreversible. That baby is my baby," Jake said. His blue eyes were flinty and serious. His mouth set in a line.

"It's mine, too, if I remember correctly," Astrid said.

"I'm just saying, I want what's best for you and the baby, and Dean wants to take you on some doomed rescue mission."

The waitress refilled our coffees.

"Jake, I'm sorry that you're type B, that you'll never get to have kids, I really am. But that doesn't mean you'll be a good dad. Just because it's your only shot doesn't mean you're actually fit for the job."

"Screw you, Grieder!" Jake snarled.

"Guys, please!" Astrid said.

"We need to take this outside," Niko said. "People are looking at us."

My blood was pounding in my ears. Maybe this would be it. Maybe we would have it out for once and for all.

"If you really loved her, you'd go home to your mom and let me get her safely to the farm!"

"I'd leave Astrid over my dead body," he spat.

"That's how I feel," I answered him.

"GUYS! You don't get to fight over me like this! You don't get to decide where I go or what I do! Just 'cause I'm pregnant doesn't make me property!"

A deeply tanned woman with too much makeup lifted her coffee cup. "You tell 'em, honey!"

"I'm going with Niko," Astrid continued. "You guys do what you need to do."

I went into the bathroom and splashed cold water on my face.

I looked at myself in the mirror.

I looked older, bigger. Less than two months had gone by since the hailstorm that started it all, but there were huge changes written on my face and body.

"Do you ever feel different?" I'd asked Astrid one day, out on the green.

"How do you mean?" she asked me.

"Like . . . stronger," I answered.

"I don't know," she had said. "My body feels so weird, it's hard to tell what's what."

I didn't know how to bring it up, the changes I'd experienced in my body. My muscles had somehow filled in during the time at the Greenway, like I was on Miracle-Gro. Neck, arms, chest, all wiry as heck before now had real muscle tone.

I wasn't sure if it was some residual effect from the compounds or if it was the demi-steroids that Jake had convinced me to take after he nearly bashed my face in. But I only took those for a couple days.

There was something else—my eyesight.

It was fixed. Cured. I'd arrived at the Greenway in glasses, nearsighted. My vision was bad enough that my parents had

DAY 33

started a Lasik fund for my eighteenth birthday gift. But since I'd gone O, I saw fine. Really—my vision was perfect.

It had to be some benefit related to exposure to the compounds.

I wondered if that's what the Army scientists were researching.

I also wondered about Astrid's baby. The way the first doctor at Quilchena said it was too developed for a four-and-a-half-month-old baby. And then Kiyoko had said the same thing, two weeks later. Was the baby stronger and bigger because of Astrid's exposure?

I leaned in closer to the mirror. My nose had a lump on it, from where Jake had broken it. The break made me look tougher. Maybe handsome, even. When I looked in the mirror I expected to see the kind of underweight-yet-also-puffy face that had stared back hopelessly for my sixteen years. My new reflection showed strength. And yet . . . it was hard to look that guy in the face for too long.

I was shifty, even to myself.

Maybe that's what happened when you killed someone. Maybe I'd never be able to look at myself again.

Jake came in.

"Niko's found a ride," he told me. "So wrap up your beauty regimen."

I could not like the trucker, who introduced himself as Rocco Caputto. That was his real name. I don't see how anyone could like the guy. Rocco was medium height, and pretty thin with gangly loose joints. He tried to be tough, which was dumb, because he looked about as threatening as Batiste. He had a thick mustache and a Jersey-gangster-ish accent that was almost cartoonish.

"Get you four to Kansas City? Hundred bucks up front for each of you. We eat when I say we eat. We stop when I say we stop. And if any of you try anything, my little assistant here will help you to change your mind."

He pulled back his Windbreaker to show a large handgun in an underarm holster.

It really was too big a gun for so small a man.

"We're not going to give you any problems," Niko said, in a placating tone.

"But we don't have four hundred dollars, either," Jake said.

"No? Aw, too bad."

"We can give you one—"

Jake interrupted, finishing Niko's sentence. "Twenty-five. We can give you one twenty-five total."

Jake must have assumed that Niko wasn't the most shrewd negotiator. He was probably correct. Niko was too honest for a guy like Rocco.

"One twenty-five for four kids?!" the trucker whined. "Come on!"

"No problem," Jake said. "Someone else will take us. Kansas City's not even that close to where we want to go."

Jake turned and walked back toward the restaurant. We followed him like lesser dogs in his wolf pack.

"Oh, for Pete's sake," Rocco Caputto said. "You have any gas credits?"

"Probably," Jake bluffed. "We haven't used any this week. Have you guys?" He turned and we all shook our heads.

"One twenty-five and all your gas credits and let's go," Rocco said.

"But can we all fit?" I asked. I don't know, from the movies it seemed like there would be one driver seat and maybe you could fit two people next to him in the front. I didn't want to

DAY 33

ride for four hours in the back with whatever it was he was trucking.

"Can you fit?!" He laughed. "Evidently you've never ridden in a Freightliner Century Class! I have bunk beds in the back! Can you fit."

It was true. The cabin of his truck had a driver seat and a passenger seat, then behind it was a little sleeper area, with a bed and a pull-down bunk over it.

"Look here," he said, pointing out the features. "Here's where I keep my clothes and I put little baggies in this cubby here to line my trash can. I got a cooler I keep my food in and an alarm clock and I even got a little bureau here. Only don't go looking in my drawers. Especially not you, miss."

"Believe me, I won't go looking in your drawers," Astrid said.

I muffled a laugh.

She winked at me.

I had to hand it to Rocco Caputo. His truck cabin was clean. Really organized and tidy.

"Don't you guys go making a mess. For one twenty-five, you better leave the place exactly how you found it."

He got into the front seat and started making preparations to go.

"Let's pull down the bunk and, Astrid, you can get some rest," Niko suggested.

That was a good idea. She looked worn-out. The blue circles under her eyes seemed more pronounced than usual.

"Okay," she agreed.

"One of you can sit up with me," said Rocco. "And the other two can sit on the bottom bunk."

I volunteered to go up front. No way did I want to be sitting on a bed with Jake.

* * *

The truck roared down the highway.

I settled into the passenger seat. It was really comfortable—
upholstered in a soft tan material. Very cushy. There was a risk
I'd fall asleep.

"Ride to KC'll take about eleven hours," Rocco said to me.
"Stop to refuel and I'm up to Chi-town."

"What are you hauling?" I asked, making conversation.

"Canned goods. Vegetables and whatnot," he answered. "Since
the wave, food goes east. No food comes west, that's for sure. I run
supplies, mail, people, anything and everything."

"What's it like back there?"

He drove in silence for a while, then he said, "It's jacked up.
It's jacked up big-time, Sam."

We'd given him fake names. Niko's idea. I was Sam. Astrid
was Anne. Niko had given the strangely unfitting name of Phillip and Jake was Buddy, which fit perfectly.

Did Niko secretly want to be a *Phillip?* Did he want to
trade his serious, all-business demeanor to be someone who
wore plaid pants and ate pâté and, I don't know, lettered in
badminton?

I think in the time that I'd known Niko he had made maybe
four jokes. None of them funny. A Phillip he was not.

"I lost my ma," Rocco told me. "Flushing. She was about
eighty though, so, I don't know . . ."

This awkward admission made me feel for the guy.

"I'm sorry for your loss," I said. Maybe I'd have to revise my
opinion of him.

He relaxed back in his seat and checked the side mirrors.

We were going seventy-five, easy.

"I do a lot of people-movin' is what I do. Lot of people want
to get out of the East Coast and get west. Anywhere. Any town

127

DAY 33

with electricity and running water. People have given up on finding their people. Given up on their houses—half the houses are molded up or got sewage in the basement. People just want out. Refugees are everywhere and all of 'em trying to get somewhere else."

I hadn't given much thought to what life would be like in Pennsylvania. Maybe Niko's uncle wouldn't want us, after all. Maybe the old farm was already overrun with refugees.

Rocco interrupted my train of thought: "You know what I get paid in sometimes?"

"What?" I asked him.

"Tail," he boasted.

It took me a second to realize what he meant.

"Yup. Girls and women in all sizes and shapes. People gotta get where they need to be."

No. It was not possible to like Rocco Caputo.

After an hour, I traded with Jake.

Niko was leaning back against the wall of the cabin, half asleep. Astrid was asleep on the top bunk, her back turned outward.

"Want to lie foot to head?" I asked Niko. "Maybe we could get some sleep."

It was a little weird to lie in the narrow bunk with Niko. And a little gross to lie in that bed at all, when I thought of what the trucker had done there with the poor refugee women, but I was tired.

Up front, Jake and Rocco got along perfectly well, which didn't surprise me at all.

Before I fell asleep, I heard Jake ask Rocco about the drifts.

"I tell you what that's about. It's the cleanup. You got FEMA and whoever in there, cleaning up the blast zone and they're sweeping up clouds of dirt and everyone's in a tizzy. I been all over the area and I ain't seen nothin'," Rocco said. "Here's what I think—those refugee camps are big money, BIG money for the people running them. They don't *want* people to go home. Think about it!"

"What about the Army, though? I mean, they all wear those protective suits. We even bartered for one for our friend"—a tiny beat here while Jake remembered Niko's fake name—"Phillip. You saw it."

"You got taken, my friend," the trucker laughed. "Those outfits are PR, nothing more. Take a look at 'em. They're paper-thin. All for show."

"Really?" Jake said.

I didn't believe that. Why would the Army go to that expense?

"I guess we got ripped off," Jake said.

"Happens to the best of us," Rocco conceded.

"Hey, I been wondering, why do they call it Kansas City if it's in Missouri?" Jake asked.

"Now, there's a good question," Rocco said. "Midwest. It's all a bunch of retards."

Yeah, they got along just fine.

DAY 33

CHAPTER SIXTEEN

JOSIE

WE'RE IN OUR ROOM. THE KIDS ARE PLAYING ROCK CHUCK, A game Freddy invented using some small rocks and bits of gravel the kids picked up in the courtyard.

Rock Chuck involves setting up obstacles on the floor and then throwing the rocks to knock down the obstacles. Sort of like a pathetic DIY Angry Birds, which I used to play when I was their age.

Mario is playing Rock Chuck along with the kids. They asked me, too, but I refused.

Mario wants me go to the clinic.

My stupid knuckles don't look right. Swollen, too red. A little whitish ooze growing under the skin near the cut parts.

"Promise me you'll stay here?" I ask him.

"I'm up next," he grouches. "Of course I'm staying here. Where do you think I'm going to go? Fly to Mars?"

That gets a laugh out of the kids.

I roll my eyes. "You know what I mean."

I don't want him going to the fence to try to tell the reporters I am here. He had whispered the secret of my identity to one of his heavyset paramours at Plaza 900. We have to wait and see.

Mario shoos me off so I go to the clinic.

They house the clinic in Rollins, by the north side of the 0 containment compound.

Going there means an endless wait in a nasty line.

The doctor had told me to come, sure, but that doesn't mean I can skip to the head of the line.

The clinic is a suite of maybe four rooms—built to accommodate the colds, flus, and drinking concussions of the Mizzou undergrads housed in the Virtues.

Now it is besieged by malnourished trauma victims suffering all sorts of horrible injuries and maladies.

As I understand it, there are a handful of prisoners with medical training—0 types who can be of service. They work shifts along with a couple of Good Samaritan doctors and nurses who are paid by the state to care for us.

I get in line behind a woman with a lined face and streaked blond hair. Her hair is the kind of frosted and tinted blond-girl hair that takes hours in the beauty shop.

She has two inches of dark brown roots and the whole mess is greasy and tied back with what looks like a piece of old mop string.

She turns and looks over her shoulder at me.

I carefully study my weeping knuckles, avoiding eye contact.

"You were out there," she said. "I can tell."

Her breath stinks of crazy.

DAY 33

I'm sure mine does, too.

"I was out there." She tries to smile. "We lived in Castle Rock. And the day the compounds hit, my husband, he just melted away in a pool of blood. We had our own company. We sold insurance. All kinds. Health, auto, home, life, you name it."

I look up at the ceiling.

"I think of all our policyholders. They must be phoning me and Dave day and night. But what can I do? Dave, he melted away. There was just bones and meat and blood and I just lost it. I mean, I really did."

I wish that she would stop talking to me.

She is looking away and it is almost like she is talking to herself now.

I sniff my knuckles. They smell, hmmm, sourish.

"I have a five-hundred-thousand-dollar life policy on him, but I don't know if I'll be able to collect. Proof of death? How will I get that? He was a pool of blood, like I said. He was blood and bones at the end. His blood was hissing like it was on fire."

Please let her stop talking to me. I put my fingers in my ears, but I can still hear her.

"I don't feel right, still. I don't feel right in the head," she says, as if explaining why she is waiting on line. "And you don't, either. None of us do. And I don't know if we ever will. I just don't know."

She is looking into my eyes and I know she won't leave me alone until I answer.

I lower my arm, withdrawing it from contact.

"Yeah," I whisper. "We're all broken."

"I know it." She nods. "That's the truth."

* * *

She and I inch up the line a ways.

My stomach is starting to growl.

And then Aidan comes for me, crying.

And I know Mario has gone to the gates.

I run, Aidan at my heels.

"He was trying to get their attention about the article thing," Aidan says as we run.

It is like the other day, a crush of prisoners at the gate, all yelling to the four or five reporters on the other side of the second gate, who are yelling questions to them and recording it all.

I see that Venger and a couple others are already there with the tranq guns.

"Where are the others? Get the others!" I shout to Adian.

At first I don't see Mario and then I see he has fallen and is getting crushed down to the ground.

"Mario!" I scream and I dive into the tangle of bodies, some of them falling, now from the darts, other pushing and fighting and still screaming to the reporters.

"They're killing us in here!" one man is shouting.

"We're being starved to death!"

I have a hand on Mario. He is unconscious and I try to get myself over him to protect him from the crush of bodies. One by one the people go dead and limp as the darts fell them.

My rage comes up. An electric fence of adrenaline hums up to fighting pitch. I want to hurt the people, to push them back and make them pay for hurting my Mario, but I shout in my head at my own self.

PROTECT HIM—stand your ground and keep him safe.

DAY 33

Then there are only a few of us still conscious and I see some soldiers come and move the reporters away from the fence on the other side.

I am crouching over Mario now.

"Mario, Mario, can you hear me?" I ask.

His head lolls back on his shoulders as I lift his torso. His legs are pinned under the body of a fat lady. He has blood on his head, but not necessarily his.

I can't tell if he's been hurt or is just tranquilized.

I get down on my screaming knees and edge him up from under the tangle of bodies. With my hands under his arms, I drag him over the others.

"Mario! Mario, it's me!" I yell over the chaos.

I see that his arm is hanging wrong. The hand flapping off to the side in a way hands can't, when the bones are intact.

I pull him as carefully as I can, though I stumble on the bodies on the ground. I step on legs and arms and hair. Just a few more bruises for them when they wake.

I pull Mario over the other fallen prisoners and lay him on the ground. The arm is wrong. Clearly wrong.

The guards back off and are now pulling bodies off the pile and laying them in rows.

Lori and the other kids swarm over Mario, kissing him and crying.

"Wake up! Wake up!" Heather screams.

"Get back! Don't touch him!" I shout. "His arm is broken!"

"What do we do?" Lori moans. "Oh my God! Mario!"

And then I see that his breathing isn't easy. He seems to be gasping.

I bend down and listen to his mouth.

"Shut up, you guys!" I holler.

I listen, is there a rasp? A wheeze?

He might have a punctured lung or something.

"We need to get him to the clinic. Right now," I tell them. "Lori, help me. I'm going to lift his body and you stay at his side, holding his arm. Try not to let it flop around or grind the wrong way."

"What do you mean 'grind the wrong way'?"

"Don't let it grind any way! Now on the count of three."

We lift him.

Unconscious bodies are heavy. But not as heavy as dead ones.

DAY 33

CHAPTER SEVENTEEN

DEAN

I WOKE TO THE SCREECH OF BRAKES AND ROCCO'S LOUD VOICE, "Pit stop number two. Vinita, Oklahoma. Wake up. We leave here in fifteen minutes."

Pit stop number one had been three hours earlier in Durant, Oklahoma.

We had spent twenty-five dollars on four ham sandwiches and a pint of warm orange juice. Our money was not stretching the way we'd hoped . . .

We would have ninety-two dollars left, after we paid Rocco Caputo.

"I'm gonna hit the head, guys. See you inside," Jake told us.

Jake got out with Rocco while the rest of us woke up.

Astrid gave a sleepy moan from her pull-down bunk. "Are we there yet?" she asked, half joking.

I stretched up in between the two front seats, where there was a bit more room.

The gas pumps for the big rigs were set off at a distance to the rest of the gas station/minimart.

I watched Jake talk to Rocco as they walked toward the minimart. I knew that Jake didn't really share Rocco's view on the world. He was just getting along, making our trip easier by gaining Rocco's trust. Jake could get along with anyone. It had saved our lives back at the Greenway, when cadets invaded the store. I shouldn't begrudge him it now.

But I did. I really didn't want Jake to do anything right or good. I wanted him to screw up time and time again until Astrid got it that *he* was the loser. I wanted her to see that he was an unreliable, macho jerk-off braggart.

Was that so wrong? (I already knew it was.)

"Do you want me to help you down?" I asked Astrid. She was sitting on the bunk, with her feet hanging over the edge, rubbing her face with her hands.

"I feel like I could sleep for another year," she said, yawning.

"Any more cramping?" I asked.

She shook her head.

"Feel tight, really tight, but not crampy."

"Do you want me to go get you a snack so you can keep sleeping?"

"Nah, I need to pee."

Niko came up front with me, rooting through his backpack. He took out some money.

"Let's just get one really big bottle of water. It's cheaper if we share," he said.

I moved back to help Astrid navigate the footholds molded into the side of the trailer.

"You know," she said. "I'm hungry again. Starving."

137

"We can get Astrid a snack, right, Niko?" I said, just as he said, "Guys?"

Suddenly the air was pierced by a high, thin whistling sound. It seemed to be coming from—from inside the truck cabin.

Then Niko yelled, "GUYS!"

Astrid and I stepped forward and looked out the windshield.

The light was weird, like before a thunderstorm. Then I saw it.

A black mass, skittering across the ground. Then up in the air, moving, writhing. It moved like a flock of starlings. Up and down, swooping and settling and spreading out, then contracting.

A living black cloud—maybe the size of a football field.

Niko was pulling his suit up. Thank God he still had it on and tied around his waist.

"Your suits! Your suits!" he stammered.

"Are the windows shut?" Astrid asked.

Where was my backpack? I'd been using it as a pillow.

"Who knows?" Niko shouted.

"Masks first!" I said.

Our visors, with their built-in air-filtering mouthpieces, were at the top of the pack.

I handed Astrid hers and put mine in. The rubber felt weird in my mouth, but I drew in a breath.

Filtering the air was the most important thing for Astrid and me. But for Niko, he had to get the suit on and seal it up, otherwise he'd blister and burn.

Astrid and I fumbled with our suits, pulling them up. I realized the whistling sound was coming from the suits! There was a little plastic eyelet, the size of a dime, at the lapel and it was now shrieking and giving off a bright red LED light.

The drift was making its way through the neighborhood behind the gas station, swooping and diving, getting closer.

Niko zipped his mask closed. He was safe.

I saw the red light on his suit turn green and the whistle died out.

Astrid had her suit on now, was shoving her feet into her sneakers. I zipped her face mask to the body of the suit.

"Hold still!" I told her. Her light went green.

Me next.

"We have to get Jake!" Astrid shouted. She didn't have her mouthpiece in yet.

"No way!" Niko said. "Jake's fine. He's in the store!"

The drift was encompassing the minimart, now, and would be on us in a second.

I got my suit up and Astrid zipped my face mask down. Green.

Through the side window I saw Jake and Rocco sprinting toward us, chased by the swirling black soot.

And I saw, behind them, a man step out of the minimart with a gun.

BANG! He was aiming for Jake and Rocco! He must be AB, and now paranoid and freaking out.

The drift was hitting the windshield with a zinging, scouring sound.

I saw Rocco stumble. Had he been hit?

I took the filter out of my mouth so I could talk. "I'm going to help!" I shouted. "Stay here!"

Before Niko could stop me, I had the door open and was running to Jake and Rocco.

Rocco had not fallen from the shot.

He was blistering.

Maybe if we got him inside the truck—and I saw Jake stop and go back to Rocco.

BANG! The man with the gun had fired way off to the side

DAY 33

of us. I saw the bullet spark against the sign giving the rate for diesel fuel.

Jake was leaning over Rocco's fallen body. There was blood. Lots of blood. We had to get him inside, quick.

"I'll help you!" I shouted, the words mashed up because of my mouthpiece.

But Jake wasn't helping Rocco up. He was sliding the handgun out of Rocco's shoulder holster.

Jake took the gun and fired a shot back at the minimart guy. The *BOOM* of the gun was shockingly loud, at that range.

"Help me get him inside!" I shouted to Jake.

"It's too late!" he answered and I saw he was right.

Rocco was already gone, the grit had seared into his face and arms. His body was starting to bubble.

Bile rose in my throat. By then Astrid and Niko were there.

"I told you to stay inside!" I shouted.

BANG! The shopkeeper shot toward us and Jake took another shot at him.

"Come on!" Jake shouted.

BANG! The shopkeeper shot again and there was this tremendous light. A fireball blossomed from the gas pump right next to the truck and then the sound, a *WHOOOOOSH-POW* of an explosion, as the fuel tanks under the ground exploded.

As soon as we could get up, we ran.

CHAPTER EIGHTEEN

JOSIE

THE NURSE TELLS US WE HAVE TO WAIT IN LINE.

"He's an old man," I say, my arms trembling. "His arm is broken and his breathing is all wrong. He might have a punctured lung."

The nurse feels for his pulse.

"Listen—," she says. "He's very old—" Starting to say, what? That he was too old to be worth treating? That he was too old to save?

"I know Dr. Neman," I stammer. "The doctor. She's my friend."

"Dr. Neman is not on duty," the nurse answers. "You'll have to wait—"

"Listen," I tell her. "I was lost and wild. I was eating out of his trash can. I had killed these men and I was lost to the world and he called to me. He brought out a cup of hot chocolate and reached out to me. I could have killed him. But he believed in me. Do you understand?"

"Be that as it may—" She is reaching for the phone now, probably thinking about calling security.

"He said, 'You put on this mask and you can have this cocoa,' and he tossed a mask over to me. And I knew that he was offering me a way to come back to the human race. Some part of my monster brain knew that it was a chance and it was my last chance."

Now I am crying and Lori, standing behind me, is crying, too. The rest of the kids, too, probably.

The nurse wants us to move out of the doorway but I'm not budging. Mario's gaspy breathing is my metronome and I tell her the rest.

"I put the mask on. And after I calmed down and started to be able to think again, he handed me a note.

"See, my friends had left me behind. They had to. My . . . my boyfriend, he had to take the others, five of them, all kids, to safety. So he had to leave me behind.

"But he left a note.

"And Mario gave it to me and I read it."

"I am sorry!" the nurse says. "But we don't have the supplies to spend on this kind of a case—"

"He gave me shelter," I weep, my arms shaking, shaking, shaking. "He fed me and let me rest and gave me new clothes and a safe place to be. And when the bombs fell, up top, we thought we were done for. We prayed through the night, asking God for the chance to live."

"I don't have the authority—," she says.

"He begged God for me to have the chance to find my friends," I sob. "Don't you see? He's a good man. He's all the family I have left."

"Rah!" she shouts in frustration. "Fine! Fine then. Come this way."

I step forward, my arms screaming now.

"Tell your friends to go away," she snaps.

I choke on a gasp of relief and Lori leads the kids away.

"Put him here," the nurse says, pointing to a blood-stained cot between two holding other people—a squat man with a bandage around his waist and a sleeping woman whose head is wrapped in gauze, stained yellow at her eyes.

"What happened here?" says a Latino guy wearing a T-shirt and jeans with a stethoscope around his neck.

"Dr. Quarropas, I'm sorry. But the girl insisted—"

"She was right to insist. This guy must be eighty years old!"

"I know," she snaps. "But he's not the most treatable—"

"Don't," he says. "I'm a doctor. I won't hear that crap about treatable cases. Not one more time."

"It's not coming from me—," she protests, but he isn't paying attention anymore. He bends over and listens to Mario's breathing and opens his mouth gently to look inside.

"Doesn't sound good," he says. "What happened to him?"

He opens Mario's eyes and looks in with a pen light.

"There was a mob at the gate," I say. "He got trampled. Maybe hit with a tranquilizer but I'm not sure."

"Probably sedated. What's his name?" the doctor asks.

"Mario Scietto," I say.

"Mario! Mario!" he says. "Can you hear me? Mario Scietto!"

Mario lays there, looking like a broken bird. He looks very small, laid out next to the two people on either side.

The doctor takes out a minitab.

"New file," he says into the phone.

So minitabs work again. At least for people running the show.

This was the first I had known.

"Mario Scietto. Late seventies, early eighties, question mark. Sedated by Etorphine dart. Crushed in mob."

DAY 33

He listens to Mario's chest with his stethoscope, shaking his head.

"Compound or transverse fracture ulna, radius, left arm. Fractured ribs question mark."

A gasp escapes from my lips. Dr. Quarropas looks up, as if focusing on me for the first time.

"You need to go," he says.

"Is he going to be okay?" I ask.

Suddenly I see stars, the room goes slanted in my vision.

The doctor puts his hand on my arm. A part that is bruised from my midnight journey on the Men's hall. I wince, the pain making the room straight again.

"Are you okay?" he asks.

"I'm fine."

For some dumb reason, I put my hands behind my back. I don't want him worrying about my stupid knuckles when Mario is in danger.

"They're not feeding you well enough. You look like you'll blow away. And what's wrong with your hands?"

"Nothing," I say.

He gives me an expectant look.

I show him my knuckles. There is definitely some greenish pus around the edges.

"How'd this happen?"

"I had to clean something," I say. "I scraped them."

"Rhonda," he calls. "Where's the roll gauze?"

"We're out," she calls back.

"Squares, then, I'll tape them on," he yells.

"We're out of tape."

"Jesus!"

"Is Mario going to be okay?" I ask again.

"I think so."

The doctor crosses to a small sink and motions for me to follow. He runs warm water into the sink and motions for me to wash my hands with antibacterial soap, all the while talking about Mario.

"He's going to sleep for a good long while now, and while he's out, I'll set his arm. I'm going to examine his rib cage, too. We're going to do the best we can."

He pats my knuckles dry with a paper towel and then he holds a spray over my hands.

"Cough," he whispers.

"What?"

He coughs, loudly, and I join in. While we cough, he sprays my knuckles, dousing them with a foam that congeals, almost immediately, into a flexible kind of rubber flesh seal.

Rhonda comes to the door.

"Oh my Lord," she says. "Tell me you are not using Dermaknit on this girl. You know that is our last bottle!"

The doctor winks at me.

"She was headed for a nasty infection. Had to be done."

I am sure I was looking at him with the fish-mouthed gawk of a zombie but I couldn't get used to being handled like I mattered, like I had some rights to humane treatment. And being joked with, like the world was a place in which people could still joke and be merry and tease each other and cough to cover up the sound of a spray.

He is being playful and kind. I must have been looking at him like he was from Mars.

"I think your friend will be fine," he says, the smile slowly fading from his face. "Why don't you come visit him tomorrow."

"Now, you heard the doctor," the nurse says to me.

"Hey!" a man from the head of line calls in. "When's my turn?"

"I'll need your help in a moment to set this fracture," says

DAY 33

Dr. Quarropas to the nurse. "But you can bring in some patients so the line doesn't go nuts."

The nurse puts her hand on the small of my back and shows me out of the room.

"You got what you wanted," she says to me. "Now get out of here."

CHAPTER NINETEEN

DEAN

OUR BACKPACKS WERE GONE—THEY'D BEEN IN THE TRUCK.

Jake didn't have a suit, but since he was type B, that hardly mattered.

The rest of us had our suits.

Drawing air through the mouthpiece was awkward, but it worked, even at a sprint. And the fact that you were basically holding the mask to your face by having the mouthpiece in your mouth meant the whole face mask/visor didn't jar around too much. It was surprisingly stable. Even at a full sprint. Japanese design.

Jake was in the lead. He led us across a low field of brown grass into a residential neighborhood.

I ran behind Astrid and I did it on purpose. I thought I could block a bullet if the guy shot at her. Probably dumb, I know, but that's what I did.

Small, nice-looking houses were on either side of the street.

Jake dodged behind a minivan and waited for the rest of us.

"Everyone okay?" he asked.

We nodded, all of us catching our breath.

The thing was, those mouthpieces made it hard to talk.

"You okay, Astrid?" he asked her. She nodded, clutching her belly.

She bent down and at first I thought she was going to be sick, then I saw that her sneakers were untied. She had pulled them on over the feet of her safety suit without tying the laces.

Thank God she hadn't tripped.

"Follow me," Jake said. "We'll just, uh, we'll find a car."

He started edging down the street.

There was screaming, from one of the houses. A horrible, nerve-jangling sound.

I looked to Niko, Should we help?

He shook his head and followed Jake.

Then we saw a young woman in the street.

She was in front of a small white house that was nestled between two larger houses made of brick.

She was muttering to herself and carrying an armload of stuff, miscellaneous stuff to an idling Mazda sedan parked at the curb. She wore exercise clothes and her brown hair was coming out of a ponytail and sticking to her mouth.

There were things on the ground behind her—a picture frame. A tub of mayonnaise. Straw hat. Couch pillow.

She threw the armload into the back of the car and scrambled to retrieve the fallen items and shove them in, too. Then she saw us.

"Stay back!" she screamed. And I saw a big knife in her hand. A chef's knife.

She'd been carrying it while she held the stuff, which was why she was dropping it everywhere.

Also, she was clearly type AB and fully, wildly paranoid.

We were a hundred and fifty feet away.

"No! No! No!" she cried. She backed away from us—from *us*—and then we saw a man behind her, moving fast.

I spat the mouthpiece out and shouted, "LOOK OUT!" and I rushed forward, trying, I don't know, to save her.

But the man got her before we did.

He was broad shouldered, bald with a pot belly, and he was O.

He stalked toward her from behind, his arms and white button-down shirt splattered with blood. Head down, eyes gleaming with the call to murder.

O, O, O—I recognized it.

"Shoot him!" Astrid screamed, screaming to Jake.

But the O man had his hands around the woman's throat, crushing the life out of her. Crushing her throat.

Her eyes bulging and it was awful, awful, awful.

I cried out in anger and wanted to fight him, then, but Niko was pulling me back.

The man got a hold of the lady's knife and stabbed her in the chest.

He stabbed her again and again, like a kid lost in play.

Niko dragged me away, Jake was helping him now, and they got me back to the woman's Mazda.

The man looked up at me. He was grinning madly, licking at his chin, where some blood had sprayed.

Astrid revved the engine of the car and then Jake pushed me into it as Niko hopped in the front passenger seat.

Astrid put the car in gear and we drove away.

DAY 33

Jake struggled to pull the door closed.

We were sitting on the woman's stuff. Crammed in on top of piles of odd items.

I looked out the rear window of the car and saw the man resume stabbing the woman with her chef's knife.

I shouted in despair.

CHAPTER TWENTY

JOSIE

I STUMBLE BACK OUT INTO THE HALLWAY FILLED WITH THE waiting sick.

A cut across the face. A woman holding a sprained arm.

Human beings, needing help. Dirty and scared and beaten down.

Locked up because of a blood type.

Mario is going to be okay. That's good. I don't know what I will do if Mario doesn't make it.

What are his chances? Alex could tell me. Alex could calculate it for me if he were here.

I cross through the courtyard, going back to our room.

The thirty or so bodies at the gate are laid out in rows now, sleeping it off. A guard stands leaning against the gate, making sure that no one robs the bodies of the sedated prisoners.

They will wake up in three or four hours, eyes dried and bloodshot, heads pounding.

DAY 33

They'll drink lots of water and feel groggy for the rest of the day.

Tonight they will go to sleep and have wild, vivid dreams. We will all hear them hollering in their sleep tonight.

The day I got shot—the same day I blocked the blow Venger meant for Mario, Mario and the kids dragged me inside. They babysat me in the rec room until I woke up.

That night I dreamed I was waiting for my parents in a train station.

Vaulted ceiling, marble hall—a classic train station. And I was skulking about, trying to stay hidden as shop vendors, with their little stores set into a colonnade against a wall, set out bottles of water in trays of ice and placed food in display cases—pastries, scrambled eggs, yogurts.

In my dream I stole a bacon, egg, and cheese on a roll and I was eating it, ducked down behind a trash bin and then there were these loud train whistles and suddenly the station was full of busy, bustling crowds.

I saw my parents there, dressed up for traveling like from a black-and-white movie. My mom wore a long coat with velvet buttons and my dad had on a suit and a fedora.

And I wanted to call out to them.

But I was so dirty and I had stolen food—I was ashamed of myself.

And they had Gram with them, and she was shuffling along as fast as she could. She walked like Mario walks. Mom and Dad were patient, as they are, but I could tell they were all in a great hurry.

I couldn't go to them. I knew they wouldn't want me anymore.

I enter the downstairs hallway of Excellence. I know the kids will be waiting in the room to hear about Mario.

I hurry through the Men's hall.

The last thing I need is to run into one of my attackers from the night before.

I am relieved that I don't.

I push open the door at the end of the hall, leading to the stairs—unlocked during the day.

Stepping in, I hear movement. Clothing rustling, breathing.

It isn't unusual to see people making out in the shadows sometimes.

But I stop.

Looking down the stairway leading to the basement, through the slats of the stairs, I see a familiar body—a familiar sweater.

It is Mario's sweater and it is Lori down there.

I freeze.

"Nice," says a voice. Brett. "You're so pretty. Don't be scared."

She has her hands up and he is putting them down, kissing her. Making her shut up by kissing her.

"Hey!" I say.

I am down the half a flight in a heartbeat.

"It's okay, Josie," Lori says. "I'm fine."

I see tears on her cheeks. Fine?

Her shirt is messed up and her hair, too, and she is crying.

And I see Brett is not alone. ANOTHER Union "Man" is with him.

That makes me so angry I can barely breathe as VRAAAAAAAUGH my blood ramps up.

"You had your chance, Josie." Brett says. "Lori understands a good deal when it comes her way."

My blood is pounding in my ears and making it hard to hear. Hard to think.

"They're going to protect us. All of us," Lori tells me. "It's okay."

DAY 33

"IT IS NOT OKAY," I shout.

The squat, pug-faced teenager with Brett pushes me.

"Keep it down, Rabbit," he sneers. "This is a private party."

God help me, I can't stop myself.

I slam the heel of my right hand into his nose.

Blood sprays and the kid squeals.

"Jesus Christ!" Brett yells and I grab him by the hair and throw him into the cement wall.

He is down and I am kicking.

"Stop!" Lori screams. "Stop it, Josie!"

I am O. God help me. Full blown and I will kill them. Attacking a fourteen-year-old? Molesting a girl? Little Lori? I will kill them.

"STOP!" Lori slaps me.

I turn on her.

"Breathe, Josie," she says.

She wraps her arms around me.

"Shhhhhh," she says.

Pug Face moans.

Lori hugs me and drags me up the stairs, away from the fallen Union Men. One step at a time.

Brett curses at me.

"We'll get you, Josie Miller," he says. "You're as good as dead."

CHAPTER TWENTY-ONE

DEAN

THE WIND HAD SHIFTED AND NOW THE DRIFT WAS HITTING THE windshield.

Astrid turned on the windshield wipers.

The black grit lay like a film on the glass, then was wiped away. Clung, was wiped, clung, was wiped.

I looked at the particles of drift that had clung to the side window. Each was tiny. Dust-speck tiny   and each a little perfect square. Much smaller than a grain of sand. Not cubic, but flat. Flat black death, particled out.

Beyond the window, we were passing through the streets of Vinita. We saw fires, people coming, screaming out of their homes.

Through the dark, sifting sandstorm people were dying and trying to save each other on every street.

"You've got to turn around," Jake said. "Get back on the highway."

Astrid pulled over abruptly, driving the car up onto the sidewalk.

DAY 33

"I can't breathe," she said, her words coming thickly through her mouthpiece. "Gonna throw up."

Within the zipped suit, she popped out her mouthpiece.

"That's not a good idea, Astrid!" Niko said, sharply concerned.

"I'm gonna hurl!" she wailed. She started to unzip her suit.

I leaned across, into the front seat and stopped her hand.

"Astrid!" I said. "Look at me."

Her body and face were completely sealed within the suit.

She looked up and through the clear visors of our two suits, she locked into my eyes.

"Breathe," I told her. "It's okay. There's enough air in the suit. Breathe."

"Don't let her take the suit off!" Jake added.

"She's gonna be fine, Jake," I said without breaking eye contact with her. I kept my voice steady. "Just breathe, Astrid."

Maybe it sounds dumb, but this space, right here, this connection between us, was the foundation of our relationship. She knew that she could count on me to be there. Yeah, I had been a total nerd who had a crush on her and we were an unlikely pair. But she knew I was there for her and that meant something.

What were we saying to each other, through the plastic?

Her: I'm scared.
Me: I know.
Me: I love you.
Her: I know.
Then: And it's going to be okay.

Astrid put her mouthpiece back in and settled back into her seat. She tried to swipe at her tears, using the gloves of the suit, but it didn't really work.

"You're crushing my leg, man," Jake complained to me.

I shifted back into the backseat.

"Somebody else should drive," Astrid said. And Niko and she climbed over each other to switch places.

We didn't dare to open the car doors—not with the drift still peppering the car when the wind changed.

Niko got us on the highway, headed north.

When the air was clear, we felt it was safe to take off the masks.

Astrid put her head in her hands. I didn't need to see her shoulders shaking to know she was crying.

She was sitting in front of me so I put my hand over the seat back and patted her on the shoulder.

"That was horrible," I said.

"That poor woman," Astrid choked out.

"They should be warning people!" Jake said, struggling to keep his voice even. "Everyone thinks they're rumors, but the drifts are real!"

"It's the military," I said. "They must be keeping the story quiet. But why?"

"To keep people from panicking," Niko said, his eyes on the road. "To keep them from evacuating."

"Why would they do that?" Jake asked.

"I don't know," Niko said. "Maybe because there's no place left to go."

Jake and I had to do some moving around and reorganizing to get comfortable in the backseat.

"That poor woman was nutso," Jake said. And it was true. She had loaded a totally bizarre selection of household items into her backseat.

DAY 33

There was:

An oscillating fan.
An industrial-size carton of Goldfish crackers, which Jake started to eat immediately.
Four giant photo albums, dated 2019–2023.
A set of jumper cables and, man, she was thinking ahead, snow chains for the tires.
A large makeup box/kit kind of thing.
A six-pack of protein shakes and a variety of snack foods.
Two unopened canisters of tennis balls.
A houseplant.
A box of dishes that had broken when she threw them in the car.

"And lookee, lookee!" Jake crowed. "Mama was planning ahead."

He brandished a half-full bottle of scotch.

He uncorked it and took a swig.

"Jeez, Jake," I said.

"Is that really a good idea?" Niko asked.

"We just saw Rocco Caputo die. We almost got shot and then blown up by a truck. We saw some poor crazy woman we don't know die. We saw a man hacking her body to bits with a kitchen knife. I think getting wasted is a GREAT idea. I really do."

And he chugged. Straight scotch. Ugh.

"That's enough," I said. "Give me the bottle."

"You want some?" he asked.

"No, I'm going to put it away."

"You're not my freakin' nanny, Geraldine!" Jake yelled.

"Quiet!" Astrid snapped.

"You heard her!" I said, making a snatch for the bottle.

"Both of you shut up!" she yelled. "I HEAR something."

All four of us fell silent.

All I could hear was the engine droning and the thud of my own heartbeat.

"Never mind," she said. She relaxed into her seat.

Jake took another drink from the bottle and then munched on a handful of Goldfish.

"You don't care that Jake's getting drunk?" I asked Astrid. "That doesn't bother you?"

"I wish I could get drunk myself," she said. She sounded miserable.

"I wonder if we can make it to Missouri on this tank of gas," Niko said. "We have three-quarters of a tank."

I sat back and looked out the window.

Miles of drying farmland blurred past.

"I wish we could have saved that woman," Astrid said.

"I know," I told her.

Astrid reached over and turned on the radio. FM and XM stations were all down, but there was some of that funny, fuzzy AM radio to be had. There was nothing on the radio about the drift.

"Hey, Astrid," Niko said. "I know it's probably pointless, but would you try the GPS?"

I shifted around in my seat, getting comfortable.

In my lap I held what looked like an empty fishbowl. Seemed like the floor mat was damp—something wet pressing against my leg, though the moisture didn't seep through the leg of my safety suit.

Maybe there was a dead fish down there somewhere.

I stared out the window and after a few minutes I realized my hands were still shaking.

"Don't you think we should try to warn people?" Astrid asked Niko quietly.

DAY 33

Jake took another swig of the whisky.

I could swear his eyes were red. I could swear he was crying there, looking out the window.

"We can't save everyone," Niko said. "But we can still get Josie out of Mizzou, if we're lucky."

I knew I should sleep but I couldn't.

We drove for a couple hours, putting mile after mile between us and Vinita, Oklahoma. The roads were clear—not much traffic at all.

We rolled down the suits, knotting them at the waist as the soldiers had done.

We caught part of President Booker's weekly address:

My fellow Americans, history will judge us by how we handle this series of devastating crises. Those of you in a position to help must ask yourselves: Am I doing enough? Can I stretch out a hand to one more survivor? Can I make do with less, so that those in dire need can live? And to those of you who have found yourselves homeless, and have lost beloved family and friends—I tell you this: Your government has not forgotten you. Medical care. Food. Water. Shelter. We are working to provide these for you. And once we have regained stability, we will begin to rebuild. Housing. Industry. Purpose. We will overcome this disaster, working together, sacrificing much, never forgetting that America is stronger than ever, united we stand. Divided? Never!

And then the "Star-Spangled Banner" started playing.

Nothing about the drifts.

Did he not know? Was that possible?

If the Network had been running, everybody would know. There'd be images and videos and alarms going off all over the online world.

But only the government had access to the Network now.

It made me feel scared. What else were they keeping from us?

"They're gonna impeach Booker," Jake snorted. "The drifts. The NORAD thing. The way he's handled everything."

"No, they're not," I scoffed. "Who told you that?"

"Rocco."

"Are you serious? He was a right-wing idiot—"

"Hey!" Jake said, pressing a finger into my chest. "Don't speak bad of the dead."

And he held my glance for a moment. His head wavered as he tried to look me in the eye.

Then he threw up his hands and laughed, trying to play off his serious tone.

"I'm just joshin' you, man," he said. "Sometimes I think you're really lame, Dean. A real wet blanket—"

"Oh God, shut up, Jake," Astrid said from the front seat.

"Let me finish, now, let me finish," he drawled. "But then I see you're not such a d-bag. There. See? I had something good to say."

I chuffed a laugh. Some compliment.

I didn't respond. Maybe he'd fall asleep. He was drunk enough. Heck, maybe he'd fall out of the car.

"Anybody want some Goldfish?" I asked. "There's also a box of Golden Grahams and some kiddy applesauce squeezer thingies."

I tossed up some juice boxes into the front seat, too.

We ate, we drove. Niko said we were at least four hours from Mizzou, though we'd need gas before then.

DAY 33

We still had our gas credits, whatever that meant. I realized we still had our money, too. We'd never paid Rocco.

Niko encouraged us all to get some sleep.

I guess I drifted off because I woke up to Astrid saying, "There! I heard it again! Didn't you hear it?"

"I didn't hear anything," Niko said and he shut off the radio.

"Pull over," Astrid commanded.

"What is it?" I asked.

"Just pull over, Niko. Right now."

Niko pulled onto the shoulder and cut the engine.

We waited. Jake snored. I started to ask Astrid more about this phantom sound but she cut me off, holding her hand up. Her head was cocked.

And then I heard it.

A soft, muted thumping. Coming from behind me.

And a wail. "Mommy!"

CHAPTER TWENTY-TWO

JOSIE

WE STAY IN THE ROOM UNTIL DINNER.

Lori won't let anyone leave.

"Look," she says. "We go straight to Plaza 900. We eat. We come right back."

"Why?" Aidan wants to know. "What's wrong? What happened?"

"When's Mario coming back?" Heather adds. "He should be back by now. He should be here."

"You heard what Josie said, the doctors are doing their best and we can go back and visit him tomorrow."

I lay on our bed and look at the wire frame and the stained mattress on the bunk above us.

It was bad, what I had done.

I can see that.

The part of my mind that is still reasonable and well oiled murmurs and tuts inside my head:—Am I suicidal? Is that why I had beaten those boys?

DAY 33

I am done for.

Or am I just a dumb animal now, going on instinct, defending Lori because she is my tribe?

My actions mean she is in for it, too.

In trying to defend her, I have probably doomed her.

And then the darkest, secret voice whispers that we're all doomed anyway and it's not my fault.

And that feels good to hear, even if it feels a little dirty to think it. It is true, after all.

The dinner tone comes over the PA system.

One chime—time for the first group to head to Plaza 900. That is us.

There is no talking, no whispering from the kids.

They are simply scared to go to dinner without Mario. They have no idea of the danger I have put us in.

We all hold hands. Aidan's hand like ice in my right. Heather's like ice in my left.

Entering the cafeteria it seems to me that a hush falls over the room.

There is no sign of Carlo or the other Union Men.

We walk to the line.

Lori says we should all stay together at all times.

Maybe she thinks the presence of the little kids will keep the Union Men off us.

We go to the line and get trays.

People shush as we approach.

It is eerie.

A man gives me a little salute and a woman with him pushes his arm down and hurries him away from us.

We get our food.

"Where's your fella?" the cafeteria lady asks me.

"He's in the clinic," I tell her.

"Aw," she clucks. Then she leans forward to whisper. "Look, he asked me to do something. I don't know. Can you tell him I'm still thinking it over?"

"Yes, ma'am," I say, looking away.

She presses an extra dinner roll into my hand. "You tell him it's from Cheryl."

"I will," I say.

Cheryl gives all the kids extra spaghetti and, what's more, an extra meatball each.

A little boy named Jonas runs over to Aidan.

"You guys are in some kinda trouble!" he says cheerfully. "My daddy said the Union Men is out for you all!"

"No!" Aidan retorts. "That's dumb. We gave them oatmeal just yesterday and ALL our sugar! They're on our side now!"

If only.

We go ensemble to a table. People go back to their eating and talking, but we get a lot of glances.

The food tastes like tomato-covered wood pulp, to me, though I see the little boys eat up their large helpings with gusto.

So the word is out that the Union Men were going to come for us. It explains the death pall we'd brought over the cafeteria.

"I'm not going back with you," I say quietly to Lori. "You take the kids and you get back to the room and lock the door."

Lori looks at me, her eyes red, her thin brown hair limp around her pale face.

"And you'll do what? Hide somewhere?"

DAY 33

There is sarcasm in her voice and for the first time, I actually see the girl.

She isn't as pasty as I thought. She has some spirit.

Maybe she will make it.

"I'm going to fight them," I say.

She shakes her head, her mouth set in a grim, determined line.

I slide my hand into hers so she'll really look at me.

"The thing is, I've been ready to die for a long time, Lori," I say quietly and my throat gets a little constricted, eyes a bit watery, maybe.

But it is the truth.

"No," she says. "We can make it to the room. We can make it one more night."

"And then what?"

She squeezs my hand hard.

"You are going to make it through the night so you can see Mario in the morning and then you're talking to the reporters and getting out of here, Josie Miller."

I look at her for a beat.

Maybe she really will make it.

The kids are done eating now, and starting to fidget.

"My tummy hurts," Heather says.

It was likely the extra meatball.

"Let's go," Lori says.

We rise and then a skinny mother, a woman from our hall, stands up at the table opposite us. She elbows her kid—a teenage girl I've seen shuffling around. The two of them, and three more people from the table behind them, get up.

"Are you headed back to the dorm?" the lady asks us.

Her voice is narrow and shaking.

These are the first words she has ever said to us, and she lives right on our hall.

"Because we're headed back, too."

And as we start to walk toward the door, people cram the last plastic forkfuls of pasta into their mouths and chug their milk.

Soon we have an escort of fifty or sixty people, herding us toward the dorm. I recognize one of the men—he is the guy who had fought to get me free, when I was trapped in the Men's hall. Patko.

As we walk, whispers come to us.

"We'll help you any way we can."

And, "Don't be scared, kids. It'll be all right."

The skinny mother grabs my hand and squeezes.

"We're praying for you," she says.

DAY 33

CHAPTER TWENTY-THREE

DEAN

"THERE'S A KID IN THE TRUNK!" ASTRID SAID, SCRAMBLING TO release her seat belt and open her door.

I practically fell out of the car.

Niko was frantically reaching around the dash, trying to find the trunk release button or knob or whatever.

He pulled it and *thonk*, the trunk came up and I skidded around the bumper and there was a little girl. A toddler with black hair matted down by sweat. She had skin the color of caramel and big brown eyes. She wore a sweater dress and little white shoes.

The toddler saw Astrid and me standing there and burst into sobs.

Astrid stepped forward and took the girl in her arms.

Astrid looked up at me. "Juice box. Now."

I grabbed a juice box as Niko came around the car.

"Whoa," he said.

"Yeah," I answered, putting the straw in and handing the box to Astrid.

The crazed (now-dead) mother of this child had made a nest for her little girl in the trunk of the sedan.

There were blankets and two or three sippy cups.

There was also a large pack of diapers pushed to the side.

"We tailgating?" Jake asked, stumbling to us. Then he saw. "Hey, who brought the baby?"

He patted the back of the toddler. She pulled away from him and cried all the harder.

"Mommy," I said, nodding to the trunk so he could see the nest of bedding.

"Wow. That's . . . that's . . ."

"Sad? Horrifying? Tragic?" Astrid offered as she bounced the little girl.

"Lucky we found her in time," he said.

"Okay, okay," Niko said. "We need to think. We need to get off the road and think."

"I need to change her first," Astrid said.

I got a whiff of the kid. Yes. She had to be changed.

Astrid held the girl on her lap and we drove to the next truck stop, fifteen miles down the road.

"What's your name, sweetie?" Astrid had asked her, but the girl wasn't talking. Maybe she couldn't talk yet. It was hard to tell how old she was. Maybe two? Maybe less?

In the backseat, I picked up one of the photo albums that we'd thrown behind the headrests.

The album started with the mom we'd seen hugely pregnant, being hugged by her husband. Some of those kind of sappy naked-belly photos with the man placing his hands reverently on her giant, round globe of a stomach.

DAY 33

Then there were photos of the hospital waiting room. Parents milling around. Two families, one black, one white, waiting it out with expressions of nervous excitement. Some older kids playing around with bubble gum cigars.

There was the dad, grinning broadly, coming to tell them the news.

There was the mother, holding the little, squished-up, squalling baby.

Lots of photos of an older boy holding the newborn. A cousin? A brother?

Some embarrassing photos of breastfeeding.

And amid many, many photos of this baby girl dressed in many cute outfits, some of which featured headbands, tutus, and/or animal ears, was the girl's birth announcement:

Our baby girl has arrived!
Rinée Lea Manning
Born May 14, 2022 at 11:56 p.m.
7 pounds, 9 ounces • 20 inches

"There's a birth announcement in here," I said. "Her name is . . . Rin-ee?"

"Rin-ee? How's it spelled?" Astrid asked.

I spelled it, complete with the accent.

"I bet that's pronounced 'Renée.' Is your name pronounced Renée, sweetie?" Astrid asked the girl.

The toddler nodded and in a very soft, quiet voice she said, "Winée." It was the first word we'd had out of her.

Niko pulled into the parking lot at the service station. It was one of those big ones, with a bunch of chain fast-food restaurants inside. There were plenty of cars clustered in the spaces near the station. Who knew how much food there was to be found inside.

Niko parked at the far end of the lot—away from the rest of the cars, near the place where the asphalt ended and a small wooded area began.

We all got out of the car.

It felt good to be out in the air. The afternoon was turning gold—it would soon be time for dinner, if we could afford any.

Astrid rested against the car, the toddler squirming to get down.

"Okay, okay," Astrid said.

The girl went right for a puddle about ten feet away.

"I'll watch her," I told Astrid. She looked like she needed a break.

Rinée looked up at me with some suspicion. When I offered her my hand to hold, she marched right away from me and headed to the puddle.

"What are we going to do?" Astrid asked Niko.

Rinée jumped in the puddle, splashing her legs with the muddy water.

"Ew!" I said with a smile. "Yucky."

"Yuck!" she repeated.

"We can't go on with her," Niko said. "She has to go back."

"We can't go back to Vinita," Jake argued. "What about the drift?"

"Maybe it's moved out by now," Astrid said bleakly.

"Yuck!" Rinée yelled, splashing again.

She bent down to pat the water with her hands. That was just too gross for me.

I bent and scooped her up.

She screwed her face up, like she might cry. I twirled around, spinning her in the air.

DAY 33

She laughed.

"Moy," she said.

"Moy?"

"Moy woun'!"

More around. Okay. Rinée could make her desires known verbally. That would be helpful.

I twirled her again and her laugh broke out—like a bell ringing. Oh, it was a sweet sound.

I laughed with her.

"We have to take her back, Jake. She has a dad. He's probably worried sick."

"He's probably dead!" Jake shouted. "Let's be honest!"

His face went all red and then he burst into sobs.

"Like her mother. She'd be alive—," he cried. "She'd be alive if I had just been—smarter, faster, I don't know, BETTER, I could have shot that guy and she'd be alive."

Astrid had crossed to him by now and was hugging him.

He sobbed into her neck.

I can handle this, I thought. She's his friend. She's comforting him.

Then he cupped her head, her beautiful blond hair, cropped short, and he kissed her.

"Down!" Rinée demanded. I let her slide out of my hands onto the ground, where she started dancing in the puddle again.

Astrid pushed Jake away, slowly and then harder. He stumbled back.

"Jake! What's wrong with you?" she said.

But hadn't she stayed a moment?

She'd let him kiss her.

I walked into the woods, my hands in fists.

"Dean?" Astrid called. "Dean!"

Screw her. Screw them both.

* * *

There wasn't even a good tree to sit against and think. They were all weedy, with trash blown into the roots in places.

I stumbled into the woods until I couldn't see any of my "friends," or the parking lot.

I finally found a tree sufficiently thick to lean against.

I thought about Alex. I'd left my brother, who I loved dearly, so I could get Astrid to safety. I'd taken this risk—a huge risk—for what? What if she and Jake got back together? She had the right to do that, after all. We weren't married.

I'd left my brother for nothing.

I cursed my stupidity long and loud.

Niko came and found me a while later. He had the gun Jake had taken off the trucker with him.

"Hey," he said.

I nodded toward the gun. "Going hunting?"

"No . . . Look, I think I'm going to go ahead alone," he told me. "I'm going inside to see if I can hitch a ride."

"Okay," I said.

"If I can't hitch, maybe I'll steal a car," he said, talking more to himself than to me. "If it comes to it, I guess I could walk."

"Well, maybe I should come with you," I muttered.

Niko looked up at me, totally surprised. He brushed his long, straight brown hair out of his eyes.

"I mean, if Astrid wants to be with Jake then I should let them have each other. I'm just getting in the way. And you might need my help."

"Dean," Niko said. "That is the stupidest thing I have ever heard you say. Really."

I heard distant squeals of laughter from Rinée. Jake was probably swinging her around now.

1 7 3

DAY 33

"You love Astrid, I know you do. Why would you leave her with Jake?"

"Because . . . because she loves me. Some. She loves me some. Not all the way, like I love her. And I know, she needs time and she's been through so much, but maybe she'll never love me like I love her!"

I brushed the back of my hand over my eyes.

"I'm pathetic. I left Alex because I thought I should protect her. But what if she doesn't end up wanting to be with me? She never shows it. She doesn't even act like she's my girlfriend most of the time."

"Dean, do you know what love is?" Niko asked me.

I looked up.

That was a jerky thing to ask. The kind of question that gets a guy punched, but I knew Niko. He could be awkward at times.

"Love isn't how the person makes you feel or what they do for you. It's how you feel about them," he said. He stood there, all backlit with the dappled sunset.

I was kind of thunderstruck.

"Love is how you feel about the other person. Everything else is just details," he said.

I let my head rest back against the scrawny tree trunk.

"So do you love her?"

I nodded.

"Then stop worrying about Jake and stop worrying about making her love you the same way and just do your job."

"My job is to love her, you're saying?"

"And keep her safe."

"I've been acting like an idiot," I said.

"Yeah, pretty much."

I got to my feet. Niko handed me the gun.

"You should have this. That O guy could still be around. You should have it to keep Astrid safe."

"You don't want it?"

He shook his head.

"I'm less of a threat if I'm not carrying a gun, I think," he said.

His profile was facing me now and he was thinking of something.

Niko Mills. Here he was, saving my butt again.

"Good luck," I told him, extending my hand.

"You, too," he said. "I'll see you on Red Hill Road, in New Holland, Pennsylvania."

"Red Hill Road. New Holland, P-A."

Niko and I walked back up to the car together.

Astrid was sorting through some of the things in the car. She had set out on the parking lot the fan, the box of dishes, the houseplant, and other stuff she obviously thought we didn't need. Rinée was busy digging with a spoon in the dirt of the houseplant, slowly scooping it all out onto the asphalt and patting it with the back of the spoon.

"Dean," Jake said, getting up to his feet. "I'm a jerk. I'm an a-hole. You have to forgive me."

"It's okay," I said. "I can see how it happened. Let's just forget it."

I went over to Astrid.

"You're okay? You sure?" Astrid asked me quietly. "I'm so mad at him."

"You know what? I've been acting like a jealous idiot. I'm sorry," I told her. "I'm better now."

Astrid looked relieved. Maybe even a little bit impressed.

I clapped my hands.

DAY 33

"Let's get this baby back to her daddy."

Rinée looked up and clapped her little hands, echoing me.

Astrid hugged Niko for a good, long time when we said good-bye.

Jake shook hands with him.

I swept him into a big hug.

We all promised we'd see each other soon. God, how I hoped that would be true.

Then I drove and Jake rode shotgun.

Astrid and the little girl slept together in the backseat, which was much more spacious now that Astrid had thrown everything out.

For dinner we had protein shakes.

There had been exactly $217 between all of us. We'd split it down the middle—half for Niko and half for us. It felt like Niko should get more, since we were taking the car, but he insisted on the split.

We wanted to make our $108 last as far as we could.

We had had to get gas at the station. That had been weird.

The attendant had to call into an 800 number. He made me give my social security number to a crabby lady, who then informed the attendant that my credits for the week had already been used.

The attendant looked at me like I was dirty.

Someone had hacked my account and had used all my credits and I got treated like scum.

Jake's account, with his luck, was completely untouched.

The guy gave us the full measure of Jake's available gas credits, which was about a half a tank.

That would get us back to Vinita and then some.

"Hey," Jake said to me in the car. "Remember that time we got high? Back at the store?"

"Yeah," I said. "That was pretty fun."

"Man, what I wouldn't give for a couple of Obezine now, right?"

"I guess."

"If we were settled. You know, safe," Jake said.

"I know."

I knew he was aching for another swig of that whisky bottle. Astrid had tucked it into the trunk. I'd seen her do it and I watched Jake see her do it, too.

But instead of thinking about what an addict he was, and getting myself all worked up, I just let Jake be Jake.

The sun went down and the road got dark.

After a while Jake fell asleep.

I'd driven for about an hour when I realized something.

I woke up Astrid.

"Guys, if we go back there now, we won't know who's there. We won't be able to see. The O guy could still be out."

"What do you want to do?" Astrid asked me.

"I think we should find somewhere to pull over and sleep in the car."

"Okay," she said, yawning.

I pulled off at the next exit and we were on a country highway. Fields of corn razed to a knee-high stubble on either side. The land was flat—really flat.

I wanted a sort of hidden place to put the car. Some tall windbreak trees surrounded a small farm up the road. But I didn't want to go too close to someone's house. They'd think we were up to something.

I wasn't quite sure where to go.

DAY 33

Everyone in the car was asleep.

I just drove for a bit. Eventually I saw a farm and then, a little ways down from the farm, a dirt road that seemed to be some kind of access road. There were some trees there.

I turned down the road and parked the car on grass, between two pine trees.

Through this, no one woke up.

All three of them were exhausted—one from being drunk, one from being pregnant, one from being locked in a trunk for four hours. Thank God Astrid had heard the baby when she did.

I got out.

The air was completely still.

I took my suit and mask, just to be safe. I was pretty sure the warning whistle would give me enough time to gear up.

A hoot owl was calling and the scent of pine was really strong in the cool air.

Sometimes, for a moment, your senses could spin your brain a story. You could forget about the disasters and just smell the crisp country air for a moment.

I sat against one of the large trees.

A few minutes later, Astrid came to me.

"You think the air's okay?" she asked me.

I held up my face mask. "Just to be safe."

She got hers from the backseat and then came to sit next to me.

"Is Rinée all right—," I asked and she stopped me talking with a kiss.

The moon was up and her hands were on my face, and she kissed me gently. An apology of a kiss.

I drank in the sight of her big eyes, her rose-colored lips, that hollow at the base of her throat.

"You were really great with her today," Astrid said to me.

"You feeling okay?" I asked. "Any cramps?"

She shook her head.

"I'm a little tired, is all."

She leaned against me and we looked up at the nighttime sky.

"Remember when you said 'it's a real baby,' when we were looking at the ultrasound?"

"Yeah," I said.

"I feel like that all the time. I can't believe I have a real baby growing inside me. Under my skin! A little human being! And it's going to come out and I'll be a real mother. It's surreal."

"You're gonna be a great mom," I said, sounding like a cliché.

"Pah, who knows!" She laughed. "But you're going to be a great dad."

I closed my eyes.

She thought of us as a family. She did.

I needed to let it sink in, so I'd remember it the next time Jake drove me berserk.

"Got any more names in mind?"

Astrid wouldn't let me or Jake or anyone know about the names she was picking out for the baby.

"Ferdinand, if it's a boy," she said, straight faced. "Or maybe Algernon."

"That's nice. Call him Algae for short."

We laughed together, under a canopy of pine branches and above them, the stars.

DAY 33

CHAPTER TWENTY-FOUR

JOSIE

I TRY TO GET THE LITTLE KIDS TO GO TO THE SKINNY MOTHER'S room but they refuse.

"We can fight," Freddy tells me, bouncing on his toes. "We're 0, like you."

"You're not 0 like me," I say. "I hope you'll never be 0 like me."

"Well, you're one of us and we protect our own," he insists. "We stick together."

"Yeah, I guess we do," I tell him. I ruffle his hair.

We start piling furniture against the door.

First we put the big single bed against the door. It is made of wood and heavier than the bunk beds, which are just metal.

Then we pile the bureaus on it.

Like all the doubles, we have two bureaus. Identical, made of particleboard with birch veneer. Both basically empty—none of us even have a change of clothes.

There is one old pair of men's shoes rattling around in the

bottom drawer of one of them. Mario is saving them to barter in case things got bad, food-wise.

There are also a dozen sugar packets in there, and a salt shaker he had lifted from Plaza 900 our first day there. Those could be used for barter, too.

I sit down on a free edge of the bed. My weight can add to our pathetic blockade.

We know it is nine o'clock when we hear the bell over the PA and the lights go out.

Lori tries to herd the other kids into the other room and get them into the bunk bed.

"Come on, you guys," she scolds. "What would Mario tell you to do? He'd tell you to go to sleep and you know it."

"But I'm not tired!" Heather protests.

"It's just stupid to think we're going to sleep!" Freddy insists.

Lori tries to put a hand on his shoulder and he dodges her grasp.

"You guys need to go to bed," I say, trying to help Lori.

"I'm staying up to fight!" Freddy says.

"Me, too," says Aidan. "I owe you, after how I got you in trouble with Venger."

"You don't owe me," I say. "Venger was out to get me from the start. He was just waiting for me to slip up."

"Well, I'm not going to sleep and that's final!" he shouts.

"Yeah! We're not going to sleep! No way."

"Fine," Lori says. "You want to stay up, STAY UP! See if I care."

She goes and stands by the window, looking out into the fluorescent-tinted nighttime sky of our containment camp.

I scratch my head.

"Have you guys ever heard of Mrs. Wooly?" I ask them.

Aidan looks at me askance, like I am trying to trick him.

DAY 33

"Who's Mrs. Wooly?"

"That's a dumb name," Freddy says, still bouncing on his toes.

"I tell you what," I say. "You guys get into bed—"

A chorus of nos and no ways!

"You guys get into bed and I'll tell you."

Three sets of crossed arms and defiant expressions.

"Look, it's not like you're going to sleep through the fight!" I tell them. "If the Union Men come, we're all going to know it. But it's cold in here. Look at Heather, she's shaking."

And she is.

Winter is drawing near and the temperatures are really dropping when the sun sets. I make up my mind to try to trade those men's shoes for some more blankets, if we make it through the night.

Many people have taken to wearing their blankets shawl-style during the day. The boys have resisted this so far, but their pride about it will probably fall as the temperatures do.

"Get in bed where you'll at least be warm."

So they do.

Aidan and Freddy get onto the top bunk. Heather lays on the bottom one. Lori has no intention of sleeping, I can see that, but she lays down with Heather, to help keep her warm.

"What kind of a dumb name is Mrs. Wooly?" Freddy asks again.

"You're taking the whole blanket," Aidan complains.

I tuck the blanket around the two of them.

Four sets of big, scared eyes blink at me from that bunk bed.

I sit on the floor.

"The day before the earthquake and the spill, I was on my way to school on the high school bus. I was sitting next to my friend Trish and we were just talking about . . . I remember we were talking about our bake sale to raise money for immigration reform. Hail started falling, but it wasn't regular hail. It was monster hail, giant hail. There were hailstones as big as softballs! It was like being fired on by cannons. Our driver, Mr. Green, sped the bus up and lost control. We crashed."

I can remember the smell of the ice in the air and the blood.

"Our bus crashed in the parking lot of a Greenway superstore."

"We have a Greenway in Castle Rock," Aidan says.

I nod.

"That's where Mrs. Wooly comes in. See, Mrs. Wooly was the driver of another bus, right behind us. And it had kids from both the elementary school and the middle school on it. She had really little kids, as little as five years old, in that bus.

"Mrs. Wooly loves kids. You wouldn't think it, because she can be very gruff, but she'd do anything to protect her kids."

Heather takes her thumb out of her mouth to say, "Like Uncle Mario."

Has she always sucked her thumb? I hadn't noticed.

"Yes, she is kind of like Mario, only a lot younger. So the hail was crashing in through the windows of the bus and Mrs. Wooly was scared that her kids were going to get hurt. She did a crazy thing."

Not a peep from the bunk bed, so I know I have them.

"She drove her bus through the front window of the Greenway!

"But remember, I was still in the crashed bus outside, and it was lying on its side so the hail was coming down through the windows, right on top of us. I got hit on the head and that's where I got this scar." I run a hand up to the dark gash, the flesh still depressed under my fingertips.

"Mrs. Wooly made the kids get out of her bus and wait

DAY 33

where it was safe, in the store. By this time, the engine of our bus had caught fire. It was going to blow and we were all going to die."

Gasps from the bunk bed. The slight shimmying of excited bodies.

"And then Mrs. Wooly backed her bus up, out into the parking lot. And she used an ax to chop open the lock on the emergency door. Then she helped us get out."

I pause, not for dramatic effect, but because I remember Niko half dragging me down the aisle.

And then Astrid holding me on that bus. She held me in her arms like I was a baby.

I don't think I ever thanked her for her kindness to me on the bus and now it is, of course, too late. Far too late.

"Then what happened?" Heather asks.

"Did the other bus explode?"

"It did," I say, shaking my head to clear it. "Mrs. Wooly drove us into the store and the crashed bus exploded before we even got inside. She saved our lives, no question."

"Wow!" Heather murmurs.

"We were snug and safe in there," I go on. "We had all this food and even lights and heat. And all the clothes we could want. Imagine that!"

"Oh man," Lori says. "I would kill for clean underwear."

"And toys? Was there toys?" asks Aidan.

"Aisles and aisles of toys," I tell him. "And candy!"

The questions stop and I can see all four of them, luxuriating in the idea of a safe place filled with games and sweets.

In the Greenway I had spun fantasies about Mrs. Wooly rescuing us in a tricked-out bus and the kids dreamed about returning to their lives and parents.

In the Virtues I told a real account of Mrs. Wooly's actions and the children fantasized about living in the Greenway.

Imagine that.

Lifted up by my real-life fairy tale, the kids drift off to sleep.

I go and sit out on the bed against the door.

Maybe a half hour later, Lori comes to sit with me.

"Do you think Mario's going to be okay?" she asks me.

I shrug.

"He's tough," I answer. "But he's old."

"What do you think is going to happen to us?" she asks me.

"Please," I say. "Don't."

"Don't what? Don't talk to you? Don't try to be your friend? God, what is it with you?"

I shush her. She is going to wake up the kids.

"You think you have it so much worse than the rest of us," she complains. "You're all high on yourself."

I laugh.

She is so totally wrong.

"You're not even going to answer me?"

"You should go to sleep."

"You know, if you had just let me do what I had to do with those boys, none of this would be happening."

"You wanted to have sex with those boys?" I ask her.

She wouldn't meet my eye.

She stands there at the window, arms crossed against the chill, the unearthly glow of the floodlights outlining her goose bumps in blue.

"No," she says. "But I could do it. To protect us. It wouldn't be the end of the world."

"Mmmmm, you don't know that. It might be the end of the world for you. Sometimes you can sacrifice too much—"

DAY 33

"It's all right to do things you don't want to, if the outcome is worthy."

"No. It is possible to sacrifice too much," I repeat. "It is."

She still wouldn't look at me.

"I'd do anything to protect those kids."

"I killed to protect my kids," I say.

And like a film being projected on the empty Sheetrock wall of our crummy double suite, I see Robbie, gun raised at Niko down at the end of a darkened aisle.

I see the crazed O soldier in the woods, headed for Max.

Oh, the joy I felt when I ripped that face mask off and inhaled, filling myself with rage and lust. And how strong I was when I bashed his head in.

And the father of the boy.

The father who had laid a trap and caught my friends.

My little loves, my devoted Niko, my old-new family, trapped down in the bottom of a pit and that daddy shining a flashlight on them, considering whether to let them live or die.

I sunk my teeth into his neck like a vampire and took out a hunk and he bled out, looking up at the no-star muddy sky.

I had enjoyed it.

Lori comes and stands beside me, wrapping her arm around my shoulders.

What sign of my distress had I given?

Maybe she could see the scenes playing in the reflections of my eyes.

They come around midnight.

First, the rattle of a hand on the lever.

Right, as if we might have left it open by accident.

Then the sound of fingers on the keypad.

Lori and I look at each other.

This is it. If they have the combination, we are dead.

Rattle, rattle, rattle. No.

They don't have it.

"Hello?" comes a singsong voice. "Anybody home?"

And sniggers. The sniggers cut off by an elbow to the stomach, maybe.

Knock-knock.

"We'd like to see Josie," the voice repeats. It has to be Carlo.

And then BAM, they try to kick the door in.

"Leave us alone," Lori screams.

By this time the kids are up and watching from the doorway to the other room.

BAM, BAM! They try the door again.

The bed shakes and the bureaus rattle.

"Hey, we just want to talk to you, Jojo," Carlo says, the singsong lilt in his voice. "Not so nice what you did to Brett and Juani."

"Go away!" I shout. "I'm not coming out."

"You messed them up real bad!" comes a different voice.

"Leave those kids alone," comes a shrill female voice. Maybe the skinny mom. "We all know you're up here! We'll tell on you!"

"'We'll tell on you,'" one of them mocks. "Who are you going to tell, Venger? He's the one who let us up here!"

"Yeah! And anyone who helps Josie is in for it. You should all know that now!" roars another one.

We can hear them striking several of the other doors in the hall.

"You leave that girl alone!" comes another voice.

"Room Three-Oh-Four. Write that down, Ray," Carlo says loudly enough for them all to hear.

Then BAM, BAM, BAM, they are hitting our door with something, maybe a chain, and the metal is bending, a little, near the lock.

I push against the bed with all my might.

DAY 33

The bed shakes with each chain lash on the door, but the lock holds.

Lori and the kids scramble to help.

The Union Men cannot get in the room.

They stop trying and my ears ring with the sudden silence.

There comes a polite knock on the door.

"Oh, Josie," Carlo calls.

"What?" I say.

"This door is fully and truly locked. So we'll catch up with you tomorrow."

CHAPTER TWENTY-FIVE

DEAN

WE SPENT THE NIGHT IN THE CAR.

Astrid cuddled with Rinée in the backseat and I reclined in the front seat.

Jake was crashed out in the passenger seat, snoring like a bear, his head lolling against the window. If I hadn't been so tired, it would have kept me up.

Rinée woke us up, crying.

"Shhh," Astrid told her. "It's okay." But there was no soothing the kid.

"We're out of juice boxes," I said. I rummaged around for something the girl would eat. Actually for anything that would get her to stop crying. My nerves felt like they'd been sharpened on a honing blade and the crying, screaming now, was going to put me over the edge.

"What about a protein shake?" Jake suggested.

DAY 34

But we tried that and she wouldn't take it.

"Come on, sweetie, let's take a walk," Astrid said.

She opened the door and Rinée wailed louder, pushing against Astrid. Astrid set her onto the ground and the toddler stormed away from the car.

"Do you want me to go?" I asked Astrid. She nodded.

The circles under her eyes were starting to worry me. It looked like she hadn't gotten, maybe, the best night of sleep in the world, curled up in the backseat of a Mazda with a twenty-two-month-old.

I followed Rinée as she wandered around. It was chilly, almost downright cold.

"Let's go get a blanket, Rinée," I said. "Come on, Rinée. Gotta keep warm."

I went to pick her up and she laughed and ran from me. Good, it could be a game. Anything to keep her from crying.

A cup of coffee sounded good to me, even though I didn't like the way it tasted. I needed something to open up my brain.

Finally she allowed me to scoop her up and I blew a raspberry onto her neck, causing her to giggle. I realized she was wet—really wet.

Coming back to the car, I saw the trunk open.

Jake's face peeked over the top and he saw me and then dropped back down.

As I walked up he shut the trunk.

"Found these," he said, holding up a bag of frosted animal crackers. "I thought I'd see if there was anything she might like . . ."

And he was sort of palming a protein shake behind his back.

He must've seen my eyes dart to the shake.

"Breakfast. It sort of tastes like last night's dinner," he joked.

I smiled. Nodded. What Jake did was not my concern. He could sneak whisky all day long. I didn't have to rat him out. I didn't even have to hold it against him.

"Where's Astrid?" I asked.

"Went to pee."

Astrid came back and changed the baby (I was going to have to learn how to do it. And soon. Blecch.) and we got on the road.

I drove, Astrid tried to keep Rinée occupied, Jake sipped whisky out of a protein shake bottle.

It's a weird thing, to have someone doing something that he's covering up in your presence. There was this huge lie going on right in the car and neither Astrid nor I said a thing.

I'm sure she could smell the booze. I could.

Jake told us about his days in Texas, back before he moved to Monument. He told us about the championship football games and about the BBQ dinners the backers threw for the team.

Breakfast was cold sandwiches from a gas station. Forty-two dollars. We were getting low on money.

I had the thought that maybe Rinée's dad might give us a reward or something for bringing her back. Then again, he might think we were kidnappers. Would he believe us, about how we'd found her in the trunk?

Jake chatted on and on. Astrid laughed at his cocky monologue.

I didn't feel much like banter.

I was thinking of Vinita. What we'd seen and what we might encounter.

I found Rinée's house by driving to the gas station in Vinita and going from there.

DAY 34

The charred remains of the service station were still smoking, twenty-four hours later. If I had stopped, we could have seen Rocco Caputo's bloody, skeleton prostrate on the asphalt, but I didn't care to stop.

What I didn't see was any trace of the drift. Nothing in the air, nothing skittering along the ground.

I kept remembering an eyewitness report I had read about a drift in a falling-apart copy of the *National Enquirer* back at Quilchena.

The man's description of the drift fit perfectly with what we had experienced. Of course it was hard to take seriously, back then, because the story it ran next to was about how aliens had triggered the Megatsunami with a rock-melting submarine.

The drift article had discussed a theory that the drifts were a fusion of the magnetic blackout cloud and the blood-type compound. That the thermobaric bombs the Air Force had used to destroy the compounds and the blackout cloud had locked them together.

The "grains" I'd seen were square in shape. Alex had described the blackout cloud as being tiny airborne magnets. There was some force keeping the particles together. Otherwise, they would disperse. It all seemed to make sense.

I wished I could have discussed it with Alex.

The mood in the car grew grim as I turned onto Rinée's street. The child was oblivious—Astrid had found a pacifier jammed in the seat-back pouch. Even though it seemed small (do they come in sizes?), Rinée was thrilled to have it and was lulled into a daze.

Some of the houses looked fine. Others looked like they'd been in a tornado—windows broken, clothes and junk on the lawns. A car with a crushed trunk sat half on the sidewalk and half in the street.

"This is just wrong," Jake said. He was fully blotto by now. "The government. To not warn these people. It's wrong."

"Yeah, yeah. We know," Astrid told him. She knew about the whisky. She had to know.

I parked in front of the house.

"If he's home, we give him the girl and we leave, that simple," Astrid said.

"And if he's not home?" I asked.

"If he's not home, I don't know."

I cut the engine in front of the house I remembered as Rinée's.

There was no body.

There was blood staining the walkway and the dry ground and turf.

There was no body.

But there was a trail.

I made a sound—kind of a moan or some guttural expression of fear and grief.

Astrid put her hand on my shoulder. "You don't have to go out there alone," she said.

"Heck, no," Jake said. He put his hand on the handle to open the door, but his hand missed it. "We're a team. Me and the Booker."

Ah, Booker. My old nickname, meaning a nerd and also, somehow, a liberal, like President Booker.

But Jake couldn't even open the door he was so drunk.

"It's okay," I said, patting him on the shoulder. "I got this."

I pulled up my suit, took my mask out, and put it on.

Astrid leaned forward to help me zip it closed. She put her mouthpiece in, too, just to be sure.

The air looked crisp and clear, but still.

Jake had his face in his hands.

DAY 34

"I'm sorry," he mumbled. "Something's wrong with my gut."

"Hey, it's okay. I really mean it," I said.

And I really did. I didn't have to judge him anymore.

I had stashed the trucker's handgun under my seat and I picked it up now, my hand shaking.

Rinée started crying. Maybe the masks scared her. Maybe she was picking up on the vibe.

I opened the door.

No whistling from the suit. No red light.

"That's a relief," I said.

I took off the mask and tossed it back inside.

I went up the walkway, stepping over Rinée's mother's blood.

The trail of matted blood led off toward the next house. It was clear where she'd been dragged.

I knocked. There was no answer. The door to Rinée's house was unlocked.

"Hello," I called. "I'm Dean. And, uh, we've been keeping your daughter safe. We're here to give her back."

No answer.

I just stood there blinking for a while. I was going to have to search this house. I was going to have to search it for Rinée's dad, who might be dead or hiding.

The entryway showed the chaos and disarray that had overtaken the woman's mind. There was stuff everywhere, including—dear God!—a ziplock bag stuffed with one- and five-dollar bills and change.

I picked it up. Didn't hesitate. We needed that money.

I checked each room. The basement. The closets. No one.

Back at the car, I just shook my head.

"Shoot," Astrid said.

"Let's just go to Texas," Jake said. "Leave a note and give my mom's address."

"No, we should stay," I decided. "The air is fine. And Rinée's dad may come back. There's no sign of him inside. We'll stay here and wait."

Astrid nodded and closed her eyes, her hands on her belly. She looked exhausted. A day or two of rest was what she needed.

"There's just one thing I want to do first," I said. "I need to follow a trail. Make sure we're safe."

DAY 34

CHAPTER TWENTY-SIX

JOSIE

AFTER WE'RE SURE THEY ARE GONE, LORI HEADS BACK TO THE other room to sleep with Heather.

I pull off one of the bureaus and sleep curled up on the foot of the bed, but not very well and not for long—they could come back.

I wake up while the sky is turning the color of silt, the sun trying to bring some gold and warmth into our bleak world.

Instead of taking the other bureau off the bed, which would wake everyone, I carefully lift the bottom of the bed frame and shift it to the side.

I wish that I had a pencil so I could scribble a note on the wall, or something to leave for Lori, to say that I am sorry— some gift that would make her understand that I do care for them, and that it is my caring for them that forces me to leave them.

They have a chance, without me.

Mario will recover and come back to protect them, I pray. But even if he doesn't, with the goodness of the skinny mom—and the other people who had come to our aid at Plaza 900—the kids will be okay.

Lori is tough enough to keep them safe.

Even if she has to bargain her body for their safety, they will be okay.

There is only one thing that I know to be true—if I am near them, I will bring danger.

So I will escape now. Or I will be killed while trying to escape.

And, dear God, wouldn't that be a relief to everyone?

It would be to me.

I grant myself one last request: I want to say good-bye to Mario.

The door to the stairwell is unlocked. Of course it is—the Union Men bribed Venger to leave it that way.

I slip down the stairs, the only sound the worn-out treads of my orthopedic shoes on the steps.

God bless Mario's wife, who had the same size feet as me.

I have to go through the Men's hall to get to the front door. It is dank in the hall. Most of the doors are closed, and the few that are open give glimpses of heavy bodies asleep on the floor or beds.

In only one room is a man awake.

A light-skinned man sitting on the floor, playing solitaire.

He looks up as I pass, startled.

Then sees who I am.

"Good luck, girl," he croaks, and waves me on.

*　*　*

DAY 34

I stick close to the buildings as I cross the courtyard.

We aren't allowed out of our rooms until six, breakfast time.

I have to skirt Gillett and Plaza 900 to get to Rollins, and the clinic.

I see a guard leaning against a building. He has a thermos of something hot and steamy and doesn't notice me.

I enter Rollins and walk down the long hallway outside the clinic. It is odd to see it empty of the sick and injured. There are stains on the floor in intervals. I don't stop to ponder what from.

The door is shut and locked, of course, but someone has to be in there taking care of the patients.

I knock on the glass.

After a moment, Dr. Neman, the woman from the courtyard, comes to the door. "We open at nine," she says and then she squints through the glass at me.

She opens the door.

"You're the girl Venger was punishing, right?" she says.

I nod.

She runs her hand through her hair. I guess she thinks I'm there about my stupid knuckles.

"Come in," she tells me.

It is warmer in the clinic than in the rest of the building.

"What are they feeding you all? You're skin and bones," she says. "Sit down and I'll take a look at your hands. Isn't it a little risky to be out before the morning bell? I mean, do you really want to give Venger another reason to discipline you?"

"My knuckles are okay, actually. Dr. Quarropas saw me yesterday."

"Well then, what on earth—" She seems tired and pissed.

"I had to come because you have my friend here," I say. "I'm here to talk to my friend, Mr. Scietto."

Dr. Neman gets a look of clenched-jaw irritation.

"You're here for a *visit*?"

"Please," I beg. "The Union Men are angry with me, and if I'm going to see Mario, it has to be now, before they can find me—"

She throws up her hands, doesn't want to hear any more about it.

She picks up a minitab and it glows under her touch.

"He's not here," she tells me, reading it.

"What do you mean?"

"Mario Scietto? He was released last night," she says.

"But . . ."

I push past her. Maybe she is thinking of the wrong guy.

"He's not here," she calls after me.

I peer into the room, to the side, where I had set Mario myself.

It is true.

He is not there.

In his cot is the pug-faced Union Man. The one I beat.

His face is black and blue, swollen. His eye crusted shut.

The gash on his nose is bandaged with a folded paper towel and masking tape.

I look down and retreat, backing up into the entrance room.

"But why did you release him? He might have had fractured ribs. When did you release him?"

"I'm sorry that your friend is gone," she tells me brusquely. "But I am busy."

"Can you please check his file?"

With irritation, she brings up Mario's file on the screen again.

"Dr. Quarropas discharged. There's a note." She moves her fingers on the screen, bringing up the note. "'Mr. Venger brought

DAY 34

in the boy in there and suggested strongly that Mr. Scietto be discharged.'"

I whirl away from her.

"You're welcome," she snaps.

I turn back. "What time was he discharged?"

"Oh, for Christ sake," she snipes.

"He didn't come back to the room and that means he spent the night somewhere on campus!" I shout. "You killed him when you turned him out. You killed him."

"He was released at eight-ten p.m."

That would have been during Group 3 dinner.

Dr. Neman looks up at me, her mouth set in a bitter frown. "We're not killing people," she says, her voice steely and angry. "We're trying to save you and you all are making it IMPOSSIBLE!"

I back away.

She is right, of course.

CHAPTER TWENTY-SEVEN

DEAN

NOW I WAS FOLLOWING A TRAIL OF BLOOD. IT WAS EASY AND IT was horrible.

I tracked the red-brown swath over the gravel of the neighbor's driveway to the front stoop. There was blood on the handle and around the doorframe.

I pushed it open. Somehow I didn't think to announce myself.

I went in gun first, like some TV cop. My heart was hammering hard and I saw my gun hand was shaking again.

Kind of modern-styled, the house. The blood trail went straight down the hall into the kitchen.

There were no bodies there, either, but the kitchen was spattered with blood everywhere, sprayed over the counters and floors.

Bile flooded up. My stomach heaved. I went out the back door and puked off the stoop, down onto the trash cans.

It was the smell. Meaty, metallic, thickening into a rotting sweetness.

DAY 34

The *godforsaken* trail continued outside, only wider. What had happened here?

I kept my head down and walked. Started running, actually. Get it over with.

The trail led to two cellar doors, set at an angle at the base of the house to the left of Rinée's family. I had gone to the house on the right, gone clear through and was now entering the house on the other side.

I grabbed the handles and flung the doors open.

"Hello?" a voice called. "Hello?"

"Who are you?" I shouted. "What did you do?"

"Here," I heard a voice say. "Please help me."

Here is the vision that will haunt me for the rest of my life.

There's a single utility lightbulb hanging from the ceiling and a wash of sunlight coming from behind me.

Stained wooden plank steps lead down into a basement with cement-block walls. Tools on a pegboard on one side. Shelves with Tupperware marked "Christmas" and "Crafting" are on the other. In the center of the floor are the bodies of two women, both stabbed and mutilated as only a madman could do, and behind them is the bald-headed man, kneeling and weeping.

"I'm so glad you're here. You see, I think I killed these women," he said. "I had . . . I had some kind of an episode and I murdered them."

I tried to talk but no words came out. Mouth too dry.

"I think I killed these women!" he repeated.

"It wasn't your fault," I told him. "It was chemicals. Chemicals in the air."

"I volunteered. Every Saturday. Reading to kids. Teaching them. Serving soup, cleaning up. I volunteered."

I needed to leave. I needed to get away from this man, this dark hole of a basement. Away from the bodies. Every sinew, every cell of my body strained toward the doors behind me, begging me to leave.

"I drove a hybrid. I put solar panels on the roof."

"I have to go," I said.

"Please." He got up on his knees. "Please help me."

His voice was low and serious and sane.

"I need your help. Please. I can't do it myself. I've tried."

"Do what?" I asked him.

"I need you to kill me."

I cursed and stepped back.

He rose on his knees and edged toward me, his hands clasped, begging.

The gun was so heavy in my hand.

"I can't live with this. It would be a mercy. A mercy. Please."

He cried and begged and I backed away.

I walked back to the car. I felt like I was moving through cement—or like I'd been filled with it. I felt like my heart was so leaden that I'd never feel light again.

"What did you find?" Astrid asked me. Her blue eyes were clear and full of concern.

And then, from next door, there came a muffled shot.

"I found the O man," I told her.

DAY 34

CHAPTER TWENTY-EIGHT

JOSIE

I TRY TO THINK. WHERE COULD MARIO BE? HE HADN'T COME home.

Had he tried to come back to the room and failed?

Had he knocked and we didn't hear him?

First I run back to Excellence. He would have tried to get back to the room.

He would have been in pain from his arm and his ribs, if they had ended up cracked.

He'd have a terrible headache from being sedated and would be thirsty.

I sprint through the courtyard. Dawn is breaching the horizon now, bringing a peachy light to the courtyard.

I don't care about being seen. I have to find Mario.

I burst into the lobby.

Still empty.

I push into the Men's hall. People are up now, a few coming out of their rooms.

"Hey! Look who's here," says one of the lowlifes I had fought my way through.

I weave my way down the hall, looking in the rooms.

Someone puts a hand on my arm.

"Union is looking for you," Patko says. "You'd better get out of here."

I shrug him off.

"Has anyone seen Mario?" I yell. "The old guy who takes care of us?"

"Ain't seen him," says the maggoty one. "But I can take care of you good, rabbit."

I push past him and head back to the front hall.

Not there.

Where would you go, Mario? Where would you go?

Maybe Plaza 900. Head for a crowd, try to find someone to help him. Try to get help from Cheryl, maybe. Or get a drink of water.

I make my way to Plaza 900.

"Hey!" a guard yells. "What the heck?"

"Sorry," I yell, trying to sound meek. "My friend's missing." And I keep running.

The guard lurches to his feet, starting after me slowly, but gaining momentum as his bulk accelerates.

I hit the front doors to Plaza 900. Locked.

I pound on them.

A sob tears out of me.

Mario is injured and somewhere on campus and it is my fault.

The guard comes into my peripheral vision. "You're not allowed to be out, miss. You're gonna get in trouble."

DAY 34

"Please," I plead. "My friend is old and he got turned out of the clinic and I think maybe he's in there."

"Well, you'll know when it opens, won't you?" He grabs my arm and pushes me toward the Virtues. "Which one are you from?"

"Please," I beg him. "He's old and alone and hurt."

I see a spark of conscience flash across his eyes.

"And he's very kind. Please let me try to find him."

"Aaugh, go on. I didn't see ya," he says, and turns his back on me.

I spin away from him and head around the other side of the building.

There have to be more doors going in.

I see two steel-gray doors. One of them is ajar.

A white truck is pulled up near the double doors.

A white-uniformed man brings out four flats of dinner rolls.

I nod to him, like I am somehow supposed to be there, and dodge inside.

"Hey, miss!" he calls.

And then I am in the giant kitchen. It smells like old Sloppy Joes and there are patches of grease on the counters and floor. The steel counters are cleaned off only in spots. Trash is on the floor in places and food, too. It looks like the kitchen staff are doing the best they can and failing. Like all of us.

Mario isn't in the kitchen and he isn't in the dining room. I am looking along the floor and in the corners.

I ignore the "heys" and questioning glances from the workers.

I can't find Cheryl, but see another one of the ladies who liked Mario. What was her name? Josefina? No.

"Have you seen Mario?" I ask her. "The man I come in with—"

"No, *m'ija*, he missing?"

I nod.

She hugs me. Says something comforting in Spanish.

I tear myself away from her.

I have to find him.

Mariana, I remember. That was her name.

I go to the lobby of Plaza 900.

Not there. Not in the restrooms, Men's or Women's. I look in the stairwell.

Someone must have taken him in, I tell myself. He must be in the room of some good-hearted person and maybe they're sending word to the kids right now.

I start back across the courtyard. That has to be it.

Maybe he is in our room right now, while I am tearing around the campus, overreacting.

I enter the front hall of Excellence and a man grabs my wrist. It is a bald, fat man, one of the men who had assaulted me before.

"Girly, your grandpaw showed up."

"Where?" I ask him, spinning around, grabbing his sweaty hand in both of mine. "Please tell me!"

"Ladies' room," he says, jerking his head toward the two restrooms off the front hall.

"Thank you!" I shout as I push away from him.

My poor Mario is on the floor, under a vanity counter right next to the door.

His body looks shriveled and tiny. Weak and endangered.

His head is lying on the floor. There is a little stain, made from drool and blood, near his mouth.

"Mario!" I say, too loud, and then I regulate my tone. "Oh, Mario . . ."

He is very hurt.

DAY 34

He needs quiet, and in the stillness, now I hear his breath. The inhale strains but the exhale is worse. Windy. A wheeze.

How, how, how could they have let him go?!

I kneel down.

"Mario, Mario," I murmur. Tears run down my cheeks. I brush them away. I put my hand on his shoulder.

I see his arm has been set in a light cast.

He opens his eyes.

"Ha," he croaks. "Josie."

He closes his eyes again.

I put my hand to his forehead and then his face. It is cold and the skin feels papery and loose.

"I'm going to take you back to the clinic," I whisper.

He wheezes.

"Thirsty."

I get up and, of course, I don't have a cup. I rinse my hands at the tap. The soap is long gone.

I cup a little cold water in my hands.

I kneel again, my bruised knees on the cold tile, and try to get the water into his mouth.

His lips against my fingers feel dry and thin.

His breath smells like old blood and I can't stop crying.

"I can carry you very carefully," I say.

"No," he says, and he looks at me. In his eyes, he is telling me he means it.

"Josie," he gasps.

"Yes, Mario?"

"The doctor told me . . ."

A gasping inhale, the wheezing exhale.

"The experiments."

The experiments? What? He draws another breath.

"Experiments people go."

"The people they send away for medical experiments?" I ask, trying to do the talking for him.

He closes his eyes, yes.

"Army takes 'em."

He is trying to warn me about letting Venger send me away.

"I know, Mario. I won't let Venger send me there, I promise."

He purses his lips.

"You Sam Rid."

What?

"You Sam Rid."

"I don't know what you're talking about, Mario." I cry. I want to tell him how much I love him. I want him to live. "Let me take you to the clinic!" I beg.

"Listen," he says, his blue eyes snapping.

"U-S-A-M-R-I-I-D." He spells it out.

"Okay," I sniffle.

"Where they do tests. It's in Maryland."

I get chills then, my flesh creeping up my arms, all the goose bumps rippling up my limbs, climbing toward my heart.

Mario is telling me to let Venger send me away, because whatever that string of initials is—it is in Maryland, close to Niko's family farm.

His dying thoughts are to get me free.

"Get sent there."

"Okay," I say. "Okay."

I lay down on the floor, so I can be right facing his face.

He smiles at me.

His face is the only thing I see now, and I know mine is the only thing he sees, too.

It is cold on the floor and Mario is dying. I try to get as close as I can. I want to give him some of my body heat.

"Good girl. Always good."

DAY 34

My eyes are leaking onto the tile now.

"Mario," I say. "Thank you. You saved me. You did it. I'll go to USAMRIID. You got me free. Okay? You saved me."

His breaths are slowing, stretching painfully. A long, weak rasp.

"Do you know that? Do you know that you saved me?"

His eyes aren't on me now. They are focused somewhere past my head.

I see bubbles of blood in his mouth, coming up to the front of his lips, starting to make their way down his jaw.

I dab at them with the hem of my shirt.

"No, Mario, don't go," I cry.

"Good girl," Mario tells me.

His lips say, "Always good," but there is no sound from his voice.

And his breath hisses to nothing and he is gone.

CHAPTER TWENTY-NINE

DEAN

NOW I WAS WITHOUT A GUN.

And that made me feel just fine.

Maybe you'll think I was stupid to give it away, when we were still in danger. In danger at every moment. But, see, you get used to the danger. You never get used to killing.

I guess I reached the point where I'd rather die than take a life.

If you're still thinking I'm dumb, then I ask you—would you have gone to retrieve it?

Would you have gone down into that dank, bloody hole and pried it out of a dead man's hand?

I didn't think so.

We moved into Rinée's house. It was pretty messy, from her mother's strange and desperate packing effort. But there was a lot of food. They were a Costco kind of family and had a very well-stocked pantry.

DAY 34

"Anyone feel like beans?" Jake said, holding up a can that must have been two gallons big.

He was in better spirits now.

The idea of being in an actual house was pretty uplifting, I have to say. And Rinée was delighted to be home.

She wriggled to get out of Astrid's arms and went toddling through the house.

"Yook! Yook!" Rinée said, bringing Astrid item after item. A sock, a sippy cup, a stuffed Chihuahua. And Astrid would say, "Yeah, a sock." "Nice sippy cup." "Uh-huh. A doggie."

Astrid looked totally exhausted. The added task of taking care of Rinée seemed to be draining her last reserves of energy. She sat down on the couch and let her head roll back.

Then Rinée came back into the living room. I was starting to put away the items strewn across the floor. Rinée held up her two hands and said, "Mama?"

"Oh," Astrid said. "Sweetie . . . Mommy's not coming home for a while. She's not coming home."

"Awesome!" Jake said, coming in from the kitchen, holding a box of ice cream sandwiches. "Who wants a Fat Boy?"

"Mama?" Rinée asked again.

"She's not coming home. I'm sorry," Astrid said, then she broke into tears.

"Hey, you okay?" I went to her.

"I'm sorry," Astrid said. "I hate girls who cry and here I am, a breakdown an hour."

"You need some rest."

"I'm having those cramps again."

"How bad?" I asked.

"Like before." She wiped her tears away. She tried a half of a smile, but looked miserable. "Maybe a little worse."

"You should go lay down," Jake said. "Me and Dean will watch Rinée for a while."

"Yup. We'll get the place cleaned up, too. And make some lunch."

"Yunch?" Rinée asked. "Yunch?" And she marched off into the kitchen. Jake followed her, asking her if she'd like a Fat Boy ice cream sandwich.

"The pace has been too much," I said, rubbing her shoulders. "You need rest. We're somewhere safe now. When Rinée's dad comes back, let's ask him if we can stay here for a few days so you can get your strength back."

"And if he doesn't come back?" Astrid asked, saying what we both were thinking.

"Then we stay as long as we like. And we'll find you a doctor. Make sure everything is okay. Get those vitamins."

Astrid went up and took a shower, put on some of the dead mom's stretchiest clothes, got into her bed—the whole thing. I encouraged her to do it. Surely the dad wouldn't mind.

By the way, Jake?—not so helpful with Rinée.

The moment I entered the kitchen he said to me, "Dude, she's got a mess in her pants."

The diaper did smell—horrible.

And as I changed her (there was a changing table in the downstairs bathroom), he stood at the door saying, "Oh Lord, I'm gonna be sick!" and, "That is FOUL."

It was pretty disgusting, but I didn't want her to get a complex about her body. I mean, it's all natural, right? So I held my breath and wiped her down and got a clean diaper on her. It was possibly on backward, but it was on.

DAY 34

After I scrubbed my hands with antibacterial soap (twice), Rinée took me into the playroom, a little room to the side of the kitchen. There was a little wooden pretend kitchen in there with tin cups and plates and some food made out of painted wood.

I sat down on a tiny chair next to a tiny table and Rinée went about bringing me different things to "eat."

Jake was kind enough to make a stack of tuna sandwiches.

He and I wolfed down two each while we watched the TV. No. News. Of. Drifts.

It was crazy. All we saw was more footage from the East Coast about the falling temperatures and the makeshift transportation system and more rioting at the gas lines. All old news.

Rinée had a quarter of a sandwich and some apple slices.

She kept asking for more apple and saying, "Moy ean? Moy ean?" "Ean" was her word for either apple or eat.

Astrid was conked out upstairs, so Jake and I divided her sandwich between us and ate it, along with the rest of Rinée's. There were four more large tins of tuna in the pantry, so I thought it was okay to eat Astrid's food. I planned to cook her something warm, anyway, when she woke up. There was some chicken in the freezer I set on the counter to defrost. If only I had Batiste here, he'd have prepared a feast. But I would do okay on my own. Maybe chicken with rice and cream of mushroom soup. There was some in the pantry and it was really hearty meal—comfort food and also hard to screw up.

We washed down lunch with a half gallon of Grovestand orange juice.

It felt so good to sit at a kitchen table with sunlight streaming in through a window and open up a fridge and take something out and eat it.

Rinée started yawning and literally rubbing her eyes—I didn't know kids actually did that. I thought that was just from over-acting in the movies.

I carried her up to her room.

It was lavender colored, with a crib in it and one of those glider chairs. The room had a poorly painted unicorn on one wall. It looked sort of like a pastel-colored mule balancing an ice-cream cone on its nose.

Rinée reached out toward her crib—that's how tired she was.

I placed her in it and covered her up with a soft crib blanket that had sheep on it.

I went to leave and she said, "Tay. Tay, ean."

"Have a good nap, Rinée," I told her and started to close the door.

"Tay!" she demanded, starting to cry. "Tay, ean."

And I realized she was saying my name.

"Ean" was Dean and she wanted me to stay.

I sat right down on that glider and started to glide. She lay back down.

Odds are even as to which one of us fell asleep first.

DAY 34

CHAPTER THIRTY

JOSIE

I HAVE TO TELL THE KIDS.

That is the first thing.

The second thing? I don't know what the second thing is. Get sent away for testing, I suppose.

The breakfast bell had rung while I was in the bathroom, while Mario was dying.

Now everyone is milling out, headed to Plaza 900.

"Lori!" I cry. "Lori, where are you?"

I try to push my way back up the stairs, but then I change my mind and go with the crowd. Maybe they are in the courtyard already.

"Lori!" I yell. Where are they?

Then I see Carlo.

He is with another Union Man and they both see me and smile.

The people file past me as I freeze.

I glance behind me and see two more of them closing in. One of them has a chain.

The part of my brain wired for survival takes over and I run straight for Carlo. I see a flash of surprise on his face. I dodge through the people streaming toward breakfast, gaining speed and momentum and then, right as I get close to Carlo, I duck my head and shoulders and tackle a large man in front of me, sending him crashing into the two Union Men.

I veer in the other direction.

Toward Rollins and the clinic.

Away from the crowd I run free and fast.

I hear the Union Men following me and then a sweet sound.

"Hey!" a guard calls to them. "Breakfast's this way."

It is my guard. My friend from before.

"That girl's running away!" Carlo protests.

"Don't worry about her, just worry about yourself!"

So maybe there is one guard who isn't in the palm of the Union Men.

I burst back into Rollins. I pound on the clinic door, knowing Dr. Neman will be furious.

"Have you lost your mind?" she screeches. But she lets me push past her into the entry room.

Dr. Quarropas emerges from the back.

"Hey. You!" He recognizes me. "We . . . we had to discharge your friend. Venger insisted—"

"You have to send me for testing," I say, my lungs screaming from my sprint. My heart beating hard and fast. "I was exposed for a long time. I'll be good to study."

I can't catch my breath. "I'll do whatever they say. Send me away."

"This is the second time today this girl has caused a major disturbance. I'm calling the guards—"

She picks up a house phone.

DAY 34

"There's no way I'd send a minor to USAMRIID!" Quarropas objects, focusing on me. "Tell me what's going on."

"The Union Men are going to kill me. I'm the one who beat up that kid in there." I gesture to the back room.

"Nobody's going to kill anyone," he says kindly. "Look, we have meds that can help you. Let me help you."

"There's only one way for you to help me," I beg. "Send me away for testing, please!"

"There's a girl here. We need assistance," Dr. Neman is saying on the phone.

"You're not going to help me?" I ask him.

"I'm not going to send you for medical testing," he says.

I back away.

Fine.

Maybe Venger will send me. He'd threatened me with it.

"Mario died, by the way," I tell the doctors, my anger getting the better of me. "He died on the floor of a bathroom. So thanks for nothing."

"Venger!" I shout as I arrive at the courtyard. "Venger, where are you? Come and get me, you stupid, freakin' bully. You son of a pig! Come and get me!"

I walk over to the fence.

There are no reporters there—maybe the soldiers had made them all clear out for good. So much for Lori's plan.

"Venger, where are you?"

Excellence and Responsibility are eating now. The courtyard is empty.

I dig my fingers into the chain-link fence and rattle it.

There is a car parked a few feet past the second gate. A minivan, of all things.

Over my shoulder, I see Carlo and two of his thugs slip out

of Plaza 900, heading for me. One of them is big, the other is puny.

"VENGER!" I shout.

Where is he? Where are the stupid guards when you actually want them?

Then I hear, "Josie?"

A voice from beyond the fences.

I look.

"Josie Miller? Is that you?"

And I see.

A skinny man in a strange dark-brown bodysuit of some kind.

It is all one piece, with a belt built on. It is some kind of light protective suit.

Then I see the person push his hair out of his eyes.

I know the tilt of his head—the straight posture.

I know the brown hair, brown tanned face.

Even across the distance of two chain-link fences.

It is Niko.

"Niko?!" I shout.

"Josie! Josie! I can't believe it."

My Niko. He is pressed up against the outside fence. He has his fingers through the grill.

It is him. It is.

"NIKO! How did you find me?" I shout.

"The paper! Your picture was in the paper!"

"I got your note," I say. I find I am crying. "I was going to get to you. Mario was helping me—"

A sharp jang of pain as my head is jerked back.

Carlo has me by the hair.

"Who's that, Josie? Who's your friend?" he asks, as if he is asking me to be introduced to someone at a party.

He pulls my head back and pushes down so that I sink to my

DAY 34

knees. The skin on my knees screams and I feel the scabs slit open.

"Leave her alone!" Niko shouts.

"Or what, spaceman?" says one of the Union Men.

The other one snorts, "Spaceman!"

"Leave her be!" Niko shouts.

He starts to scale the fence.

"Don't!" I scream. "They'll shoot you!"

The guards had shot people trying to rescue prisoners. But I don't get to explain because Carlo punches me in the face.

It's hard to explain the counterbalance of rage—but as the blow registers, I know it hurts, but I can't feel it at all because my blood is amped up now, adrenaline flowing, and I am ready to kill him.

He leans in low. "We are going to take you to our suite now. So you'd better say good-bye to your friend."

"Somebody help!" Niko calls. He paces back and forth.

He can't believe that no one is coming to help me.

Carlo digs his fingers into my hair, as if to remind me I am in his control. I fight to think.

Can I kill the three men and somehow get over the fence?

But then I hear the voices of the kids.

They are pleading.

They are pleading with Venger, trying to keep up with him as he strides our way.

"Please," Lori says, "she was only trying to defend me and they're going to kill her!"

The kids step up to us in a cacophony of pleading and begging.

"Shut up!" Venger says. Then he makes a gesture to Carlo like *What the heck?* "Carlo, you seem to have forgotten our agreement."

"I apologize, Mr. Venger. We were just leaving."

"Those men are beating her!" Niko shouts. "She needs help!"

Venger ignores him.

"I know she put two of yours in the clinic. She's been trouble from day one. But if you're gonna take her, TAKE HER. Don't stand here with her in the light of day where the press can see." Venger gestures toward Niko.

"Again, my apologies," Carlo says.

Now people start spilling out of Plaza 900. Breakfast is over.

Some of them must have seen what is happening.

Aidan is pulling on Carlo's arm.

"Please don't hurt Josie," Aidan pleads to Carlo. "It's all my fault. Please, you can have all my food! Every day! And my sugars!"

The short Union Man pulls Aidan off and shoves him away and he falls on his backside.

I look at Aidan and suddenly, with a wrench, I realize I love that little scrappy kid.

"You leave that girl alone," comes a man's voice from behind us.

The people from the mess hall are coming close.

"Venger, this is too much," someone else calls. "Let that girl alone!"

A chorus of yeahs goes up.

"Josie!" Niko calls.

I look, see him fumbling with his pack.

There is this funny, tinny whistle.

"Josie!" He gets out some kind of mask with a visor and is attaching it to the suit.

"Now look what you've done," Venger says through his teeth to Carlo. He gestures to the mob.

"No worries." Carlo jerks me toward Excellence. "We'll just be on our way . . ."

DAY 34

And then Heather screams.

I look where she is looking.

I see Niko is pointing that same direction.

From the empty quad across the street there is some kind of a dust cloud coming. It doesn't float, the way you'd think it might—it slinks. It seems to be a cloud with weight to it—lifting and then settling again, like something alive and restless.

And then I smell it.

The compounds hit my nose and it is like coming home.

Black grit in my eyes and mouth.

A key in a lock.

One second, everything is dull and gray and then the world is on fire—everything I look at is brilliant and beautiful.

The grit is the compounds and it washes away my weakness.

The drifts go through the people in the camp like a ripple.

Voices rise in an instant chorus of rage and terror.

The desire to kill is a lightning bolt and I am full of its charge.

Venger.

Face pale with terror, he fumbles for his gun.

His hand is shaking.

He will be the first one I'll kill.

Only Carlo and the other two Union Men had set on him already and are dragging him to the ground.

"JOSIE!" comes a muffled voice, over the joyous background noises of glass breaking and doors pulled off their hinges and bones snapping.

From a million miles away I see Niko in his suit.

No, no. I need to kill and Venger deserves it.

Venger has dropped his gun and is scrambling for it in the dirt.

Carlo and the short man are on him but I dive into the fight. A few blows to the head. Fighting. Freedom. Heaven. I grab Venger's head and he begs for mercy but my blood demands he die and I say, "Shhhhhh," and I brace my feet on his shoulders to pull his head off but I see the light is gone, his eyes are dead, and I see Carlo has punched his hand into Venger's chest and is pulling out organs by the fistful.

The people who'd spilled out of the dining hall are now attacking one another. Bodies twisting and fighting and bleeding everywhere and the screaming.

I breathe in.

The colors are so beautiful.

Sky blue and grit gray and blood and brain.

I am finally living again.

Carlo, Carlo.

Carlo next then.

He still has his hands in Venger's abdomen so I pick up Venger's gun and hit him on the head with it.

I fell him and pound one-two-three-four-five. Carlo's skull, caving in under my gun hammer. Joy in my heart.

I turn to take the other Union Men down. They are fighting each other.

Then my brain says: WAIT.

And I see a guard at the gate, fumbling with his keys.

He gets it open and goes running for the second gate.

And Niko is there.

My brain wants me to pay attention to that.

My hands want a throat to squeeze.

The short man is biting some other man on the leg. I grab him up by the neck and *snap*, I twist his head to the side.

DAY 34

THINK.

My brain talking to me again and I bring my bloody hands up to my head and squeeze it.

The thoughts are painful to me.

I want to rage with the others. What a party it is.

SEE THEM—my brain makes me look.

A woman grabs me by the waist and I push her down.

My brain is winning.

LOOK and I see it: my kids.

My kids are fighting.

Lori is on Freddy, and Aidan is attacking a man alongside Heather. The man swipes at Heather and she falls to the ground. Hits her head and isn't moving and then Aidan, mouth bloody, like a newborn vampire, turns on Heather, on his own almost-sister, and starts to attack her.

NO. This is wrong.

I look back at the fence.

Niko is at the second gate. Has his hands stuck through and is trying to help the guard to unlock it.

One step. Two steps. To the kids.

My brain can make my body OBEY.

I grab Aidan by the shoulder and wrench him off Heather. He sinks his teeth into my hand.

Can't feel it.

I drag them toward the other two.

"LORI!" I shout.

She is sitting on Freddy, clawing at him.

"STOP! STOP!" I shout.

She looks up at me for a second.

Then a woman, an older woman, attacks Lori.

Freddy lays gasping and I haul Heather up, onto my shoulder.

"FREDDY, COME!" I shout.

He lays there, panting, looking at me like I am speaking Russian.

Heather on my shoulder, I haul Aidan toward the gate.

I will get them out.

Yes.

Then I will go back and get Lori and Freddy and we'll be free.

Now I am fully in control, riding the rage like a surfer, using its power to fuel my escape.

I can hear Niko's heart praying for me to hurry.

"I'm coming," I whisper to him in my own heart. "I'm coming."

I step over the bodies of the dead and dying and brawling. I slip a little, in their blood and spilt organs.

I see Dr. Quarropas and Dr. Neman and some guards coming from the direction of Rollins. They burst into the courtyard, spewing darts from machine guns.

The doctors are headed for the gate, shooting down anyone in their way.

But at the gate, Os are there. Two teenagers attacking the guard. Others attacking the teenagers.

Niko is trying to get the keys, which lie just out of his reach through the fence.

"Almost there," I tell Niko inside my heart and then I see Dr. Quarropas notice me.

I have Heather on my shoulder and I am dragging Aidan. I am going to make it to the gate.

And then Dr. Quarropas catches my eye. I don't know what he is trying to tell me before he raises up his gun and mows me down.

DAY 34

CHAPTER THIRTY-ONE

DEAN

"OH MY GOD! NO! NO!!!" ASTRID'S VOICE CAME SCREAMING INTO my dream and I shot out of the glider.

My heart was thudding like it would burst my chest. I took the stairs two at a time and found her in the living room, clutching a note.

"What is it? What is it?" I asked.

"It's Jake!" she cried. "He's gone."

"What?"

"He's gone! He left!" She pushed the note into my hand and bent into a crouch, grabbing her belly.

"Is that all?!" I shouted. I shouldn't have shouted at her, but my heart was hammering so hard.

"I'm sorry. I'm sorry," she said. "I didn't mean to scare you but maybe . . . maybe we can get him back. If we hurry, Dean!" There was panic in her voice. She opened the door.

"Okay, okay!" I said. "Just calm down. This is not an emergency."

"We have to get him back!" she cried.

"Are you okay?" I asked.

"Still cramps, but I'm okay," she said.

Rinée started crying upstairs.

"I'll get her," Astrid said. "Can you go outside? See if you see him?"

"I will. But please, calm down, can you do that?" I said.

She rolled her eyes. "I'll try. But I don't want to lose him!"

Astrid looked not at all right. The circles under her eyes were worse. She looked gaunt and so pale. I noticed that when she wasn't holding Rinée, she had her hands on her belly almost all the time, now.

She went up the stairs, slowly, to fetch bawling Rinée from her crib.

I stepped outside.

It was twilight now and I saw that, down the street, one house had its lights on. It was a small, curving cul-de-sac. Maybe six houses on the street altogether. Only two appeared to be inhabited.

Jake was nowhere to be seen.

I read the note. It was addressed to me, so it was kind of messed up that Astrid had read it first, but okay.

His scrawling handwriting slanted across the page:

Deano,
When I watch the two of you with baby Rinée, I get it. You're good at it. You were born to be a dad. I don't mean that as a crack. It's a compliment.
    What's best for her and what's best for the baby is all that matters now and it's you.
    Please tell Astrid that I will always have

227

DAY 34

love for her in my heart, but that I'm not
the guy for this job.
Me going away is the best gift I can give
all three of you. So I'm giving it.
Anyway, I've been thinking I should go
check on my mom.
Wish me luck,
Jake

I went upstairs.

Astrid was sitting in the glider, with Rinée on her lap.

"Did you even look for him?" she asked me crossly.

"I don't think he wants us to stop him. I really don't."

She just looked at me and I saw her fight her tears down.

Her reaction was so intense. For a moment, my old insecurities swarmed up—did she still love him? Did she love him more than she loved me, somehow?

"Dean," she said, interrupting my downward spiral. "I know he's a screw-up. But he's my friend."

I blinked.

"I just don't want to lose any more people."

"Yeah," I said. "I get it."

She closed her eyes and rocked Rinée, who sat sucking on her thumb and twisting the fingers of her other hand in Astrid's short blond hair.

Dinner was okay. I used the recipe off the inside of the label on the can of mushroom soup. Astrid only picked at her dinner, though Rinée seemed to really like it.

Astrid didn't seem to be in a mood for talking. I, on the other hand, couldn't seem to shut up.

"Tomorrow I'm going to take the hose outside and clean up

around the house. Then maybe make some signs and post them around, just about Rinée and that we're here."

I didn't mention the other bedroom upstairs. I was sure she'd seen it.

A room done in blue plaid with a lot, a serious lot of Legos. There were vintage Lego sets on shelves on the walls—Star Wars pieces and some kind of giant futuristic Egyptian space pyramid. It was the room of a boy. A boy who hadn't made it home.

But maybe he would.

"I think we end up staying here awhile, maybe there's a way to write to Alex and let him know where we are."

Astrid was just moving her food around on her plate. She took a little sip of orange juice.

"I could just use totally fake names. He'd know my handwriting," I went on. "And that way he won't worry."

Rinée was banging her spoon on the tray of her high chair.

Astrid leaned her head on one hand.

"Hey," I said. "Maybe you should go back to bed."

"Yeah," she agreed. "My back hurts. And my head. I guess I'm just exhausted but maybe . . . maybe we should find a doctor tomorrow."

"Yes, of course. That should be the first thing we do."

Durr, what was wrong with me.

"Don't worry about it," Astrid said. "I'm fine. Do you think you can give Rinée a bath? She could use it."

I told her I was pretty sure I could manage it. Of course, I had no idea how to give a two-year-old a bath, but I'd figure it out.

The bath was uneventful, except for the fact that I got soaking wet.

After I got Rinée down, I thought about my own shower. No way was I going to put on my dirty clothes, so I threw my own, and Astrid's, into the washer.

DAY 34

I decided not to wash the safety suits. God knows what the fabric was made of in the first place. And I didn't want to damage the whistler.

I hung one suit on a coatrack near the front door and one on a hook in the back of the master bedroom door. If another drift came through, I hoped the whistles would alert us in time.

Once I got our wet clothes in the dryer, I got in the shower.

Oh man, did it feel good. I stunk of sweat and terror. Down the drain it went, along with a lot of grime.

There was a knock at the door. But before I could say, "Come in," Astrid pushed in, rushed to the john and threw up.

I shut off the water and stepped out, wrapping myself in a towel.

"Are you okay?" I asked her.

She looked up at me and started to nod yes, but was overtaken by another wave of puke.

I pulled on a pair of the husband's pajamas. They were stupidly the wrong size. Both too wide and too short, but I didn't care.

"What can I do? Tell me what I can do?" I asked her.

"Get me some water," she said. And I did, but after that, I didn't know what to do.

She was curled on her knees, her belly nestled into the space between her legs. Her forehead pressed to the cold floor of the bathroom.

"What can I do?" I asked.

"Nothing."

I tried to get her to drink more. She'd take a few sips, then puke them back up.

"Just leave me alone," she told me.

They had Gatorade. I found crystals in the back of the pantry and I made it for her. She drank some. Then puked it up.

"Just leave me alone!" she growled.

I went to get our clothes out of the dryer. I got dressed.

"Maybe we should go to the hospital," I told her, from where I stood in the hall.

She reached out with one hand and swatted the bathroom door shut.

I spent the night sitting on the bed, terrified.

Astrid spent the night in the bathroom, vomiting and sleeping on the floor.

DAY 34

CHAPTER THIRTY-TWO

JOSIE

SOMETHING IS WRONG.

I can't move my arms or legs.

And it's very bright.

It's very bright and I don't know where I am and I can't move my limbs.

My heart is flooded with panic and everything amps up.

White ceiling, dotted with LED cans. Walls are pale green. No windows.

My arms and legs are buckled in leather cuffs, tied down on a bed. There's an IV going into my right arm. The insertion point is taped neatly—a square of semitransparent white tape against my cocoa skin. My knuckles are bandaged up.

There is also a bandage on my left hand. I can't remember why.

I hear voices arguing outside my room. They are what woke me up.

"I am telling you, Savic, this girl is the key."

I am clean.

This hits me.

Someone has washed me.

I could cry for relief and for shame.

"You cannot, you will not perform tests on an underage minor without legal consent!" Heavy accent. Maybe Russian?

My head feels light. I can't feel with my hands, but I think they have cut off my hair.

My mouth is dry, dry, dry.

"Hey!" I croak.

They don't hear me.

"How the hell do you think I'm going to find her parents, Savic? This girl has what we need, don't you see? Look, I'll get her to sign the consent form. It'll stand up. It'll be fine."

"We need you on the VACCINE, Cutlass, not this super-soldier bull crap!"

"Tell that to the Pentagon, because I'm under direct orders—"

"HEY!" I manage.

The doorknob turns.

A short Asian nurse with thinning hair hurries in. She's wearing medical scrubs decorated with cartoon drawings on them, the Traindawgs.

"Sunshine!" she says with a smile. "You're awake!"

Two doctors in white coats step in.

One of them is brown-haired. Late forties? He has rugged good looks—movie star kind of looks. Or maybe it's that he reminds me of a movie star. But I can't think which one.

The other is older. Must be the Russian. He's tall and silver-haired with a paunch and a kind of grim dignity. He leans on a cane.

"Where am I?" I manage.

DAY 35

The handsome doctor comes and stands over me. He looks anxiously into my eyes.

"You are at USAMRIID," the older doctor says. "We are a government medical research facility. I am Dr. Savic and this is Dr. Cutlass. You have been exposed to the warfare compounds. Do you remember that?"

I nod.

Then suddenly I remember—Mario dying and the drift and NIKO.

I try to talk, but my throat is too dry.

I make a strangled sound.

The nurse brings a plastic cup of water with a straw in it up to my face.

"Here you go, sweetheart. Drink up."

Somehow, she has a thick Southern accent. Sounds like a Georgia peach. Looks Chinese.

The water fills my mouth. It's sweet, clean water.

"Niko found me," I manage. "You have to take me back."

The doctors look at me for a minute, then back at each other. They begin to speak again, disregarding what I've said.

"There is a level of integration in her blood that is unparalleled," handsome Dr. Cutlass says.

He has a minitab in his front pocket and he takes it out, pulling up something to show the other doctor.

"Your ethics are on a very slippery slope, James. You know I feel this way," says the Russian.

Huh. They have completely written me off. They think I'm crazy.

"You are required to get a full release form on this girl," the Russian says. "There are rumors of people being tested against their will and those rumors have reached the president."

He says "rumors" like an accusation.

"Hey!" I say. They're ignoring me. "Look, my friend Niko came for me. I shouldn't be here! I should be back there! You have to take me back—he came all that way for me!"

Dr. Cutlass nods to the nurse.

She smiles at me kindly as she does something to my IV involving a syringe.

"It's okay, hun," she tells me. "You're safe now."

And a heavy warmth seeps up from the mattress, dragging me down into a deep, heavenly sleep.

"I'll be here when you wake up, sugar," the nurse says and she looks, for a moment, like an angel, with the ceiling lights her halo.

DAY 35

CHAPTER THIRTY-THREE

DEAN

IN THE MORNING THERE WAS A KNOCK AT THE FRONT DOOR.

"Jamie! Lizzie! Are you there?"

I guess I'd fallen asleep for a while, because the knocking woke me up.

I hurtled down the stairs and looked out the three glass panes at the top of the front door.

All I could tell through the swirly glass was that it was a black woman.

"Jamie, it's me! Open up if you're home!"

I opened the door and she jumped back when she saw my face.

"Don't be scared," I said. "We found Rinée and brought her home. That's all."

"Oh my God. Where are Jamie and Lizzie? Do you know where they are?"

"Why don't you come in and I'll tell you?" I told her.

"Tell me first, then we'll come in."

She held her hand up in a halt position toward the car. I saw a boy there, watching with his face pressed up to the glass.

"Is that—"

"Rinée's brother, J.J.— Jamie Junior," she answered. "I told him to wait. Didn't know what I'd find. I got a call from his school yesterday. Whole bunch of kids were not picked up. I went and got him, but we had to spend the afternoon at the hospital with my husband. He was attacked—I'm sorry. I'm a mess. I'm Lea, Rinée and Junior's aunt. Please, tell me what you know about my brother and his wife."

"Lizzie . . . We don't know where Jamie is, but Lizzie. Rinée's mom. She was killed. I'm so sorry."

Tears filled the woman's eyes.

She nodded.

"Is . . . is Lizzie here in the house?"

"No," I said. "The body is not here."

I didn't tell her where it was or how her sister-in-law died. I planned to, I did, but it could wait.

"All right," she said. "I can do this."

She turned and beckoned to the boy.

The first thing J.J. did after his aunt explained that neither of his parents were home, but that Rinée was safe was to shoot up the stairs in a flash and go straight to Rinée's room.

I heard his voice speaking softly, waking her up and then her crying for a moment and him shushing her.

"She's fine!" he called down.

Lea was watching me. I was pacing in the living room. I knew I should, I don't know, offer to make coffee or something. But I was worried about Astrid.

DAY 35

"Listen," I said. "My girlfriend's sick. I'm not sure what to do. She won't drink anything or eat and she's pregnant and she's been throwing up all night. Could you take a look at her—"

"Why didn't you say so? Where is she?"

Astrid was still on the floor, where she'd been all night long. Only now she was lying on her side.

"Hmm," Lea said, frowning.

"I think it's a stomach virus. Or maybe some bad chicken—"

"Go get me a spoon and some fresh whatever this is," she said, handing me the cup of Gatorade. "We gotta get this girl hydrated."

By the time I got back, Lea was on the floor, sitting cross-legged with Astrid's head and shoulders pulled into her lap.

"Find me a clock," she said. "We're going to sip one teaspoon of Gatorade every three minutes. Gonna do by the clock, baby doll. Gonna get you feeling better. You'll see."

Astrid whimpered.

"How many weeks' pregnant is she?"

"Twenty-eight, we think," I said.

"All right, okay, you're gonna be fine, tootsie," Lea said. Her voice had a calming effect. She was so confident and capable—you just naturally wanted to do whatever she said. "Hey," she said, looking up at me. "Do me a favor and fix the kids some breakfast?"

"Yeah," I told her.

In a different situation, in a different world, I might have told her that I was used to cooking for kids. That it had once been my job.

I fed the kids scrambled eggs and toast with jelly. Rinée and J.J. were cute together in a way that was heart wrenching.

J.J. was very quiet. He seemed around ten years old. I would have thought he'd have a lot of questions for me about where his parents were, but he didn't ask me a thing. I remembered how, back at the Greenway, the little kids acted sort of like this after we got stuck there. You could call it denial, but that didn't really fit. It wasn't that their minds had perceived there'd been a series of deadly accidents and they were choosing to deny they'd happened. It was as if a veil had been thrown over their consciousness— preventing the horror from creeping in at all. Like layers of gauze protecting their minds from things they couldn't handle knowing.

That was the kind of softness I saw on J.J.'s face at breakfast. All he saw was his baby sister.

I'm not even sure he knew I was there.

After an hour, Lea came down.

"I got her into bed. I don't know. I wish the hospital wasn't so packed. I'd run her down there just to have them check her out."

Off the concern on my face, she rushed to add, "I think she's going to be fine. If we can get her hydrated, she'll be fine. She needs rest."

"Is it okay for us to stay here? We don't really have any place to go—"

"Oh, you're staying here. No question." She looked at her watch. "The only thing is that I left my husband at home. He's gonna need his bandages changed soon."

J.J. was playing "kitchen" with Rinée. This was obviously her favorite game. But J.J. had a way of eating and drinking from the tiny plates and cups that made Rinée burst into peals of laughter.

It was good to hear laughter.

Lea smiled, too, listening to it. Then I could see grief or fear starting to gather in her eyes.

DAY 35

"I just keep praying Jamie's gonna make it back here. I hope he's okay. I love my brother so much."

"I know how it feels," I told her. "I really do."

I put my hand on her shoulder.

"And I should tell you," I said. "About what happened to Lizzie."

"I need to go get my husband," Lea said. And I realized she didn't really want to know. "I think I'll bring him here and we can all stay here. You two can just stay in the master bedroom. There's a pullout couch in the study upstairs. We'll be comfortable there. That way, we can all help each other and the kids will feel more comfortable in their own house, anyway."

"Okay," I said.

"Keep an eye on the kids while I'm gone?" she asked me.

"You got it," I said.

"And, later. After dinner, maybe, I'd like to hear your story."

There was a sadness in the lines around her brown eyes that made my chest ache.

Well, Astrid looked pretty much the same, to me, which is to say—horrible. But she was sleeping deeply, and I knew that was good.

I saw the spoon and the Gatorade on the table next to the bed.

Lea had told me to let Astrid sleep for an hour and then to sit with her and do the three-minute thing again.

So in the meantime, I decided to wash off the front walkway and the grass.

At first, the kids tried to come outside with me. I hesitated—what if J.J. asked me what I was doing? Would he know the dank, brown spill over the cement path was blood?

But I let them go out. They seemed to be enjoying each other so much.

I put on my suit, wanting the advance-warning whistle in case the winds changed.

The hose had a sprayer, which was pretty powerful. It took a lot of the blood away, and it was easy to get the grass clean, but in the end, I had to go inside and get a bucket and some Pine-Sol.

That stain on the walkway was deeply set.

I popped in to check on Astrid. She was awake.

"How are you feeling?" I asked her.

She made the so-so sign with her hand.

"My head is killing me," she said in a soft voice. "Do you think there's Advil?"

I found some in the bathroom.

"Can you take it with some Gatorade?" I asked.

She nodded.

"Lea says I should feed you a teaspoon every three minutes," I said. "But the kids are outside . . ."

"I'll do it," Astrid said.

"You sure?"

"I just got a little dehydrated, Dean. I'm fine," she said.

Well, her cheeks were sunken, her hair was plastered to her scalp, and her skin looked greenishly waxy. She did not look fine.

But that didn't seem like a good thing to say to my girlfriend.

Lea came back with her husband, David, just after lunch (frozen meat-lovers pizzas and sweet potato fries for me and the kids—dry toast and tea with honey on a tray for Astrid). David was a huge, barrel-chested black man with one of his arms in a sling. It was heavily bandaged at the end—where his hand had once been.

DAY 35

He seemed pretty out of it, grinning at us and walking in a funny way, like he was constantly stepping over a low door threshold.

"He's on Percocet," Lea explained.

"Come on, Davy," she said loudly. "Just up the walkway and you get to sleep again."

"Oh-kay, baby," he answered and tried to give her a kiss.

"No, no." Lea laughed. "Into the house you go."

She got him in and I guess she went to check on Astrid, because a few minutes later, she called me, her voice loud with concern: "Dean! Get up here!"

I smelled the vomit as I entered the room.

"Baby, she needs to go to a hospital," Lea told me.

Astrid was hanging over the edge of the bed. She had puked on the floor.

"No," Astrid moaned.

"She needs an IV. The Gatorade just isn't cutting it." Lea helped her sit up.

"No!" Astrid repeated.

"It's not a big deal. Dean's gonna take you in. They'll give you an IV. After they get you hydrated, Dean's gonna bring you back here. No problem."

Lea took me by the arm and led me out into the hall.

"Here's the thing—the hospitals in Vinita are full up. We waited there with David for eight hours yesterday and he had a hand hanging off him! They won't see her, just for dehydration. I think you should go on up to Joplin."

"Okay," I said, wired with panic. "Okay."

"See, I think she might have preeclampsia. It can be serious, okay? Lizzie had it with J.J. Just take Mr. Waggoner's car and go."

"Who's he?"

"The man whose car you were driving before. Jamie's neighbor."

"Oh. Okay."

The stupid, logical part of my brain was clicking away, making connections as if I wasn't in the middle of a crisis, put it together: It wasn't Lizzie's car we'd been in. That's why there'd been no car seat for Rinée.

Lizzie had been stealing her neighbor's car. The one who killed her.

Before he killed himself.

DAY 35

CHAPTER THIRTY-FOUR

JOSIE

I WAKE TO FEEL TAPE BEING REMOVED FROM MY LEFT HAND.

I open my eyes and here is the nurse again.

"Well, hello there!" she tells me. "You had quite a rest. Been asleep for a twelve hours, maybe more."

It takes me awhile to remember where I am and why I can't move my limbs.

The nurse holds up the water cup with the straw to my mouth.

I drink, grateful.

"I think somebody bit you on the hand, that's what I think. I think this is a nasty old bite wound," she says as she finishes changing the dressing.

I remember that she's right.

Aidan, little Aidan bit my hand.

Dear God, what happened to my kids?

"I am Sandy," she says. "And you are Josie Miller, according to this sorry excuse of a file. You were at the containment camps at Mizzou. Is that right?"

I nod.

"How do you feel?"

Niko came for me and watched me be attacked and then sedated and taken away. My kids were left to fend for themselves in a horrific blood rage riot. And now I'm being held prisoner in a government medical facility.

My wrists and ankles are chafed from the restraints. I can feel, now, that they've got a catheter stuck in me and it's uncomfortable. My head is pounding. My throat is sore. My hand itches and my heart is broken.

I feel hopeless. Pulverized.

I have no words to answer her question.

"Let me ask you a better question. Are you hungry?"

And I am, I realize. My stomach feels hollowed out.

I nod yes.

She laughs.

"Good." She crosses to the door and calls out, "Kelly, can you order up a breakfast for Miss Miller?"

She comes back and gives me another sip of water.

"Look, I have an apology to make. I'm the one who decided we should cut off your hair. I thought it was the right thing to do but, honey, now I feel bad. Those knots, though, the way you had it in those two bumps, they was all hard like a rock. Linnea, she's black, she said your hair had done dreaded up and we should just shear it off, but I wouldn't blame you at all if you're mad at me."

She was chatting away so nicely. It would be hard to be mad at her.

"I'm not mad," I croak.

"Well, good. You don't seem to me like the type to hold a grudge."

I turn my face away from her.

DAY 35

I am just too sad.

"There, there," she says, patting me on the shoulders. "Don't be blue."

She just stands there, fluttering next to my bed while I cry. She tucks me in, adjusts my pillows.

I don't say anything.

I can't.

"Hey now, you know what? I don't think you need to be in these heavy restraints, I just don't. Leather cuffs are for big burly men and Lord knows we've had our share of them in here. Little girl like you, I don't think you could hurt a fly."

Wrong, wrong, wrong.

"I'm going to put the tape ones on you. They'll give you more room to maneuver, and you can lie on your side, which is nice. You know, I just need to trust that you're not going to try to attack me."

She slips her hand in mine and squeezes. Her skin is soft and moist. "You're not going to attack me, are you, honey?"

"No," I say sincerely. "I won't attack you."

"That's my girl," Sandy chirps. "I'll be right back."

She ducks out of the room.

While she's gone, a man carries in a tray of food.

I can smell eggs, bacon, French toast, tea.

My mouth waters up immediately. It feels like my nose is drunk. My stomach growls.

The man chuckles.

"Go slow, now. Chew each bite ten times or you'll get sick."

Then Sandy is back with two small plastic bags containing my new restraints.

She presses a button and the head of my bed moves up.

She removes my leg restraints first.

I stretch each leg.

"That's better, isn't it?"

"Yes," I manage. "Thank you."

The food. I can hardly wait for her to finish.

I feel a surge of nervous energy amping up. I want the food.

"Almost there." She attaches the light straps to my feet and moves up to my wrists.

The lighter straps are much more comfortable.

The wrist restraints are bracelets attached to long straps that fasten to the bed rails.

"Nice, huh? They're Kevlar and silk! Can you believe that?"

Sandy wheels the food tray, which is set on a stand, over my lap. There's a little sealed cup of orange juice, a roll with two peel-top tubs of butter, a plastic-wrap-covered metal pitcher of pancake syrup and a silver lid over a plate of food.

Sandy removes the lid.

Eggs, bacon, French toast. It's all there.

My hands are shaking as I pick up the plastic fork and take my first bite of eggs.

Buttery, creamy. Can your mouth go into shock?

I force myself to chew.

Sandy watches me.

"Honey," she says, "I think you were starving to death down there at Mizzou. Did you know that?"

I look up.

I guess I did.

Back to the food.

"How's the patient?" wakes me from my post-binge nap. It's the movie star doctor.

"Fine," I say in return.

"Good, good! Excellent."

This is false cheer. He wants something from me.

DAY 35

"I see Sandy's got you on the soft restraints. That's her call to make. Fine with me."

I can tell he'd like to sit on the edge of the bed, but he doesn't.

"So, Josie, I'd like to know a little about your background. Would you mind telling me about your experience before you were picked up in Parker?"

I nod okay.

"Were you outside during the initial release?"

I must look confused, because he clarifies. "When the leak occurred from NORAD, were you outside? Were you exposed at that point?"

"No," I tell him. "I wasn't exposed until almost two weeks later. I was safe, inside a big building. When we tried to get to Denver, that's when I was exposed."

He's making notes on his minitab with a stylus as fast as he can.

Sandy comes in, under the pretense of checking my IV, but I think she mainly wants to hear my story.

"See, this little kid Max was being attacked, and I knew, at that point, that I was O. The soldier attacking him was pretty out of it. I knew I could take him if I went O, so I took off my face mask."

Sandy's listening, her expression sympathetic.

Dr. Cutlass is just nodding, writing.

"And how long were you exposed at that point?"

"About three days. It's hard to say, exactly. It was dark out there."

"During that period, do you remember . . . were you completely out of control, or were you able to make any decisions?"

Dr. Cutlass looks up at me. My answer is very important to him.

"I was able to make decisions."

"I knew it!"

"I was in control enough not to hurt my friends. That was pretty much all I could do—make the decision not to kill. But at Mizzou, when the drift hit, I found I had even more control than the first time I was exposed."

Dr. Cutlass starts pacing now, in the small room.

"This is very exciting," he says. He brings up another page on his minitab.

"Listen to what they wrote about you at Mizzou: 'During the drift, Miller tried to save two small children. When every single other inmate was intent on murder and violence, Miller was seen breaking up a fight between the children and trying to get them to safety.'"

I sit up in my bed, my bonds tightening on my wrists.

"Who wrote that?" I ask.

"A doctor there."

"Was it Dr. Quarropas?"

He looks.

"Yes, J. Quarropas."

"Are you in touch with him?"

"Not to speak of. Why?" Cutlass asks me.

"I'd like to know . . . I'd like to know if my kids are okay," I tell him.

Hope surges into my heart, catching me off guard.

Sandy, rearranging the sheets at the foot of the bed, pats one of my ankles.

Dr. Cutlass looks at me. He's thinking it over.

"I tell you what. I'll think about trying to get in touch with him and find out, but I need you to think about something, too."

"Okay," I say.

"Josie, I think that you are special. I think that you have

DAY 35

the ability to exert conscious control over your mind when in a MORS-exposed state."

"MORS?" I ask.

"MORS is the name of the warfare compound that was released in the Four Corners area," he quickly explains. "What I need from you is just a sample of spinal fluid."

He goes on to say that it's a simple procedure, and there are a few risks, but they will be especially careful because I'm such an important subject and if I agree to it, he will have me released soon thereafter and all kinds of other things he thinks will make me go along with it.

And I might have, too, if it weren't for this: As soon as Dr. Cutlass says "sample of spinal fluid," Sandy's head snaps up. She is still at the foot of the bed, behind Dr. Cutlass. Her eyes are wide, scared, and her mouth tightens into a pinched line.

And she shakes her head no. Quickly. No.

"So let's do this," Dr. Cutlass is saying. "You give me the names of those kids and I'll find out what I can. Then, if you sign the release form, we'll be all set."

"Wait. How do you get spinal fluid?" I ask.

"Oh. Didn't I say?"

I shake my head.

"We do a spinal tap. Really, this is something we do all the time."

I can't help it. My eyes dart to Sandy.

Dr. Cutlass sees this and turns to look at her over his shoulder. He shoots her a cold look. A freezing cold look.

"Hun," she says. "I'm gonna go see about your lunch!"

Dr. Cutlass turns back to me, plastering a reassuring smile up on his face.

"We do it every day," he says. "So. Tell me the names of your friends. You know, maybe I could even get them transferred to a safer facility."

I know what this is. This is a bribe.

I give him the names.

I tell him I will think about it.

I see him decide that that's the best he's going to get, for now.

"You rest up, Josie Miller," he tells me. "You and I have a lot of important work ahead of us."

When I wake up, Sandy is fiddling with my IV.

"Sandy?" I ask her. "Is everything okay?"

She nods yes.

"It's all good, my little peapod."

But I know it's not good. I know that she has an opinion about the testing Dr. Cutlass proposed.

"I've been wondering, if you're feeling better, you want to get up a bit? Go for a walk?"

"Yes, please!"

She laughs.

Then she says, "See? It pays to cooperate. Dr. Cutlass said he finds you amenable and docile. That's good news for you. Means you get to walk around a bit."

There's something wrong with her voice. It's flat, somehow.

I catch her eye and she quickly looks over to the corner, directing me to look there.

Then she puts her hand on my leg.

"Let's get these straps off," and she turns me so I am facing the corner she just indicated with her eyes.

I see it.

A little silver half-sphere, up in the corner.

A security camera.

DAY 35

We're being watched and recorded.

So she's got to say the right thing.

"We're gonna take it slow, sweet girl. But I thought I'd give you a little tour of the Zone Four testing and premium rehabilitation suites of USAMRIID."

After she removes the straps, and the catheter, I get to stand up.

My legs buckle under me and Sandy supports me. She's so short her shoulder fits perfectly under my armpit.

"Take it easy, now. Just see how standing feels. Might be I should get you a wheelchair."

"No," I tell her. "I want to walk. Really, I do."

I put my arm around her shoulders. She's small and wiry. Strong.

We have to roll around my IV, but it's okay. I can lean on it a bit.

I take two, three slow steps away from my bed.

"Sandy, before we go in the hall . . ."

"Hmm?"

"Can I see how I look?"

The bathroom has a shower, a sink, and a toilet. Everything is tiny and compact. In the golden-colored light of my tiny bathroom, I am surprised. I like what I see.

My hair is gone. Shorn off. It's very close to the skin, but I like it.

It makes me look like a grown-up. And it makes me look tough.

And when I think about it, I guess I am both those things.

I'm able to walk okay, after those first few moments.

My body feels a little sore and tired, but God knows it's felt worse.

The hallway looks like a regular hospital, but I see, after peeking in one or two of the rooms, that there are no windows.

"There's facilities in Fort Bragg and Fort Benning and other places, but they pick all the most promising cases and send them here to us," Sandy tells me as we walk.

Many of the doors are closed, but in one I see a huge, hulking guy restrained on a bed. In another there's a man visiting a crying woman, who sits on her bed in a gown like mine.

"Are we allowed to have visitors?" I ask.

"Sometimes." Sandy sighs. She points to a metal door with a large window. The glass is shot through with steel mesh. An armed guard stands on the other side.

She waves to him. He nods back a fraction of an inch.

"Every doorway to the stairwell on every floor is guarded, twenty-four/seven. Nobody gets in here who shouldn't be, don't you worry."

She pats my arm.

Her words are telling one story on the surface, but I feel like there's a subtext—don't try to run.

"The security's even tight for us. Retina checks on every floor. It's all designed for the utmost safety for everyone who works here."

She's telling me they check identity at every door. I'd need stolen eyeballs to escape.

We walk along and suddenly I get tired.

The energy just goes out of me.

"We're underground," she says, waving hello to another nurse. "That's why you don't see any windows."

There's a humming noise, getting louder, and I see we're nearing a room where a man is using an industrial floor polisher.

"I'm getting tired," I say.

"Just a bit more," she tells me.

DAY 35

I don't want to go anymore. I want to sleep.

But she keeps walking until we're right by the guy with the polisher and it's loud.

She leans into me.

"Don't sign the consent form," she says in my ear. "The spinal tap he wants to do, it's too dangerous for people like you."

I watch the man moving the polisher in a circle. He looks up and I see him catch Sandy's eye.

"Dr. Cutlass is a good man, but he's . . . he's lost . . . perspective. Those spinal taps are not safe for people like you. Other people, yes, maybe. But not Os who've been exposed. Not skinny-minnies like you. Got it?"

Chills creep up my spine. I nod.

She turns me and we head back to my room.

"And you didn't hear it from me."

CHAPTER THIRTY-FIVE

DEAN

I CARRIED ASTRID TO THE CAR. SHE WINCED IN THE SUNLIGHT when I brought her outside.

"Bye!" Rinée said.

"We're coming back," I told her and J.J., who stood gaping on the stoop, as Lea helped me to put Astrid in the passenger seat.

"Bye, Ean!" Rinée repeated. Frankly, she seemed happy for us to go.

I drove. Astrid was moaning. The motion of the car was bothering her. Every bump we hit made her cry aloud.

"Please," I told her, handing her the squeeze bottle of water that Lea had put in the cup holder. "Take a sip. Please."

She obliged me.

Her hand was trembling violently, going for the bottle.

I got us on the highway, headed north.

"Are you feeling any better?" I asked.

DAY 35

She had her head hanging down, resting her elbows on the dash.

She vomited again, looking up at me with fear in her eyes. Green bile slick on her chin.

"It's okay," I said. "It's going to be okay."

She leaned against the window and I hit eighty. If a cop pulled me over, good. Maybe he'd give us an escort.

"Almost there, almost there," I said. Though I had no idea how far Joplin was or how long it would take us to get there.

"It's just a flu," I told her. "They'll get you fixed right up."

"My head," she cried. "It hurts so bad."

Then she started shaking.

Her head whipped back and she was convulsing, arms flailing. I cursed and swerved.

"Astrid! Astrid!" I shouted.

I pulled onto the shoulder and the cars screaming past wailed their horns.

I tried to hold her. Was I supposed to put my hand in her mouth to stop her from biting her tongue? I couldn't remember and then she went limp.

"Astrid? Astrid!" I called to her.

She was unconscious.

A sob wrenched free from my chest.

What to do?

I got out. Tried to flag down a car.

"HELP!" I yelled. "Somebody help me!"

None of them stopped.

Nobody would stop!

Then I saw an Army truck approaching.

It was one, and behind it were others.

I got back in the car, belted myself in, and hit the gas.

The first truck had just passed as I got up to speed.

There were eight or ten big olive-drab trucks in the convoy and a flatbed truck carrying two of the same kind of jeeps we had seen in Roufa's cargo plane back in Texas.

I honked at them, trying to wave them down, but they sped past me.

In a flash, they were ahead and I was behind. They were leaving me, literally, in the dust.

The last truck was filled with soldiers, and as I honked and waved my hand out the window, begging for them to stop, a soldier smoking a cigarette popped his head out and looked at me.

"Please stop!" I shouted, though of course he couldn't hear. "I need help! I need help!"

The soldier took his cigarette and flicked it at me. Then started laughing and pulled his head back inside the canvas cover.

My foot slammed on the gas, like it belonged to someone else. I pushed the little Mazda for all it had, 80—85—90, and pulled up next to that last truck.

I saw the soldier in the passenger seat look at me, puzzled, and then I brought the Mazda closer and closer to the truck.

I would push him off the road, into the median. I would get their godforsaken help. I was going to get it.

The truck pulled onto the median and I heard a screech of heavy metal as it braked to a stop.

I slid out behind it, almost ramming it from behind.

Holy almighty, what had I done?

My door was jerked open and a muscle-bound soldier hauled me out by my shirt and slammed me into the car.

"What the bloody hell do you think you're doing? You wanna get yourself shot?!"

"My girlfriend and I are wanted by the United States Army Medical Research lab for medical testing," I said. "We're turning ourselves in."

DAY 35

CHAPTER THIRTY-SIX

JOSIE

DR. CUTLASS COMES TO ME IN THE LATE AFTERNOON.

Every time I see him I'm struck by his hair. It's always perfect. Wavy and brown, gray at the temples, and the soft curls combed or gelled into place.

He has his minitab and a thick manila folder.

"Josie Miller!" he says, beaming. "I heard you went for a walk."

He doesn't wait for me to answer. He wheels over my tray table and takes a sheaf of paperwork from the folder.

"I've been in contact with Dr. Quarropas and he's gathering the information on those kids you mentioned. He said he'd had . . . was it Hannah?"

He takes a silver pen from his pocket and places it on the tray. Then he shuffles past the first few pages of the form, coming to a page with a "sign here" flag pointing to a line.

"No, Heather. It was Heather. Heather's in the clinic there and she's fine. She suffered a concussion and some lacerations, but she's recovering nicely. I was asking him about the possibility of transferring the kids to a better facility, one closer to here. He's looking into it."

The doctor smiles at me, his head bobbing softly. He points to the line.

"Sign right here."

I look into his eyes.

He can't hold my gaze and his eyebrow twitches before he looks away.

"I'm not going to sign it," I say.

"Really?" he says. "Huh. Why's that?"

"I don't think it's safe."

"A spinal tap? It's a common, routine procedure. Here, look, I'll show you."

He taps an address into his minitab, shows me a Wikipedia article on spinal taps.

I read, dutifully. The article says they are a low-risk procedure.

But Sandy wouldn't warn me for nothing. She wouldn't have gone to all that trouble for nothing.

I hand back the minitab and shrug.

"You know what, we haven't talked about your release," he says, changing tactics.

I don't bite.

"I've saved the best news for last. I've been given clearance to award you a grant of twenty thousand dollars for your participation in this research."

Wow. Now I know what my signature's worth. I bet I could drive it up to fifty.

"I'm not signing those forms," I tell him.

"You will sign them. Because you are the key! You have, inside you, the information we need. Heck, Josie Miller, you're going to

DAY 35

be famous. Think of that. They're going to study you in the history books!"

"I don't want to be famous in history."

"What do you want?"

I look away from Dr. Cutlass.

What do I want?

I want to go back in time.

I want my mom. Or my dad. Or anyone who knew me from before and who can remind me of how to live.

I want some magic butter or fat or oil to go into my body and fill out each cell, so I don't feel sharp inside—every atom of me grating against the others.

I want to be a girl again.

To un-know what I know.

I want someone to hold me. Someone who doesn't want something from me.

"Tell me what you want, Josie."

"For my life?" I spit.

"Not for your life! For ten milliliters of spinal fluid."

"That operation will kill me!"

"Who said that? Sandy?"

"No!" I cry. "She didn't say anything. I just . . ."

"You just what?" he asks, contempt edging through his voice.

"I just have a feeling."

Dr. Cutlass exhales. He's pissed.

"Listen," he says. "I understand why you're angry. If I were in your position, I probably wouldn't want to help, either."

He's reaching now, for a way to connect. He's trying to be a human. And even though I know it's just a gambit, I *do* see regret in his eyes. And pain. It looks sincere.

"What happened at Mizzou, it must have been horrible. I've read the reports. You mentioned a boy," he said. "Nicko?"

"Niko," I correct. "He came all the way to Mizzou for me. And then the drift hit and Dr. Quarropas drugged me before I could even talk to Niko. He went all that way for nothing."

Despite me telling myself, yelling at myself not to cry, tears well up in my eyes.

"Well, I'll see what I can do. Maybe we can locate him."

He pats me on the arm. Rises. Then stops.

"If we were able to find him, would you sign?"

I turn my head away. He only cares about the consent forms. I had forgotten for one brief moment. I'd let him find his leverage.

I nod yes and press my face into the pillow, as best I can. The pillowcase smells like bleach and slightly burned. I cry into it for a while.

After I get myself together, I press the call button.

A Latina nurse comes in. Tall and angular. Her mouth turned down at the corners.

"Yes? You need something?"

"Where's Sandy?" I ask her.

"Sandy's working on a different floor, now. What do you need?"

I turn my head away.

"Nothing," I say.

"Where are your restraints?" she asks.

"Sandy said I didn't need them."

"Oh, she did, did she? Well, we do things a little differently on my watch." She crosses to the door and calls out: "Hector, restraints, please."

"I don't need them. I promise. I won't hurt anyone."

"You've been labeled 'uncooperative' on your file. Until you start to cooperate, you wear restraints."

"Does Dr. Cutlass know about this? Where's Sandy?" I cry.

DAY 35

I can't help it—I curl up in a little ball. As if I think by keeping my hands and feet close to me, she won't get them.

She comes over to my bedside and I think she's going to talk to me, but no, she uncaps a small syringe and taps out an air bubble.

A large man guy in scrubs enters with leather cuffs.

"No!" I shout. "Please! I promise, I'll be good!"

The nurse injects something into my drip and I fall fast.

CHAPTER THIRTY-SEVEN

DEAN

THEY WERE NOT PLEASED WITH ME, THE SOLDIERS. THEY thought I was an a-hole, and they let me know it.

Each of them wore safety suits. A heavier material than ours, but with the same baggy design. They had different face masks at their hips, too. More of a helmet, with a built-in mouthpiece instead of the ones like ours, that you held between your teeth.

They were some kind of a cleanup crew.

"You got any idea what the penalties are for interfering with the US Army, son?" bellowed the giant one who'd pulled me out of the car.

"Here comes Sarge," said a different one.

I saw that the entire caravan had stopped up ahead and an officer flanked by three soldiers was walking to our car.

Then we heard it.

BREEEEEEEEE! A chorus of tiny alarm whistles.

"SUITS! MASKS!" they all shouted and everyone moved

DAY 35

fast, the sun reflecting off their face plates and the sound of zippers all around.

And I suddenly felt icy, sick, cold—I had forgotten Astrid's suit.

It was still hanging up on the back of the door at Rinée and J.J.'s house.

The soldier who'd been holding me was zipping on his mask. I darted away from him, scrambling to the other side of the car, all the while shucking my suit.

I had to get it on Astrid. I had to get her safe.

I opened the door and she fell halfway out onto the pavement.

The drift was swooping and wheeling in the sky, about a mile or so in the distance.

I got the suit off my legs. Astrid's legs were in the car. I pulled them out. Got one leg into the suit.

The whistling died down as the soldiers zipped up.

The soldiers around us ran back up to the caravan, where they were unloading the sucker-jeeps from the flatbed trucks. I heard them shouting to one another—revving up engines.

I got her feet in and then lifted her weight up, getting under her shoulders and back, so I could tug the suit up her limp body.

There was only one whistling suit now—the one I was trying to get on Astrid.

Her head lolled back onto my shoulder.

The drift sent fingers to the ground here and there, little black twisters, reaching for what?

I zipped up the front of the suit.

"Here she comes!" cried someone.

"Ready the suckers!" came an order.

I fumbled for the headpiece. It was still in its holster, under her hip.

I got it.

"Steady!" I heard them call.

I heard a tinkling sound. Tiny tinkles, like hail. Coming closer.

Hail.

I got the headpiece on her.

I remembered hail.

Hail and blood was how it all started.

I zipped it closed, the rage blossoming in my brain.

Astrid. A girl. A girl in a suit. A green light near her face.

I pushed her back in the car, pushed her too hard, and I slammed it shut, slammed too hard.

There were men there.

Men with machines, aiming giant sucking funnels into the sky and I would kill one of them and put him in the funnel and chop him up.

Yes, a chopping machine!

I laughed.

They didn't even see me coming and I got to the first one and I grabbed him by the back of the cloth suit.

A cloth suit for protection? Not from me.

I could taste his blood in my mouth I wanted it so bad.

To the machine, I pushed him.

But he was too strong. He threw me down.

And then I was on the ground and a cloth man was standing with one boot on my chest.

Machine gun! He had one! I would get it. And then I could—

"Sorry, kid," came his voice.

And he brought the gun down on my head.

DAY 35

CHAPTER THIRTY-EIGHT

JOSIE

IT'S DARK IN MY ROOM AND THEN I'M BEING SHAKEN AWAKE.

It's Dr. Cutlass.

My heart starts to hammer. With each pound I am coming up, fighting through the layers of sludge in my head, shattering through the headache and I'm there.

And I'm ready to fight. If I wasn't CUFFED to the godforsaken BED.

I see he's got an orderly with him. Not the one from before.

Oh God, the orderly is taping up black plastic over the CAMERA!

They've come to take me and do the testing against my will.

If, if, if. If they take the restraints off, for a second, I'll take the doctor's head off.

I'll scratch up his handsome, lying face.

"Don't touch me!" I shout.

"Shhh!" Cutlass says.

"I do not give you permission. I do NOT!"

"Shut up!" he says. "That's not why I'm here. Be quiet! Listen to me!"

I'm shaking—muscles vibrating with rage and terror.

"I'm not doing the testing without your consent. Calm down." All this he says in a hushed voice.

I make myself slow my breath.

BANG. BANG. Bang. Bang. Beat by beat my heart slows.

"What kind of person do you think I am?" he asks me.

A monster, I want to tell him. A bully.

I won't apologize.

"I'm here because I have good news."

"What?"

"At ten twenty-nine this evening a young man presented himself at the gates and requested a visit."

"Oh my God, Niko?"

He nods. A big smile on his face.

"Really?"

I can't believe it. And then I realize—I *shouldn't* believe it. This is a trick.

"You sign the consent form and I'll have him brought up right now."

Could it be? Could Niko have followed me here?

He could have. He could have found out they'd taken me here and Niko could get here. Hitchhiking or even stealing a car.

"That's why I asked Jimmy to cover the camera," Dr. Cutlass says. "If I let him come up, during the middle of the night, it's completely against the rules. I'm taking a big risk."

"How do I know he's really there?"

"Hmmm." Cutlass smiles. Turns to Jimmy, the orderly, who's leaning against the wall. "She's a smart one. I told you, Jimmy. Can't fool her."

DAY 35

He takes out a minitab and dials a number.

"This is Dr. Cutlass. Do you still have Niko Mills in the office there? Put him on."

And he puts the phone up to my ear.

"Hello?" I say.

I hear his voice.

It is Niko. It *is*.

"Josie?"

"Niko? Are you *here*?"

"I'm in security, Josie. They say they're going to let me see you, maybe. I don't know. But I'm here. I'm here."

I'm crying now and we're talking at the same time. Me saying: "Niko, I can't believe you came for me." And him saying: "I can't believe I found you, Josie."

Tears are sliding down my face and I can't wipe them away because of the restraints.

Dr. Cutlass shuts off the phone. He takes out the sheaf of papers.

"So here's what happens next," he instructs me. "Jimmy will remove the restraints. You will sign this consent form, and Niko will be brought to your room and he can even spend the night here."

I am already nodding.

I don't ask what will happen in the morning.

"And of course, there will be a guard stationed outside the door."

I nod.

I just want to see him.

In the bathroom, I splash cold water on my face. I brush my teeth with the little toothbrush set they've given me.

There's a bottle of lotion, too, and I rub it on my face and arms and bare legs, which stick out from my voluminous blue medical gown like lollipop sticks.

The lotion smells like vanilla. That's good.

I wish I had a belt. I wish I had a tube of lip gloss.

I look at myself in the mirror.

A smile, a real smile, flashes on the glass.

It's happiness. A sweet burst of joy.

It feels like the first time my heart has filled with something light and pretty in a lifetime—I'm going to see my boyfriend.

I pat my hair, like there's anything to be done with it.

And then there's a knock on the door.

I open the door and there stands Niko Mills.

Somehow, I'm nervous for him to look at me closely so I just rush into his arms.

He holds me tight to his thin body.

He smells sour and sweaty and dirty and wonderful. I see his hair is caked to his head with sweat.

I see Dr. Cutlass and Jimmy in the hall. Cutlass is grinning like he bagged big game and there's a guard there, with a big gun.

Niko releases me and I step back.

There's a moment where no one knows what to do.

"We'll see you in the morning, Josie. Niko can stay here until then and I've given the order for you two to be left alone," Cutlass tells me.

"Come in," I say. It seems like a weird thing to say but the whole thing is weird.

DAY 35

He comes in and shuts the door behind him.

Niko is carrying a gray backpack. He looks . . . he looks the same. Same serious expression. He seems maybe a bit younger than I remember him.

Now that he's here I have no idea what to do.

I fiddle with my bed, tucking the sheets in at the foot and making it smooth.

"I've been so worried about you," Niko says.

I can't quite look at him. I don't know. I'm antsy. I'm nervous.

"When I saw those men beating you up . . . No one was helping you! And then the drift. It was . . . was gruesome, Josie. I've never seen anything like it. The ground was running blood."

He says all this and the energy in me won't settle down. I sort of don't want him to get a good look at me. I know I've aged. I probably look like a dried-up hag to him. Or some stranger.

"Josie," he says. "Josie?"

I glance up.

"Are you okay?"

I put my hands up to my face. Get yourself together, a part of me shouts to myself. This is ridiculous. You haven't seen him in weeks and now you're blubbering like a baby. He'll want nothing to do with you.

But another part of me is somehow softening. Letting down my guard.

Niko is here. And he comes over to my side of the bed.

He takes me in his arms and holds me.

For a long time, I just cry.

Being in his arms is my heaven.

Being in his arms can be my last meal and I'll be happy for it.

* * *

"You know you can tell me anything, right?" he says when I stop crying.

We're lying on the bed. He has his muddy boots up on it. Who cares? This will probably be the last night I spend in this room, one way or the other.

"I'm sorry I got your shirt all wet," I say.

"That? You did me a favor. I haven't had a shower in almost a week."

"There's a shower here. In the bathroom. Do you want to take one?" I ask.

He shrugs. "Maybe later."

I can tell he wants me to talk, to tell him about what happened to me since we lost each other, but I don't want to talk.

When I tell him my story, he's going to find out that I've agreed to the testing, and he'll get upset.

"Tell me about the kids. How are they? What's Canada like?" I say.

He tells me everything. About how they got to DIA. Saw Mrs. Wooly! How he sent Sahalia ahead on the plane to Canada while he and Alex found someone who would take them back to the Greenway for Dean, Astrid, Chloe, and the twins. And then about Quilchena, which sounds like a beautiful place.

Chloe sent me a message: "Quack, quack."

It's an old, dumb private joke. It make's me laugh. She's such a rascal.

Niko tells me about Captain McKinley flying him, Jake, Dean, and Astrid to Fort Lewis-McChord. Imagine it—Caroline and Henry's dad in the Air Force—pretty lucky. He tells me about the second flight to Texas and the trucker and the first drift they saw, in Vinita, and about the toddler in the trunk of the car.

DAY 35

I wish I had a clock or a phone—I don't know what time it is.

He tells me he hitched a ride with a bunch of Lutherans from Oklahoma City heading to the East Coast to volunteer rebuilding homes. Then he stole a minivan to get the rest of the way to Mizzou.

And that after he saw me there, he drove his stolen minivan until the gas ran out near Indianapolis.

Then he got a ride from another trucker. He had to give the man his protective suit in barter.

But Niko says, who cares—he's never going to the Midwest again. He won't need it.

We lie there on the bed and he strokes my fuzzy head.

He tells me he loves my hair like this. He says I have a beautiful skull. It's a one-hundred-percent Niko compliment and I love it.

"When we leave here," he says to me, "we're going to go straight to the farm. Look." He gets up and takes a paper map out of his backpack. It's the kind you can buy at gas stations.

"It's less than three hours from here! We'll be there tomorrow, no question."

He sits next to me and traces the little red lines running over the paper with his pointer finger. I-83 to 222 to 322.

I watch his finger. The nail is short, bitten down. I never knew he bites his nails. Maybe he didn't before.

I close my eyes and lie back on the bed.

"What?" he asks. "Don't you want to go there? We don't have to. We can go wherever you want. I just thought—"

"It's not that," I say.

I sit up, taking the map away from him and holding his hands in mine.

"I need to tell you something. No, two things, okay?"

"I told you, Josie. You can tell me anything."

I swallow.

"I want to say that it means everything to me that you came here to find me."

He nods. The dim light twinkles in his eyes and I love him so much.

"It is the most beautiful thing that anyone has ever done for me. And you should know that I felt broken before, before you walked in that door. I had pretty much given up hope that I'd ever feel good again, but when you came in I felt so happy. You have to remember how much that means to me—"

"Josie, what is it? What's wrong?"

"To see you," I say. "To get to see you and have this time together, I had to sign a form."

He looks puzzled. I hate what I'm about to tell him.

"Tomorrow, they're going to do a test on me. They're going to take a sample of spinal fluid. And it's possible—I was told the chances of me surviving—"

Niko is as white as a sheet.

"No," he says. "That's not going to happen."

His jaw is tight, his teeth clamped together.

"I'm not going to let that happen."

CHAPTER THIRTY-NINE

DEAN

"SIR, I UNDERSTAND THE OBJECTIVE, BUT SURELY A LOW DOSE of magnesium sulfate wouldn't affect the fetus—"

A woman is on the phone.

I'm in a car. No, bigger than a car. Couldn't remember what it was called.

We are driving fast.

"This is one of the worst cases of preeclampsia I have ever seen—" She gets cut off.

"The protein levels—this girl is in danger—" She's cut off again.

"Well, sir, that's not the problem. The fetal heartbeat is very strong."

We are moving fast and I hear a siren.

Oh. My head. It hurts.

"Yes sir," she says and she hangs up.

I open my eyes again.

I am looking up at a ceiling. In my field of vision there is the underside of a metal cabinet and a black square on the ceiling with lights flashing in it. Red, white, red, yellow. Red, white, red, yellow.

"Those friggin' jackholes," the woman curses.

"I know, I know," says a man's voice.

"Under no circumstances are we to administer any drugs to that poor girl! Not even a little magnesium sulfate for the convulsions! I mean, really?"

I feel warm and relaxed, like I am swimming in soup.

It is a skylight, I realize slowly. It is nighttime and I am seeing the sky and the red, white, red, yellow pattern is the reflection of lights. They are pretty.

"What if she dies?"

"We save the baby."

The man I can't see curses.

Astrid. Astrid. Where is she?

I turn my head and I moan.

The pain cuts through the warmth. Slices right through. God, what happened to my head?

I see Astrid there across from me, an IV in her arm and her belly exposed with some kind of belt with electrode cords running this way and that and machines monitoring and beeping. I remember her.

"Astrid," I say.

I hear movement and then there is a face above me, an Indian lady with a lined face and gray hair cut short.

"Hey," she says. "Can you hear me? Do you know what year it is?"

"Two thousand . . . ," I say, my voice raspy. "Two thousand and . . ."

I should know this.

"Do you know where you are?"

DAY 36

"In a car . . . A big medicine car." What is the stupid word for it?

"How many weeks is she?" the woman asks. "I need to know about her pregnancy. Anything you can tell me will help."

Her face bobs and stretches.

"He's passing out again," she calls up front.

Not passing out, I want to tell her, just swimming.

I hear her rummaging in the cabinet above my head.

"Don't," says the voice from up front.

"I need the info. It won't hurt him. He's been out for such a long time. It will be good for him to be awake."

She pats my face.

"Hello," she says. "Open wide."

I open my mouth a little. She puts a little pill on my tongue. I close my lips.

"This will pep you up a bit."

Then *BOOMBOOMBOOM* my heart is going like a bass drum and I want to sit up but now I realize I am tied down to the cot.

"Whoa," I say "Wow!"

"Easy there," she tells me.

"That stuff's not for kids, Binwa," the guy up front says. "He's gonna feel worse when it wears off."

The warm, relaxed feeling evaporates and I see everything very clearly.

The woman leans over me and I can see into her pores and each of her eyelashes is distinct.

Ambulance, I remember. We are in an ambulance. And we were in a drift. And I nearly crashed into an Army truck.

"Tell me about your girlfriend," she says. And I do.

Binwa takes off the restraints that were holding me to the padded stretcher.

My head is bandaged. When I sit up, I have to hold it to keep my brain from exploding—that's what it feels like. But all that matters is Astrid.

"Dean," Astrid says. I kneel next to her. "I'm sorry."

"Don't be sorry," I tell her. I start kissing her hand. I know that is a weird thing to do, but I am so glad to see her awake. "You have nothing to apologize for."

"This is good," Binwa says. She comes over. "Astrid, we're less than an hour out. The doctors are waiting for you at US-AMRIID."

Astrid closes her eyes and I think she is going out again. but she whispers, "I'm sorry."

"Why are you saying that?" I ask.

"I can't do it," Astrid says. Her eyes, still closed, are leaking tears. There is a crust of dried skin on her lips. I can see a vein pulsing at her temple.

"Shhh," I tell her and I kiss her forehead. "We're almost there."

"I want you to know something."

"What?"

"I love you," she says. Her eyes close and tears leak out of the corners. "I just want you to know that."

"I do know it. I do, Astrid."

She opens her eyes and looks at me one last time and then her eyes rolls up in her head and she start to shake violently.

"No!" Binwa shouts. "Gus, hit the siren. You've got to get us there, now!"

The siren blares. Gus drives faster. The night road is streaming behind us and my girl is dying.

"You give her that stuff!" I shout at Binwa. I looked around for a weapon. Something to make her do whatever it would take to save Astrid.

DAY 36

"Calm down!" Binwa roars at me. "Look! Look! She's coming out of it now."

I turn and see that Astrid *is* coming out of it. She is sitting straight up. She is arching her back and she is screaming.

Then we see that her legs are wet.

"Gus!" Binwa shouts. "Her water broke!"

"Niko," I say. "Hold me. Be with me and somehow we will never leave this moment. Can't we do that? Can't we love each other enough that nothing else can touch us? Can you love me that much?"

"I already do," he says. And he kisses me.

He kisses me hard and we lie back on the bed. We are kissing and crying and I am learning that bodies can express what words cannot. I see his hands are shaking as he lifts his shirt over his head. Mine are, too, as I unsnap my thin blue gown. The air makes my skin prickle in goose bumps, then Niko lies down on me and our bodies warm each other. We melt together.

His hands are tentative at first, but we find our way.

Then there is a knock at the door.

It seems too early to me.

"Are you decent?" comes a woman's voice.

"Not really," I say, and it is true. We are both naked. Niko sits up, his thin back straight and tall. He pulls on his filthy clothes at the edge of the bed. We have showered, but there is no way to get those clothes clean.

He will always be the same, Niko, and that makes me happy. I know he'll sit on the edge of the bed at ninety and pull on his pants in the same dignified way. He will always hold himself straight and tall. He is unchangeable and that is something I now understand that I love about him.

I discover I am shaking.

Niko has his T-shirt on by the time Sandy comes in.

"Sandy," I say. "You came back."

"Mmm-hmmm. Had to meet your friend. And wanted to be here for you. It's good for you to be as calm as possible for the procedure," she says, but she won't meet my eyes.

"It's okay," I tell her. "I'm going to be fine."

CHAPTER FORTY

JOSIE

HE STANDS UP AND PACES BACK AND FORTH UNTIL I TELL HIM, IN strong words, that I don't want to spend our night together planning some futile escape.

He won't hear it.

He's sure there's a way out.

But I take him by the hand.

And this is what I say:

"Niko. I gave the doctor my word. I signed the release forms. And I did that knowing the risks. Just like you came to find me, knowing the risks. And maybe I will die tomorrow or maybe you will die tomorrow. That was always the risk. Every day we have lived, that's been the risk, we just didn't know it."

I sit on the bed and make him sit next to me.

He is crying, and that is fine.

"I love you, Josie," he tells me.

"I love you, too, Niko." And I mean it. I drink in his perfect silhouette. The colors of his skin and hair.

DAY 36

My mind is sure I'm doing what is right but my heart is up in my throat.

"There has to be a way to get out of this." Niko's voice is quiet and urgent. "Can you tell them she can't do it? She's sick? Can't you think of something to get her out of this?"

Two orderlies come into the room.

"We're to take you back to the waiting area," one of them says to Niko.

"I'm staying with her!" Niko protests.

"It's okay, Niko," I say but there is a scuffle as Niko tries to grab for me and one of the orderlies reaches out and claps a big hand on his shoulder.

"Now, now. Don't go upsetting the girl. Calmer she is, better everything goes," the orderly says.

"Tony's right, hun," Sandy says. "Don't make this hard for Jojo. This is just a standard procedure and when it's done, y'all get to leave. Think of that!"

"No!" Niko shouts. "Josie, please! Don't let them take me away! Tell them you won't do it if I'm not there!"

He grabs my arm and holds me to him. I can feel his body trembling with anger and fear. It is strange to feel so resigned and distant from him, when we'd just been so close.

I wrap my arms and hug him, trying to think of how to say good-bye. How to get him to let me go.

Dr. Cutlass bustles in then, looking at a chart in his hands.

"What's the holdup? Come on, guys!" he snaps. He takes a breath and you can see him trying to rein in his impatience. "Good morning, Josie, and good morning, Niko. The OR is prepped and ready. I'd like to move forward."

"I want to come with her!" Niko says.

Dr. Cutlass looks at Niko, measuring his level of agitation.

DAY 36

"Fine," he says. "You can accompany us to the OR. Will that make you happy?"

"No," Niko spits. "Let her go. That will make me happy."

"This is a routine medical procedure," Dr. Cutlass responds coldly. "You two are overreacting in epic proportion."

We march out into the hall, our whole party.

And people, to my eye, seem to move out of our way as Dr. Cutlass, Niko, Sandy, and the two orderlies all escort me to the OR.

The calm in my mind is starting to be overturned by the alarm signals from my body.

I look down. Niko is holding my one hand and Sandy is holding my other.

And I see that Sandy has a tissue in her other hand.

She is using the tissue to blot at the corners of her eyes.

Sandy believes she is walking me to my death.

And then panic hits me.

CHAPTER FORTY-ONE

DEAN

BINWA IS TRYING TO COACH ASTRID THROUGH THE contractions and I am losing my mind. Astrid screams with each contraction and it is not supposed to be this way. This is not going how it should and I can see that from Binwa's face, which is twisted with worry and anguish.

"You do what's right for her!" I shout. "Give her what she needs, for God's sake!"

Binwa tells me to shut up, she is doing the best she can and I am not making it better.

Sometimes we hit potholes as we wail through the streets and I think I am going to throw up or faint, the pain is so bad. But Astrid's screams bring me back to the horrible, terrifying moment. Yes, they do that.

It is dawn outside and we are speeding through some small town in Maryland.

"You're doing great, Astrid," Binwa says. "This is labor. This is natural."

But I know she is lying. This is what it looked like when someone dies. Binwa is *not* doing everything she can   for Astrid.

"Your body knows how to do this. You just need to relax."

Binwa presses her fists into the small of Astrid's back when a contraction comes.

The van is going down, into a tunnel.

We lurch to a stop and suddenly people are opening the doors.

Four medics bustle in and start sliding the gurney out.

Binwa is going with them and one of the doors swings shut. I push it open and follow them. No one is stopping me. No one is even noticing me, somehow.

I trail them into the bright lights of a hospital. We'd entered through an underground entrance.

They are pushing the gurney and I run to keep up.

JOSIE

"PLEASE!" I PLEAD. "I DON'T WANT TO. PLEASE. I DON'T WANT to."

"You can't force her to do it!" Niko shouts. "Please, somebody help us!"

"James!" comes a booming voice. "What the hell is going on here?"

It's the other doctor, Cutlass's boss, Savic. He has a soldier with him. A soldier carrying a machine gun.

"Please, Doctor. I've . . . I've changed my mind," I tell him.

"She signed the consent form, Dr. Savic," Cutlass spits at the other doctor. "She signed your precious form and now it's all legit."

"No," he says to me. "You didn't sign a consent, did you? Sandy didn't tell you?"

My answer's in my eyes.

Cutlass grabs Dr. Savic by the arm.

"You told Sandy to tell Josie not to sign? How dare you interfere with one of my test subjects—"

Everything is still for a split second and then double doors at the other end of the hall burst open and in comes a swarm of people surrounding a gurney.

DEAN

"YOU'VE GOT TO DO A CAESARIAN NOW!" BINWA SHOUTS.

"Adamson wants to examine," one of them says.

"Well, where the hell is he?"

I have to hold on to the gurney. I have to hold on because my head is splitting open and I might fall down.

"Who's the zombie?" one of the ER guys asks. "Orderly! Take this kid away!"

"Get her to the OR!" Binwa shouts and I stumble, falling. I am on my knees. I reach out my hand. The gurney is sliding away from me.

Someone grabs my arm. I try to stand. I have to stand.

"Astrid!" I shout. "I'm here!"

JOSIE

ALL HEADS ARE TURNED TOWARD THE OTHER END OF THE HALL.

The gurney's zooming at us and then I hear: "Astrid? Astrid Heyman?"

Dr. Cutlass is looking at the gurney with utter shock on his face.

It is Astrid.

It's our Astrid.

"This is the Type O teen multiple-exposure pregnancy," one of the doctors with the gurney says. "The one who got away from us up in Quilchena."

They start to move past us but I scream and lean over the gurney, hugging her legs.

"Astrid!" I say. "It's me, Josie. It's me!"

But she's moaning and crying. She doesn't recognize me.

DEAN

I SCRAMBLE TO MY FEET AND PUSH AWAY FROM THE ORDERLY.

One step, two steps and I stumble to Binwa. They've all stopped.

I look up.

It is Niko and Josie.

"Josie," I say. "You cut off your hair."

They are here. Somehow in the hospital. What?

"Dean!" Niko shouts. "How the hell did you get here?"

I want to ask the same thing but suddenly I am sobbing. It all just bursts out of me.

"Jake left us and Astrid got sick and I couldn't find help anywhere—"

Josie hugs me and the doctor with them is staring at us open-mouthed.

"I'm scared," I say. "I think she's going to die."

DAY 36

JOSIE

THERE'S BLOOD ON MY HANDS. IT'S DEAN'S. THE BANDAGE ON his head is leaking blood down the back of his shirt.

Dr. Cutlass is looking at me.

"Can we go with them?" I ask him. "Our friend needs us."

"You know *Astrid*?"

There's something going on in the doctor's eyes. They're clear. Present. I feel like, maybe for the first time, the man is actually with us.

"Move out of the way!" a gray-haired lady shouts. "We've got to get this girl into the OR!"

Dean is leaning on Niko now.

"It's okay, Dean. She's gonna be okay," Niko is telling him. Dean is barely standing on his feet.

"Dr. Cutlass," I nearly shout. "We were all trapped together in a store in Monument, Colorado, for two weeks. We're like family."

They're leaving now, going down the hall and Dean stumbles

after them. He calls to Niko, "Please come with me. I'm scared. I'm scared and my head's not working right!"

"Please!" I beg Cutlass. "These two are family to us!"

"That girl is Astrid Heyman. She's the girlfriend of my son's best friend," Dr. Cutlass says. "You're from Monument?"

"Brayden Cutlass," Niko says, remembering. "Brayden's last name was Cutlass."

Dr. Cutlass grabs Niko by both arms.

"You knew my son?!"

DAY 36

DEAN

JOSIE AND NIKO COME MAYBE FIVE MINUTES LATER. A SHORT
Asian nurse is with them. She is smiling so widely her face is all
teeth.

They have taken Astrid into the OR.

"They said I had to wait," I tell Niko and Josie as they sit
down beside me on either side. "They told me to wait out here.
Astrid's having the baby."

"We know," Josie says. "You told us."

Had I? I couldn't seem to remember from one minute to the
next.

My thoughts are muddled again. Worse than before. I know
that much.

"There's something wrong with my head."

"Looks of it, you have a concussion," the nurse says, peering
into my pupils.

Josie picks up one of my hands and squeezes it.

"I never thought I'd get to see you again, Dean."

"Astrid's having the baby now," I tell her.

"We know, sweetie. It's gonna be okay."

"Everything is going to be okay," Niko says. He takes my other hand in his. "We're together now."

"That dressing needs to be changed," says the nurse, peering into my eyes. She goes off for supplies.

"I can't believe he let me out of the testing," Josie says, across me, to Niko.

"He let you out of the spinal tap. He still wants blood and spit and God knows what else."

"Yes, but none of those will kill me."

"Who wants your spit?" I ask.

"Brayden's dad."

"He works at NORAD," I say, remembering.

"He was going to do a procedure on me, but we told him all about Brayden. About how we all were together, and about how we tried to get his son to safety."

"Josie?" I say.

"Yes, Dean."

"Astrid's having the baby. And I'm scared she's going to die. I tried so hard to keep her safe."

"Of course you did," Josie says. She rubs my shoulder. It is so good to be with her. She always feels like home.

"Astrid's having the baby," I tell her.

The nurse comes back with some gauze and stuff. I lean my head forward and rest it on Josie's lap.

The nurse puts something on that stings. Then she wraps up my head again.

She also hands me a little cup with two pills in it and a big cup of ice water.

We wait.

DAY 36

Josie and Niko keep stealing grins at each other, saying, "I just can't believe he let us go."

I know I should ask them how they got there to the military hospital, but I don't want to. I just want to sit and be quiet and think about Astrid.

We sit there that way for a long time.

Then the lady Binwa comes out.

She has on an orange suit. At first I don't recognize her. But then I remember her and the ambulance ride. I remember feeling so angry at her, but now I am glad to see her.

"Dean," she says. "Dean. You're a father."

Josie laughs aloud. Niko claps me on the shoulder.

"They're working on Astrid now, fixing her up. Baby's fine. Premature, of course, but lungs are good. They're both going to be fine."

"Astrid's okay?" I ask. "She's all right?"

"She did beautifully, Dean. They stopped the seizures. Did a caesarian—had to be done. But she looks great."

"She's okay?"

"She's fine," Binwa says, pushing a piece of hair out of my eyes.

She turns to go back through the double doors.

"Wait!" I say. There is something I should ask.

Binwa turns back to us. "Astrid's just fine, Dean. And you'll be feeling better soon, too."

"No, it's not that. It's the baby. What is it? A girl or a boy?" I ask.

"It's a little boy," Binwa says. "Four pounds, eight ounces."

EPILOGUE

OUR ROOM IS OVER THE KITCHEN BECAUSE THE ROOM OVER THE
kitchen is the warmest in the house.

All that worry about Niko's uncle—would he take us in?
would he be willing to sponsor us?—disappeared the moment
we rolled up to the farmhouse in Sandy's Ford Focus.

The tension had been building on the drive. Sandy, who took
the day off to drive us here, filled the ride with her sunny chatter.
Astrid sat in the back, next to the baby's car seat (which Sandy had
some how procured). I sat in the front and worried.

I worried when I saw the sign, "Pfeiffer Family Farm—Pick
Your Own!" It sat in a field studded with old apple trees, barren
now. There was also trash in the field, lots of it. It looked like
refugees had been camping out there—there were burnt-out
circles where campfires had been lit and pits dug, littered with
bits of toilet paper.

Not very promising.

I turned back to Astrid, who was gazing at little Charlie in his seat.

Charles Everett Grieder Heyman. Charles for Astrid's father. Everett for Jake's. Grieder for me.

I still couldn't get over it. After all my worry about Astrid and her feelings for me—she put Grieder in her son's name. She had named me into his life permanently.

She loved me back.

"You okay?" I asked.

She nodded.

Charlie's tiny wise-man face was the only part of him you could see. His completely bald head was covered by a knit cap they'd given him at the USAMRIID.

As we continued up the long gravel driveway, which was pitted in parts, there were signs posted on the trees. "No room!" "All full up." "No food." "Stay out."

How many refugees had passed this way?

But as we drove on—and the road was long—the signs disappeared and the scenery changed. The fields of trees ambled up and down the hills. A wooden bridge spanned a cheerful brook. It was a big, rambling farm, that was for sure.

The doctors at USAMRIID had insisted on doing some testing on Josie, Astrid, and Charlie, as well as on me. Blood work, MRIs, CAT scans, more blood work. We set limits on what they could do, especially on Charlie, and Dr. Cutlass made sure everyone respected our limits.

Dr. Cutlass actually attended every test himself, even when they just took our blood pressure. He was hanging around, I suspect, more for the details we could give him about Brayden's last days on the earth than to make sure the tests were run right, but I didn't fault him for that. I told him everything. Well, not exactly everything. I didn't see any reason to tell him about how Brayden had bullied me. But I remembered stuff like how Brayden had built the Train, and how he'd been a good friend to Jake, when Jake was campaigning to be the leader of the group.

Dr. Cutlass seemed to change into a nice guy, right before our eyes.

They released Josie before us. Astrid needed more time to heal from the caesarian and I was still a bit scrambled from the concussion. We stayed another week.

They taught us how to take care of the baby and we also learned that he was, in fact, extraordinary. Because Astrid had been exposed to the compounds, he had been growing at an accelerated rate. The average weight for babies born at twenty-eight weeks is around two and a quarter pounds. Charlie was double that. His lungs were fully developed. His ears were fine, eyes were fine. They were studying the accelerated rate of growth.

They wanted to continue to study Charlie.

We said we'd think about it.

Finally we pulled up at the farmhouse. Niko's uncle came striding out on his long legs, arms open wide. Niko and Josie were right behind him, Josie so excited to see us she was nearly jumping for joy.

Maybe it was because of the backdrop—the weather-beaten clapboard farmhouse, an oak tree complete with tire swing, and the flock of chickens darting underfoot—but Niko and Josie already looked like farmers. Niko in a plaid shirt and jeans. Josie wearing a skirt and a sweater and a pair of Keds.

"I'm Tim," Niko's uncle said, opening Sandy's door. "Welcome to the Pfeiffer Family Farm! No trouble finding the place?"

"Followed the directions just like you said. Easy as pie," Sandy replied. Tim gave her a hand out of the car.

"Well," he said to me. "You must be Dean. I've heard so much about you."

He crossed to me, took my hand in his broad grip and shook it firmly.

"Thank you so much for letting us come here," I said.

He waved it off. "Thrilled to have you. Truly. Wouldn't have it any other way. You're family now! I mean it."

I opened the door for Astrid and helped her out.

"I'm Astrid," she said. The uncle swept her into a hug.

"Easy, Uncle Tim!" Niko said. "She had surgery."

Astrid was fine, though, grinning. She gave Niko and Josie an even bigger hug.

I reached in and unlatched the car seat from the base.

Our son was swaddled tightly, the way only a nurse can do, and was asleep.

"This is Charlie," I said.

"Lookit that," Tim said. "A real baby."

"Charlie's a sweetie, there's no doubt about it," said Sandy. She was arm in arm with Josie by now. "All the nurses at USAMRIID—can you imagine how happy we've been?—usually we just get sick people but there've been babies this year! SO many wonderful babies!"

Then a man came out of the house and walked over to us. He was short and chubby, and grinning ear to ear.

"Who's that?" I asked Niko.

"You're never going to believe it!" Niko said.

The man crossed down to us, extending his hand. "I'm

Patrick Wenner. So pleased to meet you! Really, a pleasure. Can't tell you how much."

It was Sahalia's dad!

Niko filled me in as we walked up to the house. When Niko had shown his uncle Alex's letter to the editor and told him our story, Tim agreed that the farm should be home to anyone from the group who wanted to come. Tim had been hosting two families of refugees, and had asked them to find another place to stay, so that we could have the space. He told Niko he was glad to have them leave—apparently they didn't help much around the farm, ate a lot, and complained all the time.

Tim had also contacted the Canadian government and officially requested the release of Alex and Sahalia into his custody. They were due to arrive within a few days.

Apparently shortly after that, Mr. Wenner had contacted Alex at Quilchena and Alex had told him to head straight to the farm. Alex was keeping this news from Sahalia. My brother loved to surprise people.

But I sort of wondered if this was too much. Wouldn't she want to know as soon as possible that her dad was alive and she was about to see him?

Even though Tim had offered that they could come to the farm, the McKinleys were staying in Canada, for now, and still had custody of Chloe. The Dominguez family might be moving to New Mexico, where Mrs. Dominguez had a sister. Max would be adopted by them officially.

So. We weren't all going to live on the farm in a big commune. But they'd all visit. I knew they would. The kids would love it here. I could already imagine Chloe and Max fighting over that tire swing.

Back at the hospital, Astrid had written a letter to Jake, care of his mom down in Texas. She had told him about Charlie's birth and asked that he come up and meet us at the farm. I wrote my own letter and repeated the request. I think seeing Charlie could be what Jake needs to straighten up for once and for all.

Josie had been on her own letter-writing campaign, working on getting the orphans she met at Mizzou put into Tim's custody.

After the "Massacre at Mizzou," as the papers called it, the government finally had to admit that the drifts are real. How could they not? There were hundreds dead at UMO.

The papers are now filled with stories of the drifts and the campaign to keep them a secret. President Booker has demanded a full inquiry into the cover-up, but some people think he was the one who ordered the cover-up in the first place.

The upside is that the safety measures have been set up in the areas where the drifts are still a risk. And, thank God, those O containment camps are being shut down. I still can't believe the stories Josie told us about what happened to her there.

The Pfeiffer Family Farm was the new home to me, Alex, Astrid and Sahalia, Josie and Niko, baby Charlie and, now, Mr. Wenner. More would be coming. And the farm could handle them. Lots of space. Lots of promise.

"You're not going to believe this place," Niko told me. "We've got thirty acres of apples, fifteen of plums, and fifteen of white peaches. And the farm used to have a flock of a hundred sheep. We don't have any now, but my uncle wants to start up again, now that he has us to help him."

"There's a swap meet in town," Josie said to Astrid. "We got a bassinet and some clothes. But now I worry the clothes might be too big. I don't know."

"It'll be fine," Astrid told Josie, linking her arm through Josie's. "And thank you."

Niko and Mr. Wenner were talking about farm machinery

and Sandy was talking to Uncle Tim. Was she flirting with him? Hard to tell, but he looked flushed and pleased with her attention.

Tim showed me, Astrid, and Sandy around the house with pride. There were braided wool rugs in every room. Handmade, we were told, back when the flocks were big. Amish quilts lay on the beds, and some hung on the walls, too, as decoration. "That one's been in my family for more than a hundred years," Tim told us, pointing to a quilt with a dozen ovals interlocked. "And that one was given to me by my wife on our wedding day, God keep her soul."

Beautiful kerosene lanterns with mirrored backplates were affixed to the walls in the hallway. Framed portraits in black-and-white of people posing with prize livestock and farm machinery.

"Each generation, our family got smaller. At one time there were twenty Pfeiffers from three generations living in this big old house," Tim told us. "But I guess we've had bad luck. After my sister—Niko's mom—died, there was only me to farm the place. None of my cousins wanted anything to do with the farm. It's felt just miserable here for years. I was going to sell the place and move to Florida and probably go crazy with nothing to do."

He showed us our room, with an old carved wooden bed-frame with probably the nicest quilt of the bunch. An empty bassinet standing at the ready. A pack of diapers resting on an old hope chest. A rocking chair that looked at least a hundred years old.

Astrid took my hand. Her eyes were shining.

"Can't tell you how happy I am to have this house filling up again," he told us. "Makes it seem like a home again."

I'm up with Charlie every couple of hours, it feels like. Of course I don't mind.

I give him to Astrid. She nurses him and then I change his diaper and swaddle him up again.

I rock him in the chair and he opens his nighttime-blue eyes and holds on to my finger with his tiny fingers. He yawns. I marvel at his little mouth. His small voice cooing, calling to who? Maybe he is speaking to me. Or to the blanket. Or to God.

I never knew how much goodness a newborn has wrapped around him until I held my son in my arms. I get it, why everyone wants to hold the baby. They're filling up.

Today, Alex and Sahalia will arrive.

We're all giddy with excitement.

Alex's and Sahalia's bedrooms are on the second floor. We put Alex down at one end of the hall and Sahalia at the other and Mr. Wenner in between. A little space to encourage them to . . . take their time.

We had so much fun cleaning the rooms. Niko and I hauled out the mattresses and beat them with a broom. We scrubbed the floors with Murphy's Oil Soap and dusted away the cobwebs in the corners and in the dresser drawers.

They're going to love it here.

Alex and Niko will have a dozen ideas for ways to fix up the farm and improve productivity—all of them good. And I can't wait for Sahalia to see her father.

Alex's been very specific in his instructions about how we are to handle the moment when they arrive.

First of all, only Tim was allowed to go pick them up at the airport. I told Alex (on a landline they allowed him to use at the Air Force base) that I wanted to come with Tim to pick them up, but he said he was afraid I'd blow the secret. He insisted that we stay home.

The truck only fits three comfortably, so I relented.

It's taken forever. The airport is an hour and twenty minutes away and the plane was supposed to land at 11 a.m. I don't miss minitabs too much, but I'd kill for a text right now.

Where are they? Why's it taking so long?

We're on the front porch. Astrid's rocking Charlie, who just nursed, and I'm pacing back and forth.

"They should be here by now, don't you think? What's taking them so long?"

"They'll be here soon," she tells me.

"They should have been here an hour ago!" I say.

"We're going inside, aren't we, Charlie. We're going to do what Alex told us to do."

According to Alex's plan, I'm in the wrong place. Astrid and I are supposed to wait inside with the baby, so Mr. Wenner can walk up to the truck and surprise Sahalia.

Mr. Wenner, meanwhile, is inside, pacing laps around the kitchen table.

Finally, finally, I hear the crunch of gravel on the drive.

"They're coming! They're here!" I say. (Okay, I shout.)

"Get in here!" Astrid shouts to me.

"Oh my God," Mr. Wenner says as he pushes opens the screen door and steps out. "It's really happening."

I give him a hug and my congratulations and I go to stand inside the kitchen, looking out the age-rippled glass of the window above the sink.

I pull Astrid and Charlie to me.

He's asleep in her arms, smiling and milk-drunk.

"I can't wait to introduce Alex to Charlie!" I say.

Astrid ducks her head and presses it into Charlie's blankets. She is already crying. It's very sweet.

"Look!" I say.

The truck comes into view, and God, it's going really slow, ambling over every pothole in the drive. No wonder it took so long.

I see now, that there are two figures in the bed of the truck, riding in the open air. It's kind of weird. Maybe they wanted the open-air view?

The engine isn't even cut before I hear Sahalia shout, "Daddy! Daddy!"

She jumps down from the truck bed and Mr. Wenner sweeps her into his arms. They go around and around, laughing and crying and hugging like it's too good to be true.

But it is both good and true and it makes my heart ache with old-fashioned joy to see them together.

Sahalia has changed so much. Her dad is going to be amazed at who she's turned into. Or maybe it's that she always was a kind and thoughtful person, but was just hiding behind a crappy attitude.

I kiss Astrid on the top of her head.

"Dean," Astrid says. "Look. There's another surprise." She points out the window with her chin.

Alex has hopped out of the back and he's opening the passenger door.

I peer closer to the window.

A man gets down.

I think . . . I think . . . it's my dad.

And now I stride to the door, and I open it and it *is* my dad.

I'm running now, down the gravel drive.

My footfalls crunching fast.

I see that behind my dad, still in the cab of the truck is a woman, very frail.

She needs a hand down and she is my mother.

"Mom!" I shout. "Mom! Dad!"

I reach my mother and come to a stop, my feet sliding in the gravel.

Gently, gently, I hug her. She's thin and I see, no, I feel, against my cheek, that she's suffered some terrible burn down the side of her face and over her neck. The skin is bandaged in places and shiny in others and she's in my arms. She's thin and fragile and she's in my arms.

My mother.

My dad puts his arms around the two of us and Alex wriggles into the middle and we're all laughing and crying. We're in a big knot. A knot of Grieders. A cluster. A group. A family.

My dad kisses the back of my head and Alex's grin is a mile wide. I've never seen Alex so happy and I know I never will see him happier. He did it. He reunited us.

In a moment, Astrid will make her way down the drive and I will introduce my parents to my son and my (someday soon) wife.

But right now I just let my mom cling to me.

"My sweet boy," she says. "I thought I lost you forever."

I hold my mother, taking care to be gentle, and I tell her I love her.

ACKNOWLEDGMENTS

First and foremost, I would like to thank Holly West, my editor at Feiwel and Friends. During the four years that I have been working on the Monument 14 series, Holly has risen through the ranks at Feiwel and Friends to become an Associate Editor. Holly is the one who fell in love with *Monument 14* when it was in proposal form and insisted Jean Feiwel take a good, long look. After collaborating with me on both *Monument 14* and *Sky on Fire*, Holly was given the reins to edit *Savage Drift*. I feel fortunate to work with you, Holly, and I look forward to many more years together.

Jean Feiwel, I love being one of your friends. Thank you for getting out in front of this series and clearing the way for it.

Hearty thanks to my excellent agent, Susanna Einstein, for her forward thinking (and for always having my back) and to Sandy Hodgman, for helping to bring the Monument 14 series to the world.

This series wouldn't be the success it is if not for the efforts of the Macmillan Children's publicity department. It also wouldn't be such a success if the Macmillan Children's art department wasn't so nail-bitingly awesome. And if the sales team hadn't gotten behind the series like a 40-ton 18-wheeler. Then there's the marketing department, which I just want to kiss on the mouth for everything they've done.

Are you sensing a theme? It takes a bunch of departments—scores of people—to make a book a hit. Here is my list of shout-outs at Macmillan. Thank you to: Publicist superstar Molly Brouillette! Cover artist extraordinaire KB! Lauren "Brings It" Burniac! Delightful Angus Killick! Elizabeth Fithian, who I'd follow anywhere! Allison "Vrrrrroooom" Verost! Big-thinking Kathryn Little! Brilliant Rich Deas! The GonzBargRuCron-TaylWards Hit Squad! Patient, patient Dave Barrett! Ksenia "Kickass Blog Tour" Winnicki! Courtney "Go! Go!" Griffin!

Anne Heausler, I'm honored to share you, the finest copy editor on the eastern seaboard, with countless YA superstar authors. We're all lucky to have you.

I enlisted a large crew of beta readers to help me with *Savage Drift*. Sincere thanks to: Kristin Bair, Jonathan Blake, Shyam Dewan, Greg Harrison, Lukas Lopez-Jensen, Zack Martin, Donna Miele, Ken Herndon, Tiffany Zehnal, my dad, Kit Laybourne, and my uncle, Colonel Tim Ryley.

I'm terrifically excited about the film company Strange Weather and their development of a *Monument 14* movie. Jeff Fierson, thanks for loving the book so much and for believing in it, and in me. I'm looking forward to collaborating with Andrew Adamson and Aron Werner. And thanks to my film agent, Stephen Moore, for putting the deal together and to Kim Stenton, for making sure it all lined up.

Adam Cushman and Red 14 films did a phenomenal job with the trailer for *Savage Drift*. Thank you to the Deka

Brothers, Ben and Julien, for their vision and direction. You can see the trailer at emmylayborne.com or on the Red 14 site, Red 14films.com.

(Do you think it's weird and wonderful that the film company I'm working with is called Strange Weather and the cinematic book trailer company we chose to do the trailer for *Savage Drift* is called Red 14 films? I do.)

I dedicated this book to my sisters, Herran and Renee, because they each showed some serious bravery this year. You each gave me a great gift in 2013 and I want to thank you both.

My kids love to read their names in my books, so I will write them here: Ellie and Rex, hello! I am a very lucky woman to get to be your mama. The last person I thank is the first in my heart, my husband, Gregory Robert Podunovich. Your faith in me was my constant companion as I worked on this series. Thank you.

Vancouver

Quilchena
Refugee
Camp

Monument, CO